Killing Time

Frank Tallis is a clinical psychologist and one of Britain's leading experts on Obsessional States. He has written six non-fiction books. *Killing Time* is his first novel.

KILLING TIME

FRANK TALLIS

HAMISH HAMILTON · LONDON

HAMISH HAMILTON LTD

Published by the Penguin Group
Penguin Books Ltd, 27 Wrights Lane, London w8 5tz, England
Penguin Putnam Inc., 375 Hudson Street, New York, New York 10014, usa
Penguin Books Australia Ltd, Ringwood, Victoria, Australia
Penguin Books Canada Ltd, 10 Alcorn Avenue, Toronto, Ontario, Canada m4v 3b2
Penguin Books (NZ) Ltd, Private Bag 102902, NSMC, Auckland, New Zealand

Penguin Books Ltd, Registered Offices: Harmondsworth, Middlesex, England

First published 1999
1 3 5 7 9 10 8 6 4 2

Set in Monotype Bembo by Intype London Ltd
Printed in England by Clays Ltd, St Ives plc

A CIP catalogue record for this book is available from the British Library

ISBN 0–241–140307

Contents

I

Electrical Disruption of Temporal Flow

'Still not heard anything?'

'No. I haven't heard a thing.'

Dave begins to shake his head. 'I don't know. It's not like her at all. Maybe you should call the police.'

I am able to maintain my composure.

'The police? No, not yet.'

'When then?'

'Tomorrow. If I don't hear anything by tomorrow night, I'll give them a call.'

Dave is clearly dissatisfied. I can see it in his eyes. He will continue to ask questions. 'How long has it been now?'

'Two days.'

I am lying, but *so what*? I have every right to withhold the truth.

'Two days! Shit, Tom, you really should do something.'

There is an uncomfortable pause, during which Dave assumes an expression of such intensity that I am reminded of an early Francis Bacon. The seated figure of 1961, to be precise. The atmosphere between us becomes increasingly tense. So tense, it cannot be sustained.

'I don't understand how you can be so cool about this.'

For the first time – the first time ever – I hear irritation in Dave's voice. He is clearly annoyed with me.

I respond: 'I'm not being cool.'

'. . . and you're not going to contact her mother?'

'What good would that do?'

'Isn't it obvious?'

'And if Anna's not there?'

'You should call the police.'

I cannot answer immediately. Choosing my words very carefully, and softening my voice, I say, 'Look, I don't want to worry the old woman. Not yet.'

This has no effect on Dave. He simply continues. ' . . . but Anna might be there.'

His tone is insistent. Indignant, almost. I am not accustomed to hearing Dave's voice burdened with feeling. I pause for a moment and rotate my glass. I think about his last utterance: *but Anna might be there.*

'What makes you say that?' I ask. 'Why should she have gone home?'

'I don't know. It's just the sort of thing people do when . . .'

He stops and searches for the right word. I decide to urge him on, urge him to dispense with tact and finish his sentence.

'When what?'

'I don't know. When they're unhappy maybe.'

'And you think she was unhappy?'

Dave does not reply. Instead, he turns his head away and becomes lost in thought. His expression is sullen. A careless oaf squeezes past and spills some beer on Dave's jeans; Dave doesn't even notice. There are no jibes. Not even a cutting remark, made for our private amusement. After a while, he says, now without emotion, 'Yes. I think it's a possibility.'

There are too many people at the bar. Our glasses are almost empty but neither of us feels inclined to battle through the crowd. We will be here for some time yet. Perhaps it is the appropriate moment to provide Dave with a rationale. A plausible reason for my reluctance to contact the police or Anna's mother. Even so, I must retain a certain amount of dramatic authenticity.

'Dave, I know you're only trying to help but . . .'

' . . . but what?'

'It's not that I don't want to talk about it . . .'

I hold my breath for a second or two, before letting out a lengthy sigh. Simultaneously I assume the collapsed posture of a man bludgeoned into submission. My shoulders drop and I let my chin sink to my chest. Dave perceives the change and leans forward.

'Did you have an argument? Is that it?'

I continue turning my glass, but raise my head. I nod, like a naughty schoolboy, too ashamed to speak.

'Jesus, Tom, why didn't you say?' At once the timbre of Dave's voice is different. There is a sudden release of tension, as though a taut steel wire had been cut.

'What's with all the secrecy? Surely you could have said!'

This, of course, is one of Dave's problems. He does not understand that we have *moved on*. Things are different now. I shift uncomfortably in my seat before saying, 'It's a bit of a fuck-up really. It all seems to have got out of hand.'

'What happened?'

I don't reply, and Dave continues.

'Come on, Tom, you can tell me, for Christ's sake!'

His expression has become eager.

'It's all so fucking stupid,' I reply. 'I'm sure you don't want to hear it.'

'Of course I want to hear it!'

I perpetuate the charade and simulate a further breakdown of resistance.

'You're not going to believe this, but we had an argument about mess.'

'Mess?'

Dave's voice is incredulous. The hint of a smile brushes his features.

I persevere. 'I'd laid out some of my collection – you know, my antiques – in the bedroom, and she got really pissed off with it. To be fair, she had told me to clear it up weeks ago, but you know how it is. I never got round to it. Anyway, she just went crazy. The argument got out of hand, and she left.'

3

'Just like that.'

'Yes, just like that.'

'Jesus.'

Dave considers the situation carefully before sharing his first hypothesis. His knowledge of women is encyclopedic, therefore I was somewhat disappointed with his unimaginative line of enquiry.

'Was she having a period?'

'Maybe, I don't know.'

'Does she usually give you a bad time? When she's on?'

'Not really. To be honest, I think this has been on the cards for a long time. We haven't been getting on that well.'

Dave looks down. He cannot maintain eye contact.

'Oh, I'm sorry. I didn't realize.'

We are suddenly both embarrassed. Dave and I look toward the bar, toward the line of figures, made indistinct by a heavy curtain of restless cigarette smoke.

'She has done this before, you know.'

Dave turns back to look at me.

'Has she?'

My disclosure has undoubtedly surprised him.

'Yes, only once. Went off to stay with her brother in Peckham for the night.'

'Why was that?'

'We hadn't argued or anything. She just took off. Afterwards she said she had wanted a change . . . space, I don't know . . .'

Again, I am lying, but safely.

'You know, I would never have guessed. She really didn't strike me as someone who would behave like that.'

'Well. There it is . . .'

We sip our flat beer, in synchrony. Our glasses tilt at the same time.

'She's not close to her brother, is she?'

'No. He's a smackhead.'

'So why did she go to see him?'

4

I shrug. Dave still wants answers. His need becomes palpable.

'Maybe you should give him a call.'

'He's not on the phone.'

' . . . figures.'

I am surprised by his ready acceptance of my answer.

'If I don't hear anything by tomorrow, I'll call the police. I'm not going all the way over to Peckham on the off chance that Anna's hiding out in Huntley's squat.'

Dave tilts his head to one side.

'Huntley?'

'That's his name.'

'Oh, yeah.' A vague memory rises from the depths of Dave's mind, snagging his features and pulling them upwards. 'That's right. I think she mentioned him once. Huntley. How unfortunate.'

There is a flinder of humour in these words. For the briefest moment, our eyes meet (as conspirators) and we recapture a suggestion of our suspended intimacy; this insubstantial, fragile thing hovers in the air between us before dissolving into nothingness. Dave's face becomes sullen again. As though a light behind his eyes has been extinguished.

'I suppose you're right, Tom. Call the police tomorrow.'

Poor Dave. How worried he looks. Yet, when he returns to his cold, unwelcoming bedsit his anxiety will evaporate. There will be a message from Anna on his answering-machine.

I lean my glass to one side and look down at the warm, phlegmy residue. Dave is aware of the distance growing between us and clearly feels obliged to perform a reconciliatory gesture. His features soften.

'Do you want another?'

I decline his offer.

We have, it seems, made a tacit agreement to leave the subject of Anna alone for the rest of the evening, and our desultory conversation eventually settles in the tired rut we so frequently choose to furrow. Dave asks me about my research, and I ask him about his. He complains about his supervisor, and I complain about mine. There was a time when I truly loved these discussions. As the tobacco smoke coalesced to form an impenetrable sedge around us, we would find ourselves straying toward the remote frontiers of contemporary science: emergent properties, the ethics of cloning, exobiology, quantum models of consciousness and 'smart' drugs. Nothing was beyond our reach. Dave and me. Enjoying the sense of camaraderie that is truly unique among those whose IQs and bank balances so often (and so unfairly) share the same numeric value.

This evening, however, we are both uninspired. We manage to talk about our research, complain about our supervisors without difficulty, but fail to develop the conversation any further. Dave's prodigious powers of imagination have all but deserted him. He cannot find an appropriate theme and therefore falls back on a more pedestrian topic. Dave begins to tell me about a nurse he has just met, then, belatedly recognizing his insensitivity, brings his story to a premature and unsatisfactory close. I find it hard to believe in his nurse. She is a fiction whose only purpose is to fill a painful silence.

Eventually, our conversation peters out entirely. We are able to venture one or two trite observations before being struck entirely dumb. There is nothing left to say. Our friendship has become dust. Our words, a mouthful of ashes.

We leave the iniquitous Nightingale before last orders. Immediately, we are received by the sulphurous fumes of an articulated lorry making its bellicose way down Green Lanes towards the North Circular. The night is suffused with a heavy fug. The sky is a uniform and featureless canopy. I cannot resist a quip.

'*Look how the floor of heaven is thick inlaid . . .*'

Dave smiles, but does not laugh. I am not altogether sure that Dave is *au fait* with *The Merchant of Venice*. Indeed, he seems to have read very little of anything written before 1955. His expression becomes lined and intense. 'Tom, you are OK?'

There is genuine concern in the tone of his voice, and I feel as though something has given in my chest. His sympathy takes me by surprise. I am, for a moment, caught off guard.

6

'I'll manage, I suppose.'

'No. I wasn't thinking about Anna. I meant . . .'

'What?'

'I meant *you*. Are you OK? In yourself.'

'In myself? What's that supposed to . . .'

My question trails off. I am uncomfortable with what I believe he is about to imply.

We both stop walking for a moment.

He seems about to ask another question, but suddenly loses heart. 'Doesn't matter,' he says. These few syllables, uttered in a tone that communicates resignation, also serve as a substitute for 'Goodbye'.

Dave raises a hand and walks off towards Wood Green Tube as the first droplets of drizzle settle on my spectacles. His lean, loping figure is suddenly surrounded by an aura of yellow light. He fluoresces, like the survivor of a nuclear disaster, or a Renaissance image of the Virgin Mary. ''Night, Dave,' I call after him.

It sounds ominous, this farewell. As though I am naming a new form of urban predator.

When I arrive home there is some time to kill. *New Scientist* contains an incompetent and rather misleading article on complexity, which I read anyway; however, in my head, the red light on Dave's answering-machine is blinking and I am somewhat distracted. It is difficult to focus on the page. I keep thinking of Dave's dark, empty room, illuminated by the machine's rubiginous pulse. This, I imagine, is how it must feel to be psychic. Having to wait for things that you know are going to happen. Finally, my telephone emits a familiar treble purr.

'Tom?'

'Dave?'

'Yeah. Listen, Anna's left a message on my machine.'

'She what? Where is she?'

'Don't know, she didn't say. She just said she was OK and that you weren't to worry. It wasn't very clear though, the message. It could have been long distance.'

I pause.

'Tom?'

'Sorry?'

' . . . at least you know she's safe now, eh?'

'Yes. That is a relief. Though why on earth did she call you? Why didn't she call me?'

I hope that my pointed question will unsettle him but it has no effect whatsoever. Dave adopts a gentle, confiding tone. He utters a few platitudes about relationships and experience. I hear certain phrases – 'ups and downs', 'sometimes it's hard', 'who can say?' – but I am not really listening. His premise, only thinly concealed, is that I know absolutely nothing about women and will therefore be incapable of resolving any problems that have arisen between myself and Anna. He does not say this directly, but it is strongly inferred. I am impressed by his audacity.

We arrange to meet later in the week – I must, after all, keep up appearances. When I replace the receiver my hand is shaking.

Although I hate to admit it, Dave is absolutely right. Where women are concerned, I have no judgement. I don't understand them. There is no deep, meaningful explanation for this inadequacy. If I were to lie on a psychoanalyst's couch, I would be a very unrewarding patient. I have no terrible secret to disclose, only ignorance. I don't understand women because, put quite simply, I have never had very much to do with them. Laugh, if you will, but during puberty the most important things in my life were a Junior Electronic Engineer Kit and a Chemistry Set. The latter I recall, carried an image on its lid of the prototypical boy genius, inexplicably mesmerized by a copper-sulphate solution in a test tube. That child – with his weighty spectacle frames and horribly precise side parting – was me. His appearance explained a great deal, a fact I readily acknowledged at the time. It explained the complete futility of my own sexual maturation. None of the girls in my school, with their crotch-hugging jeans, open-topped blouses and hair like spun copper would speak to such a creature. What sexuality I had would be discharged into a Kleenex tissue and disposed of, like rubbish. I despised my doppelgänger. Our identity proclaimed an intolerable truth. I would very probably die a virgin.

Now, there is nothing wrong with virginity *per se*. After all, Sir Isaac Newton died a virgin. The issue for me, however (if you will excuse the pun), is choice. I did not want a future in which the only way I might participate in 2 billion years of reproductive biology involved throwing a semen-saturated tissue into a wicker basket. This really wasn't what it was all about. I had been excluded from the Darwinian party. My DNA just didn't let me in. Flashing my pheno-type at the door did nothing – well, if I am brutally honest, less than nothing. I didn't ask to be excluded. I didn't want to be excluded. I just *was* excluded. Moreover, entry was clearly non-negotiable. Then I met Anna, and everything changed.

What can I say about Anna? Smallish, flat-chested, brown hair (which she might have washed more than she was inclined to), studious, intelligent, never seen in a skirt (though there are one or two rather long ones hanging in the wardrobe). Somewhat ill-disposed to the wearing of make-up, although not averse to perfume (I think her favourite was Sentience by someone like Lanvin or Estée Lauder). A very good cellist, or, let us say, good enough to give a spirited account of several serious chamber works. Not possessed of a great sense of humour, although able to produce a modest smile when in the right company. Two publications. One on preconscious processing and the other on implicit memory, neither yet cited by authors outside of the University College psychology department. Nevertheless, a very promising start for a first-year post-grad. Very promising indeed.

I do miss her, physically. I can't say that I miss her as a person. No, that would be altogether misleading; but I do miss her body. I miss cuddling her in the morning. I miss the warmth of her naked buttocks against my erect penis when I wake. I miss the soft, almost inconsequential mound of each breast and the way that her nipples hardened between my teeth. I have been left with a primitive, animal longing for contact.

Of course, there are some things about her that I don't miss. The fact of the matter is, she had become something of a nag.

'Come on, Tom, get up now,' she would say. It was quite useful having her there to coax me out of bed on those days when I was due to see Béla (my awesome Hungarian supervisor), but on weekends I found her exhortations intolerable. I realize that four o'clock in the afternoon would be considered an inappropriate hour to rise by the majority; however, I was extremely tired. Anna even began to take (what I thought to be) an unhealthy, almost obsessive interest in my personal hygiene. 'You haven't shaved today,' she would say. I wanted to reply, *So what? So what if I haven't fucking shaved?* Though I never did. I simply replied 'Oh, right' and retired to the bathroom.

Needless to say, she objected when I began to assemble Locke's apparatus.

'Look, we haven't got room for this in here.'

'Yes we have.'

'No we haven't.'

'We have, I'll put it by the bed.'

'What!'

Her expression would collapse in despair.

'Look, I'll dismantle it once I've seen it working.'

' . . . and when will that be?'

'Soon. Really. I only need a few more parts.'

I never disclosed what Locke's apparatus was really for. I had told Anna that it was a reconstruction of an early lighting system produced by the Edison company in 1878. Her understanding of proper science is lamentably incomplete and she was quite happy to accept my explanation without further questioning. Although I imagine she had become quite accustomed to my little 'projects'. I suppose, by that time, they were all much the same thing as far as she was concerned.

Arnold Autoloycus Locke, AA to his friends, was an extraordinary character. I knew nothing of him before I came across his 1883 paper in the *Proceedings* of the Cavendish Society (a short-lived fraternity of engineers and self-proclaimed *natural philosophers* who enjoyed the patronage of the wealthy and eccentric George Cavendish, heir of the Cavendish textile empire). A. A. Locke had been invited to speak at the third and I believe final meeting of the society. It was at this meeting that he presented his experimental findings on the electrical disruption of 'temporal flow'. His work was not well received, even by the notoriously radical Cavendish audience. Nevertheless, his presentation (in a slightly modified form) was published in the *Proceedings*, prefaced by an unprecedented disclaimer authored by the president of the Cavendish society, Sir Robert Maplethorpe (the inventor of the Maplethorpe lens). This, in itself, precipitated a considerable amount of heated discussion by Cavendish illuminati concerning the aims and objectives of the society. An unholy row broke out at the 1884 Founders Colloquy, and the society never fully recovered from the internecine struggles of the following year.

That, really, is about as much as there is to say about Locke and his contemporaries in the Cavendish Society. Yet this brief, almost dismissive biography is the result of many hours' toil. Of course, my research was hardly exhaustive. Nevertheless, I feel confident in asserting that there is – in all probability – not much more to discover. Locke was fated to leave the faintest of impressions on the world, a ghost's footstep, the merest suggestion of concavity in the sand. However, unknown to him, his purchase on history was secured – albeit precariously – by his contribution to the Cavendish *Proceedings*.

I could so easily have missed the Locke paper; it was located in the basement of the DMS Watson science library, on the lowest shelf of a bookcase partly concealed by an open door. Indeed, it was necessary for me to close the door to reach it. The publications in this neglected section seemed to have no unifying theme. It was as if I stood on the most remote shoreline of nineteenth-century science, staring at the flotsam and jetsam that had been trapped in an obscure coastal inlet. I examined one or two volumes of bound papers before lifting the Cavendish *Proceedings* from their hiding-place.

The first was a rather poor collection of articles on geology, the second so inauspicious I have no recollection of it. The Cavendish volume looked, on the outside, no different from the others. A rather battered cloth cover, barely holding together three journals (the middle one had almost worked itself loose). The pages were yellow and smelt damp. Most were stained with brown archipelagos of varying sizes, and some, sadly, were torn. I flicked through the last journal and was immediately arrested by the title of Locke's paper: 'Electrical disruption of temporal flow and the fixture of anomalous impressions using a procedure after Daguerre'.

I am something of a collector of academic curiosities, particularly so with respect to the nineteenth century. I have photocopies of some quite extraordinary papers, for example, Algernon Brightwell's 'The expression of humour in the Irish wolfhound' and William Healey's 'The Dorset homunculus', to say nothing of James Hunt's hilarious Anthropological Society address of 1865, entitled 'On the Negro's place in nature'. All splendid examples of post-Darwinian idiocy. Locke's paper seemed to be a worthy addition. Another amusing example of a Victorian gentleman scientist arguing well beyond his data and educated well beyond his intelligence. I made a copy of it there and then.

It is strange that I never discussed the Locke paper with Dave. Well, that is to say, not directly. On more than one occasion I coaxed him into discussing the implications of Locke's work, but simply in order to test his opinions. Nothing more. Dave has, without doubt, a first-class mind and extraordinary powers of imagination. When given a theme, his extemporizations are a joy and a delight. Although Dave will probably make a significant contribution in the field of organic chemistry and genetics, it will be at the expense of speculative fiction. He could have been – indeed might yet become – a very competent creative.

Why did I keep the Locke paper a secret? When I reflect on this,

I feel distinctly uneasy. Yes, I suppose it's true that I had a great deal on my mind (just at that time). But, subsequent to discovering the Locke paper, I showed Dave one or two other acquisitions. Otto Weininger's *Sex and Character*, for example. If I were a psychologist, I would most probably posit some unconscious motivation. That I had some unacknowledged intention to build and use Locke's apparatus with a specific purpose in mind, and that necessarily Dave should remain ignorant of its existence. I for one have never been convinced of psychology's value. All that I can confirm with certainty is that my reticence to share the discovery of the Locke paper with Dave was uncharacteristic. Unusual. I do not believe in fate, the conspiring of astrological signs or, for that matter, a divine hand, pushing and shoving human lives along the incorrigible track of predestination. Nevertheless, if I wanted to claim that fate had ever played some part in my life, it must have been then.

I have no idea why I did not show the Locke paper to Dave; he was, after all, just about the only person I knew who would, or could, appreciate it. Discussion of my *acquisitions* had become something of a ritual for us. It marked a unique point of intellectual coincidence. Anna never really understood our jokes. I can remember sitting in the Nightingale with Dave and crying with laughter as we read certain passages from 'The Dorset homunculus'. Anna would look on, bemused. Then, after a while, she would say something like, 'But it's really stupid,' which would make Dave and I laugh even more. She would then give a little (really quite attractive) smile, which communicated dismay and warmth in equal measure. She could so easily have said '*Boys!*', like an overindulgent mother, admonitory, yet hopelessly weakened by affection – and she would have been right. The fact of the matter was, when with Dave, I became *one of the boys*. For the first time in my life in fact. It was good to feel like *a bit of a lad*. Drinking and joking with *me mate*. Dave made all this very easy.

I wonder, would it be wrong to say, that, initially, I rather worshipped Dave. After all, his entry into my life was nothing less than heroic.

13

It had been a muggy, hot day. The kind of day that causes anger to rise exponentially. The kind of day when it is unwise to be in the centre of London, where tempers fray and frazzle (at the best of times). I had gone to the Students' Union bar in Gower Street, to slake an improbably tenacious thirst. It was early evening, and there was hardly anyone there.

After I had been given my drink, I turned around without looking properly and knocked into a man standing behind me. He was a tall, heavily built individual, whose substantial mass was almost flab but not quite. His glass jogged and the beer slopped and cascaded down his shirt-front and jeans. 'Fuck!' he said very loudly, looking down at a fair reproduction of the consequences of incontinence.

'Oh, I'm so sorry,' I said, hoping to appease him, although there was little use.

'You fuck-wit, look what you've done!'

He glared at me. I noticed that he was standing between two rather thin women with pinched expressions. This was a bad sign.

'Look what you've done!'

'Yes, I can see, I'm really sorry.'

'So what are you going to fucking do about it?'

I began to tremble. I didn't know what he wanted me to do. I rather foolishly put down my orange juice and then prised a compressed paper tissue out of my pocket. I reached out, hopelessly, toward him. His clenched fist came crashing down on my arm and I dropped the tissue to the floor. The crumpled sphere absorbed the liquid and opened slowly, like a flower. I was flabbergasted. In shock. I began to whine, very quietly. 'Leave him . . .' said one of the thin women, unexpectedly.

'Why?'

'Because he's a spastic.'

The man guffawed. For a moment I thought that his attention had been diverted elsewhere, allowing me to make a pathetic and inconspicuous exit.

Instead he said again, 'So what are you going to do about it?'

It was then that Dave appeared behind my adversary.

'That's enough,' he said quietly.

The big man turned around.

'He spilt my drink.'

'I know. Do you want him to buy you another?'

They looked at each other very carefully, as though trying to estimate each other's weight to the nearest kiwi fruit.

' . . . if not, then perhaps you should leave him alone.'

There was a long pause. Dave appeared supremely confident. There was something too relaxed about his posture. As though, unbeknown to us, he had a Kalashnikov magically concealed up his sleeve. The big man registered Dave's disconcerting *laissez-faire* and, inferring danger, with little grace conceded defeat.

'Ah, fuck him, let's go.'

He and his small but devoted entourage sloped off toward the door. Dave suddenly called out. 'Hang on.'

The man stopped and looked around.

'What?'

'How about an apology?'

I started to mumble 'That really won't be necessary', but my reply was drowned out by the big man's response.

'Fuck you . . .' He swung his head forward and burst through the swing doors like something resurrected from the Triassic era. The two women followed like debris caught in a gust of wind.

Dave smiled and shrugged.

I was really very impressed.

'Thank you,' I said, like a girl.

'That's all right. He's a complete arsehole. I enjoyed it.'

'Are you a karate expert or something?'

'No. Should I be?'

'If you behave like that on a regular basis, then yes.'

Dave laughed. And so did I, dizzy with relief and admiration. We retired to a nearby table and found that, against expectations, we got on rather well.

By the end of the evening, Dave was – now I understand somewhat typically – regaling me with stories of his sexual exploits. I nodded sagely, happy to sun myself in his benevolence, delighted to be included in such an adult and intimate conversation. This is one of Dave's most distinguishing characteristics. He is always happy to talk about sex, which is, after all, the essential glue of male bonding.

Prior to making Dave's acquaintance relationships with my own gender were always fraught with difficulties. At Cambridge I was able to master some aspects of the male-bonding process, but never all. Yes, it was relatively easy to sit by the roadside with other mathematics undergraduates, affecting a devil-may-care attitude by swigging cider while discussing Fermat, but talk of sex – beyond innuendo – was never possible. This was, of course, because sex and the study of mathematics do not seem to go together. In this respect Newton has set a precedent. English students, drama students, foreign-language students, even medical students, all seem to get laid without difficulty. Mathematics students, on the other hand, simply masturbate in dim rooms feebly illuminated by their glowing acne.

There is something so unfair about this. We are by far the most naturally gifted of all students. Given a couple of weeks' study, I think I could craft an essay, as well as any English undergraduate, on window imagery in *Wuthering Heights*. Yet, given twenty years of study, I doubt whether most English undergraduates could resolve the most basic of mathematical problems. We are intellectual athletes. You can as much pretend to be a good mathematician as pretend to be a competitor in the Olympic games. It is simply not possible. Yet we are the runt of the academic litter – 'nerds'. It makes me so angry. Even now.

There were many times when I found myself sitting on the stairs at parties gazing through the bannisters at my more trendy university contemporaries, consumed with envy. From my vantage, I would observe a young woman who I considered to be (for that moment at least) the very model of absolute beauty. I would be transfixed by the bounce of her small breasts as she moved to the rhythm of some intolerably bad but unanimously praised pop group. The fact that she was not wearing a bra would be betrayed by prominent nipples that disturbed the sweep of a skin-tight T-shirt. *Dear God, my heart would break.* I would peer through the bars of my cage, trying to summon the courage to approach her, my heart racing, my head swimming with cider, my throat sore from inhaling the stale, opiate exhalations rising from below, and then, after several hundred rehearsals of potential opening gambits, I would watch my nemesis – usually in the form of a tallish, thin-looking arts student with a short leather jacket and black 501s – materialize beside the object of my desire and, almost instantaneously, press his mouth against hers while cupping a breast in an eager hand. She would, of course, mean nothing to him. It was not unusual to see the same young man, later the very same evening, pressing another of my fantasy inamorata into a dark corner, his hips, moving backwards and forwards, simulating the act that underscored my hopeless inadequacy. How I would rage, inside.

Why are attractive young women content to be used by men who have nothing more to recommend them than the right haircut or wristwatch? Why are they happy to be treated with utter, undisguised contempt by any individual socially sanctioned as fashionable? I, who would have been prepared to die for them, wasn't even worth registering. Indeed, for most women I worshipped from afar I simply did not exist. They would look through me as they scanned the room for regulation trainers.

Sex, therefore, was another country. A foreign clime. That is, until I met Dave and learned that the details of sexual relationships could be discussed without the conversation immediately disintegrating amid hoots of laughter and screeches reminiscent of the monkey house at London Zoo. When Dave talked about sex it seemed to be a perfectly natural development in an ongoing conversation. He could carry a narrative from first glances exchanged in the Students' Union building to fellatio on a floor in Camden without changing gear. It just happened that way, and when it did, it was unremarkable. Part of life. This was a rather different approach to my colleagues' in

17

Cambridge, who shared the view that women were projections from another universe.

In Cambridge, a conversation might start with 'I saw Lucy today.' To which the response might be 'She's got terrific tits.' At this point, various comments of a lewd nature would be made and everyone would feel obliged to join in. There was always something hysterical, or fevered, about the swift crescendo of howls and yawps that ensued. As the hubbub subsided someone might mention Liapunov exponents and we would steer our conversation toward nonlinear oscillators, like men who had spotted land after many years lost at sea. The crisis had passed. We, quite literally, sought safety in numbers.

They were a useless bunch, the Cambridge crowd. Bright, yes. Very bright. But a more jaw-drop-embarrassing brigade of wank-merchants never walked God's earth. Their puerile jokes, tired old piss-takes and diabolical choice of knitwear are still enough to make me sit bolt upright and screaming after so much as a visitation in my dreams. I am far, far, far from fashionable, but even to my untutored eye, my colleagues seemed to be hell-bent on breaking every known rule of colour coordination (irrespective of host culture). Moreover, they all seemed to have engaged in some Faustian bargain whereby they forfeited muscular control in exchange for cortical supremacy. I never saw one of them open a yoghurt carton without later using half the contents as a fashion accessory. En masse, they would appear over the other side of Trinity quad like a band of juveniles who were exploring the group possibilities of chemically induced motor neurone disease.

No wonder I was so unhappy in Cambridge. Imagine being counted a member of this unhappy – socially condemned – crew. And imagine trying to discuss the possibility of forming a sexual relationship with individuals to whom adulthood had presented an unassailable barrier to emotional development.

Dave, on the other hand, made sex 'normal'. Pedestrian almost. More importantly, he made it possible. Sex was not for other people, it was for him and, by association, I supposed sex might also be for me. I had never before been able to speak openly about my feelings. Particularly my feelings of inadequacy. Dave could be trusted. For one man to admit weakness to another, in most situations, is much the same as the ritual surrendering of the jugular among pack animals. It is not the starting point for discussion but rather an invitation to abuse or mock. It was never like that with Dave.

Of course, if it hadn't been for Dave, I would never have had the courage to pursue Anna. I had occupied a computer terminal adjacent to hers on several occasions but we had never exchanged more than an embarrassed eyebrow flash. Anna was a plain girl, I realize that. But to me, at that time, she appeared rather beautiful (albeit in a rather subdued, understated way). She was the kind of woman I might have approached, if I were not possessed by the spirit of the boy genius on the chemistry set. When I saw her I imagined myself to have assumed the appearance of that dreaded figure. Out of the corner of her eye she would perceive me, a two-dimensional cardboard cut-out, glasses like scaffolding and a side-parting so deep and wide that it appeared to reveal underlying bone tissue. No, I could never have said a word to Anna, not without Dave's encouragement (and hairdressing recommendations).

'What's the problem?' he would say.

'She won't be interested.'

'How do you know? Can you mind-read, or what?'

'No.'

'Well, then?'

I held on to my incapacity, my social infirmity, with both hands.

'Dave, she won't be interested. It'll be really embarrassing.'

'So, what if it is embarrassing?'

'I'll feel like shit.'

'So what, it's only a feeling. Feeling like shit. It passes . . .'

He would then raise his glass, sip, and think for a few moments.

'You take risks all the time. Every time you step off a kerb you

19

could be killed. Why are you happy to risk dying but not happy to risk rejection?'

'Rejection is worse than dying.'

'Fuck,' he would say, with great affection, shaking his head at my incomprehensible lack of confidence. 'What a stupid fuck!'

One evening, after Dave had spent the best part of three hours persuading me to ask Anna out for a drink, we stumbled out of the Nightingale and walked across the road to a nearby recreation ground. Dave, quite drunk, pointed at the sky.

'What's that then?'

'What?'

'Those stars there.'

He was tracing a constellation with his finger.

'You know what they are.'

'Yeah, but do you?'

'Of course I do.'

'Well, what are they?'

'Andromeda.'

' . . . and the smudge?'

'The Andromeda galaxy, of course.'

'Right! Two million light years away. Two fucking million. Those photons, hitting your retina, left that galaxy two million years ago.' Dave placed a hand on my right shoulder, to steady himself, before continuing his oration. 'When your hominid ancestors were recombining the very DNA that you carry in both, yes both, of your testicles . . . and . . .' He lost it for a moment and then placed his other hand on my left shoulder. 'Tom. Two million years. Nothing . . . Nothing is important. Not really. Not when you really, really think about it. Fucking . . . ancient Egypt, Copernicus, doing a Ph.D. Against two million years . . . don't mean a thing. You see, life . . . life will just pass you by. You've gotta take risks, otherwise . . . it'll be gone. Two million years . . .'

And he was absolutely right. Somehow, his inchoate plea penetrated my defences. I not only understood the argument, I felt it. I would have to talk to the girl with dull brown hair. I could no longer afford to lead such an impoverished, pathetic, lonely life.

'You're right, Dave,' I said. 'And, I'm going to do things differently, from now on.'

'You bet!' he said, and then proceeded to project vomit in the direction of the Andromeda galaxy in the style of an ornamental fountain (as might be found in a garden of opulence such as Versailles).

The first time Anna and I made love was at her place. That, of course, was when she had *her place*. She had asked me to help her with some statistics. This sort of thing had happened to me once or twice before; numerate and computer-literate young men are remarkably popular with female post-graduate psychologists (let me tell you). However, nothing had come of these earlier invitations. As the evening drew on I began to feel that I might have my hopes dashed yet again. We talked, and talked, but the conversation remained peculiarly sterile. More like enumeration than discussion. Each taking turns to describe likes and dislikes.

Finally, we sat at her computer, together. My thigh was pressed against hers. I was ostensibly explaining to her the basic principles of cluster analysis and showing her how to write a command file; in reality, I was focused on the heat that licked around my outer thigh. I was able to formulate the correct sequence of words, but my awareness was firmly located in my trousers. I felt the pressure of engorgement. My penis, straining against my underpants. When the statistics instruction was completed, Anna leaned towards me and kissed my cheek. She lingered, for a moment, but it was enough. My mind filled with a vision of a spiral galaxy hung in the impenetrable blackness of space and I rotated my head until our lips met. Of course I had no idea what to do. She, I believe, expected me to take some kind of lead at that point. A senseless expectation if ever there was one. So, we remained in that position for some time. Eyes closed, lips touching. Like a shabby, mutant Rodin. Then I felt the warmth of her tongue slipping between my lips as she gently prised open my mouth.

Two days later Dave and I sat in the Nightingale, and for the first time in my life, I felt normal. For the first time in my life, I felt like a person. Not the boy genius. Not the emotionally bankrupt son of ageing, suburban parents, but an *ordinary bloke*. Dave was delighted by my conquest. He slapped me on the back, bought me more drinks than I could realistically consume and requested a comprehensive account of what had transpired between myself and Anna. In that supreme moment of bonding there was no embarrassment. No reluctance to disclose the most intimate detail. I discussed the folds of Anna's genitalia with Dave like a connoisseur. I was a grand Lothario, louche and reprobate in the extreme. A debauch without parallel. It was as though I had spent the greater part of my life engaged in an anthropological study of cunnilingus. If there was such a thing as a chair in clitoral studies, it would have been awarded to me without question (although, in actuality, what I mistook to be Anna's clitoris at that time was very probably her pubic bone).

Dave, cognisant of my sudden transformation, now felt at liberty to divulge the more technical aspects of his arcane knowledge. The result of numerous encounters in student halls and bedsits around north London (and one on the Old Kent Road). There was no method to this disclosure. He described peeling back the clitoral hood to reveal the epicentre of a woman's sexuality and exploring its diminutive geography with the glistening tip of his tongue. He described probing the vagina with wet fingers, in search of the fabled Grafenberg spot. He described musk-scented, soft white thighs, and gaping pudenda, weeping honey. Our conversation was like a rich banquet. How fondly I remember that evening. It was the evening on which I joined the human race. Even now, thinking about it, I cannot help feeling some affection for Dave. Yes, even now.

It was a strange experience, becoming human. At first, I couldn't really handle it. My life had become fragmented. On the one hand, I continued working on my Ph.D., devising mathematical models to describe the motion of liquids, playing chess with Béla and gossiping about the personal shortcomings of distinguished academics in his circle; on the other hand, I spent a great deal of time kissing Anna's pink genitalia or attempting to insert a spittle-covered finger through the dark, rather tense circle of her anal sphincter. The two did not seem to go together. Anna told me that Freud ascribed most human ills to the basic conflict between our lower and higher selves. I concede, he had a point.

I couldn't hide my distraction from Béla. He detected a problem immediately.

'Tom, you are not yourself. You are – what is that stupid expression?' He paused for a moment, before saying in his best exhibition-standard Transylvanian accent, 'Away with the fairies.'

'Oh.'

'Now, Tom, leave your fairies! Concentrate!'

But I couldn't concentrate. It had all become rather difficult. As much as I would try to focus on some formula or other, my mind would simply choose to re-create, in imagination, the sensation of Anna's lips closing around my penis. One afternoon, Béla got quite annoyed. He told me to go away and not come back until I had recovered the use of my 'brine'. This oblique reference had nothing to do with saline solution but a great deal to do with my diminishing cortical prowess. I must say, it was pretty demoralizing. Moreover, I felt bad about offending Béla. I had wasted quite a lot of time and had to work extremely hard to catch up. Perhaps it was because of all this hard work that I began to get my headaches. Horrible, throbbing headaches that made me feel sick for days at a time.

I was always visiting Anna in her little flat. It was above a hairdresser's shop in Canonbury. The rent was really beyond her means, but she liked the area and was prepared to make sacrifices to stay there. Sometimes, I would just sit and look at her. The fact that I had acquired a girlfriend still seemed to need frequent verification. I particularly enjoyed looking at her when she played the cello. Most of the time Anna's face was inexpressive, neither happy nor sad, as though her limbic system was stuck in neutral; however, when she put resin on her bow her features would become more animated. The anticipation was clearly visible. Then, she would take a deep breath and exhale as her bow made contact with the string. Her face would assume a series of expressions that reflected the spirit of each phrase. Sadness, yearning, hope and resignation. This was an unexpected pleasure, contemplating Anna.

One evening is particularly vivid in my memory. The rain was falling heavily outside (drumming on the windows) and the gas fire emitted a soft, soporific hiss. Anna was playing Bach's beautiful D-minor suite. 'Sarabande,' I believe. I didn't know what it was then (indeed, like most people, I was quite unfamiliar with the repertoire for solo cello). It occurred to me, at that moment, that I never wanted to be separated from Anna. Ever. I needed something '*of*' her, with me, all the time. Something essential. Without letting her see I let my arm fall and pressed the recording button on the radio–cassette. I had previously taped and listened to a science programme on Radio 4. The tape had been rewound and was ready. This would be my essential Anna. Something to listen to while I worked. Something to fill the emptiness that threatened to become physical pain when we weren't together. After the menuettos, Anna stopped, but I left the tape running anyway. I would have an evening with Anna. Her music and her voice, for all time, whatever happened. Was this love? Well, I suppose it was. Love was worse, far worse, than I had ever imagined. I had been unmade. I was, now, half-formed. Love had injured me, yet I was happier (and sadder) than I had ever been in my entire life.

Although I recovered some of Béla's good will by the spring, things took a turn for the worse again in the summer. Anna and I had moved into the flat in Wood Green. It just seemed a sensible thing to do. We were spending most of our free time together and it was senseless living in two small flats in central London when we could live in one big flat – for half the rent – further out.

I was finding it so hard to concentrate. My mind felt sluggish and heavy. Anna seemed to lose momentum too. Her mother, who lived – indeed, still lives – in Bournemouth, would leave messages on the answering-machine. Her voice became more and more irritated with each call.

Do call back, Anna!

Look, I would so appreciate a call!

Anna, it's Mum again. Do you think you could possibly give me a call?

But Anna didn't call. Or couldn't. Well, not for many months, anyway. She became a somewhat inconsiderate daughter. In that first, overwhelming wave of infatuation we become dislocated. Dislodged from the positions we had previously occupied, leaving only outlines of our former selves in the real world. We were very happy for life to continue, without us. We would get back on top of things in due course . . .

Sometimes, we would set the alarm for seven, wake, prepare breakfast, and simply get back into bed again. A kiss would prompt a caress, and before long we would be making love. Afterwards, we would lie together on the bed, not talking, just looking at each other, or at the ceiling. The air, heavy with sweat. This was how we lived. The victims of love in idleness.

One day, while we lay together, steaming and naked after sex, I watched two flies tracing eccentric trajectories around the light shade, and it occurred to me that they too might be having intercourse. Why this should have made me wonder, for the first time, about Anna's previous sexual experiences, I really can't say; however, the impact of this consideration was both painful and confusing. I felt a curious churning in my stomach and in my mind's eye I saw Anna, supine, accommodating a shadowy figure between parted legs. Rather stupidly, I turned my head to avoid looking at this ghastly image, but of course it remained at the centre of my awareness. At that moment

25

I wanted to interrogate Anna. Ask her outright – *How many? Who? When? Where? Which way? Why?* But I couldn't. It seemed inappropriate. Instead, I rolled over, and positioned myself on top of her. She had been slumbering, and she opened her eyes and smiled. I pushed my erection into her and began to move up and down, with spite. Anna winced, and I was glad. I wanted to punish her for enjoying sex with other men.

'Gently, Tom.'

I stopped. She stroked my back with such care, such affection, that I felt wholly ashamed.

'Sorry . . .'

'It's OK, just do it gently.'

You know, when I think of her words – *just do it gently* – I feel quite unsettled. Less sure of myself. It is almost as though I can hear her voice: *Gently, Tom.* I hope that I have been correct in my assumptions.

Even though I finally managed to join the human race I remain an odd person. My oddness has, to a greater or lesser degree, always been present. I am particularly odd insofar as ordinary things frighten me. The things that most people accept without question are, paradoxically, the very same things that leave me with a deep sense of disquiet. For example, I can remember – quite distinctly – becoming aware of my own existence as a child. The act of introspection itself disturbed me. I suppose it was my own insubstantiality that made me uneasy. The fact that, at any given moment, I seemed to be nothing more than a few thoughts. A few poorly articulated questions about my essential nature, hanging in the diffuse nebula of my own awareness.

'Seeing' bothered me too. I've got used to it now, but I can remember learning about the visual system at school and being quite worried about it for some time after. What I perceived as the external world was, in fact, the result of electrochemical activity in my brain (in an area roughly located just above my neck). What I perceived as light, was 'made up' in my head. A sunrise was nothing more than an electrical discharge occurring in the utter darkness of my skull. Again, my response to this consideration was fear. An unnerving sense of ectopia. Of being exposed. Things are not what they seem to be.

I suppose, the fact of the matter is this: I was (and it would be falsely modest of me to say otherwise) an exceptionally thoughtful child. Like Eliot's 'Animula', issued from the hand of God *To a flat world of changing lights and noise*; a little, enquiring soul. And the world, the ordinary world, is a terrifying place for those who choose to ask questions. For those who are prepared to reach out and give the fabric of reality a firm tug, just to see if it can take the strain. It's scary, when you do that as a child and, for a moment, it seems to give.

Of all the things that I scrutinized and questioned, of all the mundane, everyday things that were taken by most for granted and that I felt compelled to query, it was 'the family' that scared me most. Families terrify me. They are unnatural! Not just my family, but all families (although my family would justify many persuasive arguments for the abolition of family life). Whenever I see the members of a family together I always see one of two extremes: families are either overcontrolled or out of control. Mothers, fathers, sisters, brothers are either biting their tongues or giving them licence to kill. Saying nothing (even when speaking) or saying too much (often with silence). Families scare me. They are immoderate. They have no concept of the middle way.

When I was eleven (at about the same time as I discovered Eliot in fact) I read Aldous Huxley's *Brave New World*. It was completely wasted on me. I read it − as it were − backwards. I envied the people of this Brave New World. There was nothing dystopian about Huxley's vision to me. One of its most attractive features was the complete absence of families. I wished that I had been born in the Central London Hatchery. I dearly wished that I had been lifted from a test tube. It seemed so pleasant, clean and uncomplicated. When the citizens of Huxley's Brave New World became embarrassed at the mere mention of words such as 'mother', I knew exactly how they felt. Huxley's irony was lost on me. I, too, felt the word was obscene.

Like 'being' or 'seeing', 'maternity' was one of those taken-for-granted concepts that I couldn't help picking at. I couldn't stop toying with the scab of motherhood until it became loose and fell away, revealing an aspect of reality underneath almost too difficult to reconcile with everyday life.

I remember many interminable evenings, when my mother would occupy her favourite chair and read in front of the gas fire. I would look up from my homework and think, this is entirely ridiculous. I came out of that woman. There she sits, in her Marks and Spencer floral dress, reading her lightweight novel, drinking her milky tea. The picture of propriety. Yet, that same woman had me growing inside her like a parasite (not so long ago). Her muscles contracted and I was forced down the birth canal and out, through her vagina. She would have screamed and yelled with pain. This paragon of lower-middle-class values would have writhed, sweated and burst open, her person reduced to a split bag of mucus, blood and stringy tissue. Unbelievable really, and hardly the best way to start a relationship. Huxley's option seemed to me to be infinitely more civilized. People are not honest about giving birth. They engineer a cover-up. They obscure its brutality with frothy talk and sweet, anodyne words, with nursery colour schemes, romper suits and rattles. Big fluffy animals with huge, shiny glass eyes. People like my mother simply pretend that it never happened.

To be perfectly honest, I have never understood why people like my mother and father bother with children. They seemed (and still seem) so ill-suited to the task of procreation. Yet their fecundity is further evidence of Darwin's doctrine. Even they, with their Battenberg slices and their petit bourgeois conventions could not escape the relentless pressure of natural selection. Their DNA had plans for them, wet, bloody plans which they obeyed like automatons; and afterwards – shocked by the appalling violence of nativity – they continued to position plates in the Welsh dresser as though it had never happened. I can almost hear my mother saying, like she always did when faced with the merest prospect of confrontation, *Best leave it, dear.* Yes, *life* is best left alone.

Families don't work. Genes, from male and female gametes, can be recombined in an almost infinite variety of ways. In real terms, sons and daughters are so different from their parents they might as well be total strangers. Yet we continue to live in family units. Little communities of strangers, sharing the sitting-room sofa and enjoying the ambient flicker of cathode rays. Together.

When my parents recombined their DNA they certainly didn't anticipate Robert, my older brother. Bob was a changeling. Either that, or from an improbably early age he had decided that he was not a member of the family into which he was born. He took part in our daily routine with quiet, detached amusement; however, he was never present, as such. I cannot claim any insight with respect to the workings of his mind, though it would not surprise me to discover that he viewed my parents as a quaint old couple who happened to provide him with regular meals and temporary accommodation. Nothing more. And as for me – well, he barely noticed me.

Occasionally, I would catch my mother and father talking quietly about Bob. Their voices would become subdued and they would stand close together. If I didn't know better, I would say that they looked frightened. Every now and again I would strain to hear them. Bob was an enigma to them, an insoluble problem; however, Bob was never rude. He never misbehaved, as such. There was the inevitable conflict between my parents and Bob when he reached adolescence, but this never amounted to much, largely because my father was never comfortable attempting to discipline Bob. It was as though he were trying to discipline someone else's child. He would give up prematurely and say something ineffectual like, *I think you should talk to your mother about this.* And there, of course, it rested.

When Bob and I were alone he would sometimes take on the appearance of an anthropologist. He would inspect my mother and father's possessions as if he were visiting an alien culture. I can recall, when we were still very young, he once removed my father's tartan-framed photograph of the *Flying Scotsman* from the mantelpiece and held it out to me. 'See anything wrong with that, Tom?' he said.

I didn't know what he meant. I was sitting cross-legged on the floor playing with my Lego bricks. 'No, it's just Dad's favourite train.'

He shook his head and then laughed. 'No,' he replied, 'it's conclusive proof that there's no life before death.'

I was quite perplexed. 'I don't understand,' I said.

'You will,' he replied. Then, narrowing his eyes and looking at me more closely, added, 'But then again, maybe you won't. Did you know that when you sit like that you look like Kafka?'

He left the room laughing his head off. He could barely stand.

A week after taking his A levels – a curious mix of mathematics, art and geography – Bob left home to travel. There were some vague plans that he should return and read geography at Lancaster University, but they came to nothing. The following year we received the odd postcard from America, but he was well and truly gone. Robert was perhaps one of the most compelling examples of the power of genetic recombination I have ever known. I would have liked to have had an older brother. Someone to confide in. Someone who could have given me answers, instead of a smirk and a shrug. I am, at once, a sibling and an only child. Like I said, I am odd.

2

Trent Park

My collection of amusing scientific papers is complemented by a modest hoard of obsolete laboratory equipment. To the uninitiated observer it might well appear that I simply store junk in a suitcase under the bed. Metal discs, lengths of flex attached to wooden boxes, and glass capsules encasing tiny networks of wire. It is a kind of grotesque, overblown parody of the electronic and chemistry sets of my youth. I have once or twice considered finding a poster-sized print of a super-geek – with flabby lips and podgy hands – that I could paste on to the suitcase lid, and then the illusion would be complete.

Although I do not like to admit it (even to myself) I am very fond of my little hoard. You see, each piece speaks volumes about the intellectual climate of its day. Moreover, each piece, now abandoned and obsolete, might have played some small part in a historic scientific experiment. Who can say? My grooved copper disc – or my eighteen-inch length of red rubber tubing for that matter – may have begun its odyssey in a distinguished laboratory, Faraday's perhaps. The great man might have cast it aside at the end of a long and productive day. A technician would have tidied up after Faraday's departure and he might then have placed the small metal disc in the general store cupboard. There, in the darkness, it may have succumbed to years of neglect, until stolen by an impoverished student. Eventually, after generations of ownership and a capricious journey taking it through many lofts and suburban attics, it would have come to rest on a table, in a jumble sale in East Finchley (priced at twenty pence). Thereafter, it became mine, but only on a temporary basis. It will no doubt continue its odyssey long after my demise.

As soon as I have anything more than a derisory income, I will go to the scientific antiquities shop in Covent Garden and buy myself an object that I can truly cherish. An object that evokes the spirit of H. G. Wells and Jules Verne. Preferably a machine of some kind. It won't matter if it doesn't work; indeed, its impotent cogs and gears will then be imbued with a certain melancholy.

More important will be its late-nineteenth-century aesthetic. It must be made of wood that can be burnished to reveal a rich, satisfying grain. It must be made of brass that will catch the light and transform it into a flash of gold, as though it has captured the last rays of a *fin de siècle* sunset. It must be made of leather. Green, or red, deeply creased and fading.

You need an eye and a brain to appreciate this kind of beauty. An eye that most people don't have. I can remember showing my collection to Anna and her initial dismay. I can remember sharing my fantasy of purchasing a genuine scientific antiquity with her and being disappointed by her lack of enthusiasm. I felt quite hurt.

'You're like the Pre-Raphaelites,' I said, unable to contain my disgruntlement.

'What?'

'You're like the Pre-Raphaelites, with their towers, goblins and ghosts.'

'So, what's wrong with that?'

'They slept through the most dramatic and important scientific changes the world has ever seen.' Even as I said these words I was filled with self-disgust. I sounded like a precocious child, addressing the local Conservative party on an issue beyond my understanding (like race relations or housing). Nevertheless, I had started and I just couldn't stop myself. 'Instead of addressing these changes in their art, they simply avoided them. Ran away. Went to Never-Never land.'

'I quite like the Pre-Raphaelites.'

32

'Yes, but their work is all so meaningless.'

I was determined to make myself look terminally pompous. I took a book from the shelf and showed Anna a picture of the Papplewick Pumping Station.

'Can't you see how beautiful this is?' I asked.

Her brow furrowed. 'It looks like a factory.'

'Yes, but look at it. Look at the pump. The men who built that really knew what was going on. They knew that the world was changing, and they were celebrating it. They could see beauty in mechanization – wheels, pistons, well-oiled moving parts. They didn't run away from it, they embraced it. If it had been up to the Pre-Raphaelites to take us into the twentieth century, well . . .' I shook my head, as though ranks of Pre-Raphaelite artists were standing in front of me, shamed by my technocratic homily. In fact, I was thinking, *You sound like a wanker*, and shaking my head at this.

'I see what you mean,' said Anna. *Yes*, I thought *I bet you do.* I let the subject drop, more for my sake than for Anna's.

Later that same afternoon we drove the Skoda out to Trent Park. It was a warm day, but quite cloudy. Only a few people were around. Trent Park always strikes me as a rather odd place, the stately home – now part of a college – and the rather run-down, shabby grounds. It is as though a landscape gardener got started but simply abandoned the project half-way through. Suddenly startled by the imperfection of his vision and feeling betrayed by his muse, he must have walked away, leaving a motley group of mythic and classical figures gesticulating without purpose. Like the inmates of an open-plan asylum.

Nevertheless, for those who live in the northern reaches of the metropolis, Trent Park can be a convenient retreat. A place where one can go to escape the smell of diesel and the shrill chorus of faulty braking systems.

In order to enhance the rural illusion Anna and I left the public footpath and strayed into an area of farmland. To gain access to the farmland we had to step over a wire fence that was clearly intended to exclude the public. This was not the sort of thing I would have done before meeting Anna. I still felt apprehensive, expecting all the time to hear a shout followed by a gunshot.

We walked behind a large line of trees for a while, before crossing a field. It was quiet and empty. No sound, but for the birdsong. In front of us was an expanse of neglected wheat. The stalks had grown so high that many had begun to fold under their own weight. They were a little off-colour. Slightly jaundiced. We cut across, without saying anything to each other.

When we reached the centre Anna stopped and lay down.

'What are you doing?' I asked.

She smiled. 'Kneel down beside me.'

I did so, obediently, not really understanding what was happening. She lifted her jumper up, revealing her breasts. She didn't need to wear a bra. She guided my hand on to her stomach and up to her chest. I began to breathe quickly. I felt nervous, but excited. I bent down and began to kiss the taut flesh of her stomach. Anna began to writhe and wriggle.

'Stop,' she whispered and then sat up. She began to take off her jumper.

'Hang on,' I hissed, pulling her arms back down again. (Why we were both whispering, God only knows.) 'You can't, not here.'

'Why not?'

'We might . . .'

'Get caught?'

'Maybe.'

'No we won't.'

She crossed her arms, grabbed the bottom of her jumper and T-shirt, lifted them over her head and lay down again. She then undid the buttons of her jeans and wriggled them down to her ankles. Her body was very white. Like a cadaver. She opened her thin, bloodless legs and exposed her moist, ragged gash. It was somehow unfamiliar. More vivid. Like a wound. Nevertheless, I could smell her familiar fragrance. I lowered my head and licked her genitals like a dog.

34

She was positively fluvial. Oozing and discharging. As though some biological sluice gate had opened, allowing her to spill and pour. I snuffled and snorted, inhaling her residue. My face was emulsified. Gummy and glazed. She moved her bony hips vigorously and began to moan a little. She then rolled over on to her stomach.

She looked back at me, over her shoulder. Her face was red and her expression frantic. She was sweating, and her hair was stuck to her cheek; a strand or two had become caught in her mouth. 'Tom . . .'

I knew what she wanted, but was uncomfortable with the idea.

'No, not here.'

'Why not?'

There was an urgency in her voice that I had never heard before. She was suddenly unfamiliar.

'Because we might get caught.'

'We won't!'

'But we might! I don't want to risk it.'

'Tom.' She turned my name into an ululation that communicated her desperate need. A whining obsecration.

'No, not here.'

'We won't get caught.'

'How do you know?'

'Please.'

'No.'

'We can do it really quick.'

'No!'

She looked suddenly deflated. She lowered her head to the ground, the tension in her hips was released, and she let out a long, defeated sigh. 'OK.'

She pulled her jeans up and then recovered her T-shirt and jumper. She struggled with them for a moment (as they were inside out). Her movements were quick and impatient. I didn't know what to say; it was clear that I had made a serious blunder.

Anna was extremely moody for the rest of the day. I thought this incredibly unreasonable. We made our way back to the public footpath

35

and held a civil but frosty conversation until we arrived back at the car. I held Anna's hand but it was lifeless. It did not respond to my touch.

When we got home I tried to make amends. I guided her to the bedroom and took off her clothes. She began to respond but it was all rather half-hearted. When I ejaculated it felt like I was leaking a drop or two of semen into the condom rather than filling Anna. The spunk seemed to travel up my urethra like mercury in a thermometer. My penis shrunk immediately and I had to quickly withdraw (just in case the condom came off, releasing its meagre but potentially fertile contents into Anna's body). I felt really bad.

It was getting dark outside. We hadn't switched the lamp on and the room filled with shadows. I looked at Anna. Her eyes were closed and her breathing shallow. It suddenly occurred to me that I didn't know her at all. The image of her half-turned face, looking back at me, became vivid in my mind. That frantic, eager, pleading expression. There was something ruttish about it. A breathless, craving impatience. Like hunger. Tormented.

This was Anna. My Anna. The very same woman. Sweet, retiring and studious Anna. The same woman who sat at her old Amstrad next to a pile of journals and textbooks. The same woman who played Bach on the cello. I thought of her, carefully bowing the strings, and the sonorous voice of her instrument filling the room; but the position of the instrument between her thighs began to evoke uncomfortable mental resonances. I shut the image out of my mind with the force of a slammed door. If I slept at all before daybreak I was unaware of it.

I remember, the untimely and tragic death of Diana, Princess of Wales, put Dave into the blackest of moods. He, at such times, was perhaps at his most compelling. We took our places in a rather subdued Nightingale. The television was on and the increasingly familiar images of 'floral tributes' banked high outside Kensington and Buckingham palaces hung suspended in the pallid gloom. The country had apparently had the marrow sucked from its bone. The earth and sky had been leached of colour and vitality. The nation was spent. The nation was in mourning.

To allow the people of England to give vent to their grief, books of condolence had been strategically placed at various royal and civic foci; like singularities, they sucked at the threads of melancholy permeating the atmosphere, and held them in check. Thus the nation was saved from a surplus of dolour and misery that threatened to overwhelm and paralyse the populace. Dave looked up at the screen and peered at the broadcast of a seemingly endless queue. The old, the young, black and white, united in mourning. United in their near-obsessional commitment to release their pent-up grief in valedictory words and actions. Dave's expression had become anguished. He could hold back no longer.

'What the fuck is a book of condolence anyway? What does it mean, to condole?'

'Not so loud, Dave,' I said, with genuine concern.

Although the Nightingale was almost empty, a large man by the bar turned on hearing the word 'fuck' and looked at us with disapproval. It had become unpatriotic to swear, particularly in venues frequented by the lower orders. In fact, it had become unpatriotic to do virtually anything but voice disbelief and sorrow or, alternatively, to wear an expression that betokened the deepest and most profound contemplative state. To smile in certain quarters was as good as asking for a fight.

I tried to pacify Dave with an answer.

'I think it means to give sympathy.'

'Books of condolence,' he returned. 'Another bloody media catchphrase. God, I never thought the British public was so suggestible.'

'It is worrying,' I agreed, hoping that Dave would contain his ire.

'Have you been listening to the coverage much?'

'Well, it's a bit difficult to avoid, isn't it?'

'The crap they're talking. It's amazing. They've had people on

37

the box saying that people lived longer when she visited hospitals. That she somehow knew when photographers wanted a particular shot and would turn to give them just what they wanted. There was even some jerk saying that a shooting star had been seen over Kensington Palace . . . and, it was a sign. A sign, for Christ's sake! A sign of what?'

Again, the large man turned, and this time his gaze lingered. I wondered whether he was warming to the idea of demonstrating his fidelity to the late Princess (and all that she stood for) by punching our faces into a bloody and unrecognizable pulp.

'Not so loud,' I hissed. 'Look, Dave, people are really upset by all this. I know it's irrational, but they are.'

Dave acquiesced with a terse grunt. I looked back toward the bar. The large man was staring again at the television. Transfixed. To this day, I could swear that I discerned the track of a tear glistening down his expansive and stubbled cheek.

'Well, I can't take much more of it,' Dave went on, although thankfully in a lower and softer register. 'If this carries on I'm going to have to leave the country for a while.' He paused. 'I'll go to Ostend,' he added mysteriously. 'That should do it.'

I didn't question him about his chosen destination. It would have spoilt the effect.

I let Dave simmer on a low flame for a moment before volunteering my own, more considered opinion.

'It's all very interesting, though. From a sociocultural perspective.'

'Interesting?'

'It's an opportunity to see hagiography-in-action. Gradually, a version of her life is becoming settled in the popular imagination. She is slowly accruing supernatural attributes . . . it's all very interesting. In a few weeks she will be, in all but title, a saint.'

Dave paused to review his position. After a few moments, he said, 'You're quite right, you know, it is interesting.'

I was glad that I had diverted his chagrin. I could see that he was thinking.

'One day,' he began, 'I suspect there will be Spencerians. A sort of religious sect who model themselves on the life and works of Diana Spencer. They will be distinguished from other sects by their curious fondness for high fashion and luxury. Indeed, they will be famed for their unprecedented marriage of haute couture with compassion for the very needy.' He took a sip of his drink, and continued, 'Some critics will, of course, object to this and call it hypocrisy. But the Spencerians will know better. Diana's life would represent, in their eyes, a kind of paradox. To comprehend its incompatibilities one must achieve an elevated level of consciousness. To understand how wanton profligacy and mercy can be reconciled will be to hear the sound of one hand clapping. That will be the whole point. That will be the fundamental spiritual challenge. To make sense of her life, you see, will require such an abrogation of intellect that one will become enlightened immediately.'

Dave's despondency had found its theme. He was well and truly off.

'The average Spencerian will attempt to live a life in which there is a seamless fusion connecting ostensibly antithetical concerns, for example, manicure and global starvation. Diana's eating disorder will be perceived as a contemporary 'impro' on the old spiritual riff of fasting. Yes, she had the good life, but like any of the great spiritual teachers, she could mortify the flesh with the best of them.'

Dave had now lightened up considerably. He even smirked once or twice.

' . . . and, let me tell you, Tom. Let me tell you now. She will come again. And, unlike any messiah before her, she will come again as many. She will cometh as an legion. For, at the moment of death, no one saw the critical event. No one saw the surgeon surreptitiously placing a small tissue sample into a cryogenic canister. It will be passed, from generation to generation, like a beacon of hope. And then, when the world needs her most, she shall return, in great numbers. Unlike Jesus and these other two-bit charlatans, she will be back. Thirty-six clones, for each of her years on earth, each matured for thirty-six years. Each inculcated in the innermost sanctum of the fabulously wealthy Spencerian sect . . .'

Pleased with his creative flight of ideas, he rewarded himself with a long draught of lager. His Adam's apple bobbed up and down as he emptied his pint. He placed the glass on the table and then reached for his Scotch. 'You know something, Tom?'

'What?'

'It could happen, couldn't it?'

'Have you been drinking? This afternoon, I mean?'

'Piss off, I'm sober.' Dave never took too kindly to being told he was drunk. Even after falling into the kerbside he would claim to be undertaking an informal study of road maintenance standards. He would usually get up, brush himself down and say something like 'Not bad. Not bad at all for Haringey Council. They must be using a different aggregate mixture.'

Dave knocked his Scotch back in one, presumably to make a point, before continuing. 'No, I mean it. I'm serious. It could happen, couldn't it?'

'Well, technically, yes.'

Dave's expression changed from glee to depression. He was as unstable as an isotope. 'I'm not sure I want to live in a world where that could happen.'

'You do, Dave. And it's largely the likes of you who are responsible for it.'

'Don't knock my discipline, Tom, please, not now.'

He affected an expression of pantomime sadness and sunk his head toward his glass.

'You know, it's going to be great in the future, isn't it?' he suddenly expostulated.

'In what way? In what way will the future be great?'

'In a genetic engineering kind of way.'

'What, with all those Dianas?'

'No, that would be serious shit. I was thinking on a more practical level, here. A more important level really. I was thinking future-sex.'

'What *are* you talking about?'

'Well, the possibilities are unlimited, aren't they? Picture, if you will, the year 3098.' He stopped. 'Well, are you?'

'Yes, I think I have it.'

'Gernsback or Dick?'

'I think by that time we will have passed through Dick. More Gernsback.'

'OK, Gernsback it is. There he is, then, our man in the chrome tower. He's got the horn and he feels ready for *lerve*. His wife is sadly absent. She's pissed off. Gone to talk to her therapist, a telepathic artificially engineered dolphin in the next block called Spiteful and our man is frustrated. Virtual reality is a bit of a bore by this time, so there's no fucking about with VR visors or jacks.'

'Bit of a bore! You wouldn't say that if you'd *actually seen* any of the *Virtual London* sub-routines! Some of them are . . . very creative.'

'Yeah, yeah, yeah,' said Dave, exercising his dismissal reflex, 'I'm sure it's all good stuff and I respect your opinion, Tom, I really do. But – and it's a very big but – there is no substitute for the *real thing*. So, if you can make your virtual fantasies *real*, then that's got to be the dog's bollocks. Right?'

'Well . . .' I whined, somewhat uncertain about this point, and recollecting some of the more 'abstract' pleasures I had enjoyed while wearing a VR visor; however, Dave was eager to continue.

'Right?' He gave his demand extra emphasis by raising both palms and jutting his head forward. The gesture was a curious combination of aggression and entreaty.

'I suppose so.' I decided it would be better if I simply agreed.

'It's just gotta be true. If you've got the technology to make your fantasies real, then it's just got to be preferable to participate, rather than simulate. Right?'

I just nodded.

'So, there he is, Mr Gernsback, way up there in the chrome tower, nursing a mighty horn. A horn that throbs, showing a clearly perceptible second-by-second expansion and contraction of the helmet. This guy needs flesh, and lots of it. So, he lifts the equivalent of a remote from his bedside cabinet and points it at the wall. A panel soundlessly slides across to reveal a collection of purpose-built female biomorphs. There's a line of about ten. Their nervous systems are intact but they have no cortex. However, they each have a chip implanted in the brain stem which activates an interactive affective-motor programme called Orgiaste. Our man presses the button, and out they trot . . . He drops a pill called Stamina, which kills the sexual satiation centres in his brain. Each of the biomorphs is . . .' Dave stopped for a moment to recover data from his memory banks that would further enliven his juvenile Utopia; however, I cut in before it made his consciousness.

'Made in the image of famous women from history?'

'Hey, why not? What a collection. Marilyn, Cleopatra . . .'

'And you know who?'

'Well, why not. Even her. It was never her body I objected to. Life will be so good, courtesy of my glorious discipline. Tomorrow belongs to me, mate.' He stopped, and stared at his empty glasses. He then turned them over. Residues trickled down the inside surfaces toward the table top. 'I think they're empty,' he said.

'Would you like a drink Dave?'

'Well, now that you're asking, that seems quite a good idea.'

I stood up and pulled a solitary five-pound note from my pocket. I was about to go to the bar but, before leaving, something made me ask him a question.

'Do you think of sex all of the time, Dave?'

'More or less. Do you think I have a problem?'

'No. But it might become a problem, one day.'

Dave did not reply. My statement failed to resonate in the air. There was no sense of implication, as I had hoped. Dave was looking up at the television again, his animated expression reverting slowly back to one of horror and disgust like a wax mask, features melting in the gentle electric glow.

★

I used to enjoy making Anna happy. It wasn't that difficult, actually. Although, on reflection, I wonder if I was simply trying to buy her affection. No, that's wrong. I didn't need to buy her affection. She could be very affectionate (when so inclined). There was never any reluctance on her part to touch, or hold. Squeeze or stroke. She was always ready to give in that way. What I was seeking to purchase was commitment. Loyalty. What I wanted to secure was her fidelity.

It had taken me so long to find someone, someone to love (and have sex with), that the idea of losing her was almost intolerable. I could see myself, revisiting the hopeless condition of my youth. Lying on my bed, trousers around my ankles, discharging pointlessly into tissue after tissue (and no matter how many tissues went into the wicker basket, in the end, I was always left unsatisfied). Trying to summon the courage to start a conversation with this woman or that woman while others took advantage of my procrastination and incompetence. The living nightmare that was Cambridge! The loneliness, the emptiness . . . No, I resolved that all this should never happen again. Never!

It may seem implausible, but at heart I am a very romantic individual. I am merely incapable of expressing it. My life has been uniquely devoid of good role models when it comes to the expression of feelings. The passion was always there, I see that now, but I never got the hang of channelling it. I was often worried by the idea that I might have stockpiled my feelings, that I was perhaps seated on a powder keg of repressed emotion, and that one day it would be inadvertently exposed to a naked flame. Oh well, *Out of the mouths*, as the saying goes.

Words like 'I love you' do not come easily to me. I wonder what they mean. I wonder what I mean, by saying them. Moreover, it is difficult to be romantic when you don't look romantic. It has about it a sense of wrongness. Like overweight women who wear crop tops, or the use of blue eye-shadow or, for that matter, tartan picture frames. It just doesn't seem right. If you don't look right, you feel like an actor in the wrong part. As though you're a slapstick comic playing Hamlet.

I could not declare my undying love. Yet it was necessary to show Anna that I cared a great deal about her presence in my life. Subsequently, I took to buying her things.

Anna was very appreciative. It has to be said. She was always remarkably grateful. I imagine that this was because her childhood was associated with considerable financial hardship. Such circumstances make a lasting impression, I believe.

I remember my first significant purchase very well. We were walking down Hampstead High Street, browsing. We had visited the bookshops and were walking down the hill toward Belsize Park. Anna was quite taken by a dark-blue jumper that she had seen in Monsoon. It was nothing special; in fact, I thought it a rather dull article of clothing. Nevertheless, she caressed the material with longing in her eyes. When she turned the price tag, she was crestfallen.

'Look at the price!' she said, defeated.

I agreed that it looked nice, but let Anna tear herself away without compunction, seemingly ignorant of the strength of her desire for possession. We walked down the road, and after a while I said something like 'Oh, no, I don't think I put enough money in the meter. Carry on, I'll just run back.'

She gawped at me as though I were insane.

When I returned, Anna was standing in exactly the same place. I handed her the Monsoon bag, saying, 'There.'

Not, *Because I love you* or *Because I adore you* or *Because you mean everything to me*, but 'There'. Like I was passing the salt.

Anna took the bag and peeked into it. 'What have you done, Tom?'

I didn't reply. I just waited while she poked a hole in the wrapping to reveal the dark-blue wool inside.

'Oh, Tom, you shouldn't have. It cost a fortune!'

'Well . . .' I replied. Not really knowing how to follow it up.

'You shouldn't have. It was ninety pounds, for Christ's sake! Where did you get the . . .'

She seemed totally overwhelmed. It was quite a pleasant feeling, watching her struggle to express her gratitude. In the end she abandoned language altogether and kissed me, hard, on the cheek. She was delighted, though embarrassed by my generosity.

Later, when we were sitting in McDonald's, enjoying a scalding-hot coffee, Anna said, 'Tom, look. I really appreciate this, but it was really too much. You just haven't got this sort of money to . . .'

'Burn?'

'No. That makes me sound ungrateful, and I am. Really grateful. It was so kind of you. But, it's too much.'

'Not really. I had some spare cash.'

'You're a Ph.D. student. What are you talking about, spare cash?'

'I did. I had some spare.'

She looked at me and pulled an *Oh yeah, like hell* face. It amused me to think that she was certain I was lying. I did have some spare cash on me that day. Quite a bit in fact. Unfortunately, I hadn't thought of an appropriate way of explaining to Anna how I had acquired it. Anna had certain feminist pretensions. I wasn't sure how much I wanted to tell her. Besides, I didn't want to spoil the atmosphere.

3

Inborn Errors of Metabolism

Science is a curious pursuit. For the professional, it is not a subject, but a forest of assassins. A life's work can be rendered insignificant by a single publication. When Wagner broke from writing the Ring (so that he could divert himself with *Tristan* and *Die Meistersinger*) he did so secure in the knowledge that no one was going to take advantage of his hiatus. No one was going to sneak out of the woodwork and complete the Ring cycle before him; however, while Rosalind Franklin continued her steady and systematic enquiries into the structure of DNA, Watson and Crick grabbed the double helix from under her nose like a couple of street thieves. And what of Oswald Avery now? Who discovered DNA in 1944 but didn't realize why it was important!

Science loves to mess with the scales of justice. She (for it can only be a she) is always rigging the balance. Copernicus was not the first to displace the earth from the centre of the universe. Wallace has as legitimate a claim on the theory of evolution as Darwin. Islamic doctors knew about the circulation of the blood four hundred years before Harvey. Science always hands the prize to the man who came in second or fifth. It must amuse her. Science is nothing if not treacherous and unfair. It is not a career for the faint-hearted.

I wonder at the ignorance of those who talk of academics escaping into their ivory towers. Only someone who had the very slightest knowledge of the university system would be capable of such an idiotic misconstruction of scholarly life. When I hear those who work in the *real world* (by which is usually meant the worlds of

46

commerce and law) making disparaging remarks about the leisurely life of academics, it makes me shake my head in disbelief. I pity them, these poor, deluded fools. I pity them because, one fine day, they may decide to give up the cut-throat world of the City, and choose instead, the 'easy' option of academia. What a surprise awaits them. When I hear these men of the world describing the scholar's life, they do so with reference to another time, another age. Quiet, gentlemanly pursuits. Dreaming spires and punts lazily coasting on the Cam. Young men, gathered in the quad, exchanging invitations to dinner: *Please, do come, Monty, I would enjoy nothing more, this evening, than a decanter of port, a plate of medlars, and your fine company.* Absent-minded dons, regaling their bookish wards with Byron over tea and hot buttered crumpets. Unfortunately, the academic world is no longer like this. Indeed, I doubt that it ever was.

The groves of academe are lined with landmines. There is blood, there is gore, there is carnage. The average successful academic is a creature driven by mysterious forces, an almost primal lust for knowledge and celebrity among equals. So strong is this lust that no cost is considered too great, providing this dual trophy is attained.

The ruthlessness that allegedly characterizes those who work in the City is not beyond our understanding. It is, after all, rational. Stabbing your best friend in the back makes a certain amount of sense if it means that you can retire to a life of unimaginable luxury the following week. The academic, however, surpasses all understanding. The academic will, indeed, stab his best friend in the back, and then stop to grind his head into the earth, to meet his ends: an almost insulting salary and a pre-eminent position among a group of people so small they could barely fill a department-store lift.

To survive in academia requires the tact of a diplomat, the skills of an assassin and, so I am told, the ablation of any brain centres that are helpful when buying fashionable clothes. I have often discussed the dreadful state of academic life with Dave. The sniping, the backbiting, the plotting and the sabotage. Dave is of the opinion that,

47

compared to the average university lecturer, most City traders are, and I quote, 'Soft as shit.' I think he is right.

Rumour has it that Béla once killed a man. A colleague. When I first heard this rumour, I imagined that, if it were true, it must have happened back in Hungary. I fancied some web of intrigue, involving politically subversive activities and a struggle against the secret police. Samizdat publications and betrayal. I pictured Béla, caught on the horns of some diabolical moral dilemma. Béla, presented with a choice. To kill his errant colleague – a one-time intimate perhaps – or expose the resistance movement to the wrath of the authorities. When I found out the truth, I could hardly believe it, so discrepant was it with my fantasy.

The killing was not a direct killing. Nevertheless, a killing it was. It did not take place in Hungary, in Béla's youth, but in Edinburgh, about ten years ago. The unfortunate victim was Janos Zajos, originally one of Béla's tutors in Budapest. I don't think Béla ever liked Zajos. Béla always recognized that he was the older man's intellectual superior and bitterly resented being cast in the student role. Many of Béla's first papers are jointly authored with Zajos, even though, according to Béla, Zajos could hardly understand most of them. Béla had hoped that the old man would gracefully 'step down', as it were, and encourage his young protégé to publish the papers as the work of a single author. This wasn't to be. Indeed, Zajos insisted that, as he was the senior party, he should not only be joint author, but first author. Béla was mortified. When Béla protested, Zajos suggested, in no uncertain terms, that Béla was placing his future at the university in jeopardy. Needless to say, Béla conceded. He remained, however, an enemy for life.

For many years, Zajos continued to dominate mathematics in Hungary. He became something of a national hero and received numerous tokens of professional acclaim. I suspect that he made it more or less impossible for any rising academic to challenge his position. Indeed, it may even be the case that Béla left Hungary because of Zajos.

The two men never spoke to each other. However, after many, many years, their paths crossed. It transpired that Zajos was to address an international conference in Edinburgh. He was to take part in a symposium on Attractors. Béla was in the chair. Had Béla known that Zajos was to be invited I am sure he would have declined the honour. By the time he found out it was too late. When the old man arrived, Béla welcomed him like a long-lost relative. He kissed him and hugged him and made him feel that all was forgiven. The world had changed, and so had their relationship. As the delegates gathered in the lecture hall, Béla helped the old man prepare for his talk. He fixed a cordless radio microphone to Zajos's lapel. I understand that at that time these were quite new; Zajos had never seen one before and marvelled at its compactness. The two colleagues then reminisced about old times, and their mutual acquaintances. Mathematicians such as Grzyzgy, Keszseggel, and Csodalatos.

Soon, the hall was near capacity.

'Béla,' said the old man, 'do I have time to visit the toilet?'

'Of course,' said Béla, who escorted him out of the door and pointed him in the direction of the gents.

When Béla returned to the hall, he signalled to the audio desk that the sound system should be switched on. At first, nobody recognized the sound that filled the auditorium. A clanking sound. It was, in fact, the sound made by a belt buckle hitting a tiled floor after a three-foot drop. There then followed a hissing, bubbling noise, which the assembly immediately recognized as a jet of urine hitting a porcelain toilet bowl at high speed.

The man on the audio desk looked to the chair for guidance. Béla merely smiled.

The earth-shattering expulsion of flatus that followed was so shocking that the hall was plunged into deathly silence. Apparently, it was explosive, and arrested all conversation. There then followed a soliloquy in Hungarian, punctuated by flatulence that sounded like the crumping of erratic and distant ordnance. For those who spoke Hungarian, Zajos was apparently saying, 'Dear God . . . dear God

. . . Where is all this coming from? Dear God . . . dear God.' And so on. Never had the divinity been called upon to explain such a mundane phenomenon.

Béla made extravagant gestures at the man on the audio desk, miming that he should cut the broadcast immediately and making sure that everyone noticed that he was pointing in the direction of the gents outside. The sound system cut about a second after the toilet chain had been pulled.

Zajos took his place at the lectern. A legendary figure, whose mere presence could command the respect of the world's finest minds. A patriarch. He scanned the auditorium, before beginning, 'My dear colleagues' – he paused, then looking at Béla added – 'and dear friends, it is a great honour to be here today.'

The assembly could not suppress its mirth. Shoulders were shaking violently and one or two members of the audience had to rush from the hall. As the doors closed behind them, their laughter could be heard, echoing down the empty corridor.

The old man was completely bemused: 'What is this? This laughing?' No one from the audience volunteered an explanation. Although Zajos attempted to deliver the rest of his talk, it was an impossibility. The final straw was when one of the more disciplined members of the audience attempted to suppress his laughter by holding his breath. Unfortunately, he was asthmatic, turned from red, to blue, lost consciousness, and then fell from his seat and down the central aisle.

Béla removed the radio microphone from Zajos's lapel and quietly explained the cause of the audience's amusement. Zajos, a proud and distinguished man, was devastated. Two days later, he committed suicide. He was mourned by a young wife and two children in their teens.

To my knowledge, there is only one bound copy of the *Proceedings* of the Cavendish Society. Remarkably, the British Library does not have a copy. Given the history of science is replete with miscarriages of justice, I suppose I should not have been so amazed that a paper such as Locke's should have been completely overlooked. Some of the greatest discoveries of all time had, as we now know, been neglected for centuries; however, it is difficult to explain why Locke himself failed to promote his work after the dissolution of the Cavendish Society. Moreover, it is even harder to explain why his discovery did not merit greater public interest. One can only assume that the internal political squabbles of the Cavendish Society took a sinister political turn.

Anna was attending a British Psychological Society conference at the Institute of Education when I finally decided to have a serious look at Locke's paper. I was eager for entertainment. Béla had, that day, subjected my latest piece of work to an excoriating critique which had left my head humming and produced a gentle but tenacious ache behind my eyes.

Locke's style, as is almost always the case with nineteenth-century science-writing, was absurd and ponderous. AA referred to himself by name in his introduction, which heightened the paper's comic effect. For example, '*Soon after this, Locke contrived, by means which modesty necessitates omission, to transfer himself to London*' or '*Oh, how Locke was troubled by the momentous import of this sudden revelation,*' and so on. I smiled and chuckled my way through the introduction before coming to the substance of his paper; however, as I read on into the body of his text, it seemed to me that the ideas he was articulating began to make sense. Scientific sense. I began to follow his reasoning and, as I did so, my heart began to beat faster. I can remember suddenly getting up and pacing around the room in a state of considerable agitation.

The 'plate preparation' employed the earliest method espoused by Daguerre. This involved placing a sheet of silver-plated copper over a box containing iodine. The iodine fumes react with the silver and form light-sensitive silver iodide. When exposed to light, the silver oxide is reduced to silver in proportion to the intensity. The exposed plate can be placed over a box containing heated mercury, which produces fumes that amalgamate with the silver, so that the image becomes visible. Washing the plate in a strong salt solution renders the exposed silver iodide insensitive to further light. This all made perfectly good sense; however, the next section produced in me a terrible, dreadful sense of excitement. It mounted with every line I read. As I turned the page, I saw before me the most extraordinary set of equations. Their elegance made me gasp. The sensation was not unlike hearing a beautiful chord change or suddenly noticing a particularly rich red in a painting by Caravaggio. Something inside me, deep inside me, responded.

Making use of knowledge little more advanced than Tesla's, Locke demonstrated how to create a temporal anomaly. It was as though an engineer equipped with nothing more than steam technology had designed a calculating engine that compared very favourably with a contemporary IBM laptop.

I really didn't know what to do. For a moment my vision blurred and I became quite dizzy. I sat down and tried to do some deep-breathing exercises; this didn't really work. I had once heard that breathing into a brown paper bag could stop hyperventilation, so I sought one out in a kitchen drawer. The bag expanded and contracted like a deformed external lung and eventually I became less agitated. It was probably the rhythm of expansion and contraction that had a calming effect rather than any change in my blood chemistry. I put the bag down, folded it up into a small square and began to laugh.

I picked up Locke's paper again and went to the bedroom in order to lie down. The equations were still the same. My first impressions were entirely accurate. This was a remarkable find. What would I do with it? Would I become Locke's champion and write the definitive biography and introduction to his work? Would I sell the equations to the highest bidder? Would I recognize Locke at all? It would, of course, be easy to destroy the Cavendish *Proceedings*. No one would know. I closed my eyes and imagined my face on the cover of *Time* magazine. A pair of fashionable glasses and a seriously trendy haircut. A leaner, healthier version of myself. A world exclusive: 'Interview with a Time Lord'.

I shook the headline from my mind and concentrated on bringing myself back to the present. Of course, it would be foolish to make any claims for Locke's apparatus before testing it. I would build his machine. I would conduct the necessary experiment.

When Anna came back, I said nothing about my discovery. Instead, we sat, discussing the symposium she had attended. Unfortunately, I was not able to give her my full attention – for obvious reasons. I think she became a little irritated with my failure to engage fully in the conversation.

'I'm going to bed,' she said, finally bringing our rather unsatisfactory conversation to a close.

'OK.'

She walked to the door, then paused for a moment.

'Are you coming?'

'No, not just yet. I've got a few things to do first.'

'Must you work now? You had a late night yesterday too.'

'I did, but . . .'

'Come to bed, Tom.'

'In a minute.'

I felt slightly pressured. Harassed. Anna went on. 'You said the same thing yesterday and you didn't come to bed till God knows when.'

'Look' – for some reason I found myself hot and unsettled – 'I'll come to bed in a minute, all right?' I may have even raised my voice.

'OK. But don't be too long.'

When Anna left I felt strangely relieved. What I really wanted to do at that point was scrutinize the Locke equations (which of course I did with enormous enthusiasm). They seemed even more magical when I looked at them again. I seemed to get drawn into them. A curious, vertiginous sensation, as if I were falling through the very fabric of time and space. Each operation carried me further and further into realms of breathtaking symmetry and beauty. At the same time they demanded the utmost concentration. Pursuing Locke's line of reasoning was very much like walking a tightrope; a momentary lapse of concentration and all would be lost. The sensation was not unlike being slapped round the face. Reality would – as it were – bring you *up short*. It would then be necessary to return to the beginning and start from the very first expression. I don't know how long I spent that night, trying to scale the slopes of Locke's monumental achievement, but I eventually had to stop because of one of my damned headaches. I was not, therefore, too upset when Anna appeared in the doorway, the pleasing shape of her body visible through a diaphanous nightdress, to insist that I should go to bed.

She stretched out her hand, and she led me, like a child, to the bedroom. I took off my clothes and lay beside her, my cheek resting on her tiny breast. The light was already off. She said nothing and gently stroked my throbbing head. It was very soothing. I sucked her gauze-covered nipple into my mouth and continued to draw on it until I lost consciousness.

The next day I met Dave for lunch at King's College. We met on what we called the 'veranda', an al fresco square of concrete attached to one of the dining areas. Dave was in a rather buoyant mood, having just secured a date with one of the MBBS neuroscience students. It really wasn't necessary to be wearing sunglasses (in fact, the sky was quite overcast) but Dave insisted on wearing them. We looked out over the Thames like two grandees.

Opposite, the concrete boxes of the South Bank complex were briefly illuminated by a single burst of sunshine, before being plunged again into penumbral murk.

'How's Anna?'

'OK. Attending the BPS conference.'

'Yeah? Her work going OK?'

'A lot better than mine.'

Dave smirked.

'Still going at it all the time then?'

He took a certain pride in having brought us together; however, recently I had become uncomfortable about these 'man-to-man' discussions. Occasionally, when Dave, Anna and I met up for a drink, I would sit there somewhat troubled by how much Dave knew about Anna's sexuality. He knew about her slightly elongated left labium, he knew that she could only achieve orgasm properly if entered from behind, he knew that her pubic hair had a slight ginger tinge. I can even remember his lewd response to the latter: 'What, a minge with a ginger tinge?'

At the time, it was funny. At the time, it was all part of our *boy talk*, but now it felt inappropriate.

I changed the subject.

'Dave, can you nick some stuff for me, from the lab?'

'What stuff?'

'Some chemicals . . . mercury, iodine, that sort of thing?'

'What the fuck do you want those for?'

'I want to build a replica of Daguerre's original camera.'

'Fair enough . . . do me a list.'

And that's what I did, there and then. Dave thought nothing of it, and why should he? He was already familiar with my interest in scientific antiquities – an interest that he professed to share. I handed him my inventory.

He quickly scanned the items and said, 'One or two might be a bit tricky.'

'If you can't nick some of them, then I'm happy to provide the lab technician with a financial incentive.'

'Oh, well, in that case, there's no problem. He's such a dopehead, a tenner and he's anybody's!'

'Good.' I produced a very modest roll of notes.

Dave was quite used to sudden – although brief – changes in my financial circumstances. Indeed, he had been a beneficiary of my generosity on several occasions as a result. As I handed him two five-pound notes, he said, 'You've been freelancing, have you?'

'Yes.'

'Anything interesting?'

'No, the usual stuff.'

'The *Virtual London* crowd?'

'Yeah.'

'Christ, I wish I could freelance,' he said, with regret.

Although I recognized that Dave would be discreet with Anna, I thought it prudent to ensure that he understood my position.

'Dave?'

'Yes.'

'Anna doesn't know yet. OK?'

'Sure. Why haven't you told her?'

'Well, she's bound to ask questions.'

'So?'

'I don't think she would approve.'

'Well, don't tell her everything then.'

Curiously, I had not considered this option.

'Yeah, you're right. I should tell her. And I don't have to tell the whole truth, do I?'

'No. Be economical?'

Having displayed my cash, I felt obliged to buy the next two rounds. After a few lagers and a soggy tuna sandwich, I left.

The camera was, in fact, the least challenging component of Locke's apparatus. Its assembly would be relatively straightforward. On the other hand, constructing the core device or 'condenser' might prove to be a near-insurmountable challenge. Although some parts of the condenser would be readily available from specialist dealers, others would have to be built from scratch. Fortunately, our garden in Wood Green contained a tiny, rather dilapidated shed which would serve as a workshop. I became quite excited at the prospect. Long hours, welding and fixing. The boy genius roused from his slumber.

That afternoon I spent some time in the DMS Watson library and later made my way to Russell Square. It was a pleasant afternoon and I sat outside the sandwich bar situated in the square itself.

I intended to get the Piccadilly line back home, but first required some refreshment. The Italian proprietor greeted me with a sunny, convivial smile, and soon I was seated at a white metal table, sipping a cappuccino and observing the pigeons.

A vaguely familiar man walked by, making his way toward Senate House. His expression was very intense. I watched him as he sped toward the monolithic nerve centre of the university and became quite fixated on the question of his identity. He was very famous, but I couldn't quite place him. I had had this experience before. It is curious how famous people are difficult to recognize in the flesh. We are so used to seeing them, shrunk and flattened, that their actual size and an additional third dimension confuses the brain.

I heard a voice.

'That's that Richard Dawkins, isn't it?'

I turned, and a rather dishevelled-looking man appeared, in the process of seating himself beside me.

'Yes, I think it is,' I replied, glad that he had resolved my quandary but at the same time none too happy at his presence.

'Clever man, but only one way of seeing things. The truth, you see, is never that simple.'

'Maybe not . . .' I ventured, before burying my head in the current edition of *Nature*. The cover of *Nature* unfortunately carried a picture that caught the gentleman's interest. It was a cosmological montage, including a rather large picture of the moon.

'The moon,' I heard him say. I looked up.

'I beg your pardon?'

'The moon,' he said again, pointing at the cover.

'What about it?'

'They never went, you know, the Americans, NASA. It was all a conspiracy. A political gesture. Nothing more.'

He fixed me with a knowing stare and I was transformed into Coleridge's ill-fated *wedding guest*. He intended to tell me something and nothing was going to stop him. I wanted to get up, but simply couldn't. His face was rather drawn, his complexion yellowish and his hair far too long. I noticed, as he raised a can of Tennent's Super to his lips, that his fingers were filthy.

'You see,' he continued, 'the radiation above the van Allen belt would have killed them. You could only go up there and come back alive if surrounded by six feet of lead. And that, my friend, is simply too heavy to get off the planet. They didn't have the technology then. It just couldn't have been done.'

I couldn't look away. He kept his eyes fixed on mine. They were, unlike the rest of him, remarkably beautiful. Clear, bright blue eyes. He did not blink once.

'And the film. How did that survive? The temperature on the surface of the moon swings from between minus 280°C to above 250°C. They took ordinary film, why didn't it disintegrate? Tell me that, eh?'

'I don't know.'

'Of course you don't. You see, you haven't really thought about this, have you? You might read *Nature*, but you just accept what you're told. It's never that simple. Then, of course, there's the X-rays. Were the cameras protected from X-rays?'

He paused for a moment and looked up at the sky before turning back to hold my attention. While he was looking away I made up my mind to run for it but he had fixed his hypnotic gaze on me again.

'Do you have any pictures of the moon landings, at home, in a book? Do you?'

'Yes, I think I do.'

'Fine. Go home, look at the horizon. Where the horizon should be, there's nothing but shadow. If it was lit by the sun, you should be able to see the horizon. Well, you don't. Why not? I'll tell you why not, because it's not lit by the sun. The pictures are artificially lit. They were done in a studio.'

I really didn't need this. Yet, there was something terribly persuasive about this man's manner. It troubled me.

'Thank you, I'll take a look when I get back.'

'You're not just humouring me, are you?'

'No.'

'Because, to humour someone is to treat them with utter contempt.'

'I'm not humouring you.'

'It is arrogant and unacceptable.'

'I'm sorry.'

'You don't have to apologize. You weren't humouring me. I can see that now.'

'Thank you.'

Again, he looked at the sky, and tilted his head to one side, as though listening very carefully. 'The satellites are up there, of course,' he said. 'There's no doubting that.'

'No.'

At last, he seemed to lose interest and just sat, sipping his drink.

'Well,' I said, 'I must be going.'

He turned to look at me. 'Go on, then,' he said. 'Go home and don't forget to look.'

'Yes,' I said, getting up. My legs were shaking. 'Yes, I'll do that. Thank you.'

I started to walk off.

'Oh, one more thing, Tom.'

I stopped, my blood ran cold.

'If you want to know more, I'm always ready to discuss it with you. I'm here most days – about this time.'

I suddenly felt very angry. He had no right to invade my life in this way.

'How did you know my name?'

He gestured toward a file that I was carrying. My name was written large, in black felt-tip. I felt embarrassed. I had so clearly overreacted. I tried to feign nonchalance.

'I see . . .'

He had seriously rattled me. I walked off, quicker than Richard Dawkins.

★

59

When I got home, I had regained my composure. However, I was immediately unsettled again, by Anna.

'I think someone's taking the piss.'

'What do you mean?'

'There was a message on the answering-machine. Well, I say a message, but it was clearly a piss-take. Some guy singing "It's Not Unusual" and asking you to give him a call!'

'Bastard.'

'Do you know who it is?'

'Probably one of those jerks at Cambridge.'

'Why would they bother to do that?'

'Oh, it's the kind of thing they would do.'

'How immature.'

I wasn't feeling up to levelling with Anna.

'Did you erase the message?'

'Yes, I didn't think it was worth keeping.'

'No, obviously.'

I made a mental note that I should call Tad the following day. It could only be him.

At first, I didn't really understand why Dave and I *hit it off*. We were, without doubt, unusual companions. Dave was so assured, so comfortable in the world, whereas I, of course, have always felt myself to be something of a misfit. Yet, Dave, too, is an oddity. In spite of his confident social persona, there lies beneath it a curious longing. A longing that can (in quieter moments) become sadness. You would have no idea that this sadness was there. Well, not unless you had spent many hours with him, drinking and talking. Listening to his sudden, furious flights of fancy. Listening to his naked truths. Even though I was overwhelmed by Dave, from the very beginning I recognized a certain kinship. A certain 'alikeness' shared by those who tread the perimeter wire of social convention. A certain sympathy, common to those who can't stop prodding reality to see what it's made of.

On reflection, I feel that Dave's sexual exploits were nothing more than escapology. An attempt to lose himself in sensation. He was afflicted with the dissatisfaction and emptiness that all thinking people share. The dissatisfaction of living in a world without so-called 'spiritual values'. A world without point or meaning.

We shared a veneration of science; however, whereas the bald, stark facts of physics and biology were enough for me, Dave always seemed to want more. Even after our most satisfying discussions, Dave would wear an expression that said, *Is that it, then?* There are numerous adages about cynicism and scepticism being the last retreat of those with romantic dispositions (made wholly redundant in the modern world). I suspected that Dave, although he might deny it, would be easily counted among that number. A man so bitterly let down by the senselessness of it all that he could no longer take life seriously. His humour, like my own, depended largely on a recognition of life's absurdity.

Every now and again he would try to squeeze something more from science. Something more than science was prepared to give. I remember, after a particularly trying day for both of us, we met up in the University of London Students' Union bar, by that time a place of some sentimental significance in the history of our relationship. Whenever we visited this venue, Dave would always remind me of our first encounter by saying '*Now don't go picking any fights*' as we went in. It made me laugh every time, he would say it with such an earnest expression. Inevitably, my mirth would be overtaken by embarrassment, and I would feel ashamed that I had laughed yet again at the same joke.

That night, the bar was relatively empty. Surprisingly, the music was not loud. We could hear each other speak with moderately raised voices.

'So. What's it all about then, me old mucker?' said Dave.

He tossed a salted peanut up in the air, opened his mouth wide, purposely neglected to catch the peanut in his mouth, and instead, caught it in his beer glass. It created a small splash.

'You weren't expecting me to do that, were you?' he added.

'No.'

I inspected his glass, and no doubt furrowed my brow.

'Well, don't let a peanut dropping into a glass of beer faze you for Christ's sake. I just asked you a very meaningful question.'

I looked up at Dave.

'You're serious, aren't you?'

'Yes, I am. Tell me, what's it all about?'

'It isn't about anything, is it?' I replied.

'Are you sure?'

'Yes.'

'Absolutely?'

'No. But, very nearly.'

'It all just . . . happened then?'

'Yes.'

Dave looked down at the table, dipped his finger into his beer and drew a system of concentric circles. 'So. What have we got? Big Bang, inflation, us?'

'Yes, that's about it.'

'Nothing before the Big Bang then?'

'Meaningless question. No such thing as "before". No such thing as time before the Big Bang.'

'Can you imagine that? No time?'

'Yes, just about.'

'Fucking mathematician. I can't.'

It was at moments like these that Dave would look at me with – and I hesitate to say this – admiration. Clear, unmistakable, admiration. My ability to deal with *the abstract* impressed him inordinately.

'Mad, isn't it?' Dave continued. 'First there was nothing. Unimaginable nothing. Not even the space for nothing to exist in. Then it happened. The universe. Why then?'

I sighed.

'As I'm sure you realize, that's another stupid question.'

I was about to elaborate when he fixed me with an uncharacteristically incandescent expression. 'Do you ever have doubts, Tom? Do you ever think to yourself, maybe there is more to it?'

'No.'

'You have unshakeable faith in the pointlessness of life, the universe and everything.'

'Yes, I suppose I do. It all just happened. It might not have, but it did.'

'Yeah,' he responded. 'I suppose you're right.'

But you could see the disappointment. You could feel the sense of loss. And, without missing a beat, Dave began scanning the room. 'Not much talent, eh?'

There are some scientists who pretend. They pretend that science *does it* for them. Does it like God can. They will look a camera 'head on' in an interview and say, 'The universe is endlessly fascinating. Why do people want miracles when they are surrounded by miracles?' But, for most people, DNA is not a miracle. It is a self-replicating double helix. Although it is the symbol of life, all it means is that you're going to die. It's hard to put a positive spin on that really.

What made Dave's yearning tolerable to me was knowing that, fundamentally, he knew the truth. He wanted more, but accepted that he wasn't going to get it. This was difficult for him. So difficult, in fact, that the vaginal lubricant on his penis barely had time to dry before it was reinserted into another emollient aperture. Ultimately, Dave could not reject the evidence. He was too good a scientist. It was beyond him. Therefore, I always forgave him. I always forbore his querulous searching for the numinous. Because, in the end, he would have the courage to say, *There's nothing there.*

Religious people, on the other hand, are unforgivable. They have always been, and will always be, the special object of my scorn. They are pedlars of superstition and irrational fear. A raggle-taggle band of Dark Age refugees who, because of some unhappy quirk of history, managed to make it through the age of Enlightenment to blight the modern world. They are, also, unbelievably stupid, to a man (or woman).

I was constantly being bothered by Jehovah's Witnesses in Wood Green. I always considered them a confounded nuisance, until I realized that they had enormous potential as victims in a kind of home-based metaphysical blood sport. I would open the door and, as I did so, I would immediately be subject to a sustained verbal assault. A smartly dressed member of our local coven would make a determined effort to offer me the keys to the gates of heaven. I would listen for a while, allowing him or her to gather momentum. I would then deploy the philosophical tripwire (otherwise known as the logical half-nelson).

The argument usually went something like this.

'Yes, that's all very well. But there are an awful lot of terrible things that happen in the world. Fred West, the sexual abuse of children, people tied to electrified bedframes in South American torture chambers, and use of bad language on the radio, to name but a few. Surely, your god, your loving god, does not permit this? That would be terrible, wouldn't it? If he did?'

'Yes,' would come the reply. 'Yes, it would be terrible. But these things you describe, these are the works of mankind. These are not the works of God.'

'I see,' I would say, adopting an ingenuous expression. 'But tell me, why then does God allow man to do these terrible things?'

'Ah . . .' An exhalation of satisfaction. The Witness would inevitably have the answer to my enquiry well rehearsed. 'This is the truly beautiful thing. God loves us so much, he gives us total freedom. He gives us a choice, to take the path of good or evil. To serve the Lord, or Satan. Even though it gives him much pain to see his children hurting themselves and each other, he understands that love cannot be something that is forced. Love is something that must be chosen.'

I would nod in agreement.

'But isn't God omniscient?'

'Yes.'

'Well, that means he knows everything, right?'

'Of course.'

'Well, doesn't that mean that he also knows exactly what's going to happen?'

'Yes.'

'Then he would also know what choices we were going to make?'

'Err . . .'

'From the very beginning. From the dawn of time, he knew all the choices that we were all going to make.'

'Well, err . . .'

'He would have known the mind of Fred West. He would have known exactly what Fred was going to do. Myra Hindley, the Yorkshire Ripper, he would have known exactly what they were going to choose. He made them that way.'

I would enjoy the sudden shadow of doubt cast across the bland, open features. I would tighten my grip at this point:

'You see, you can't have an omniscient deity and free will. They are mutually exclusive. Explaining the presence of evil as a uniquely human act by invoking choice is senseless if your god is considered omniscient. The argument would only be viable if your god were semi-omniscient, but unfortunately, omniscience and omnipotence seem to be key, indeed, defining features of your god.'

At this point the Witness's mouth would work like an octogenarian ruminant's, without articulating any syllables or producing words. It always amazed me how unbelievably stupid these people were. To actually go out into the world, preaching a doctrine, without having first thought through its most fundamental tenets.

The Witness might then respond by reverting back to a dogmatic restatement of his or her beliefs. But, I would then remind them of the fatal flaw in their faith. Again, I would enjoy the return of doubt, which in some cases would gratifyingly intensify and shift in the direction of panic.

At that point I would say something like: 'So why does a wholly good creator wilfully include child murder, genocide and penile cancer in his divine creation? By virtue of his omniscience, we can safely assume that these things are entirely his responsibility. Entirely,

65

you understand? So, would you care to hazard a guess at his motive? I would welcome any explanation, however modest.'

The Witness would shift uncomfortably. Attempt a further restatement of beliefs – although perhaps less confidently – and promise a return visit, as he or she edged backwards down the path. After a while, they stopped knocking on my door. Although I did receive one further visit. Yes, there was one other.

Anna took a very dim view of my theological debates. 'You shouldn't do that, Tom. You're a lot cleverer than they are. You shouldn't undermine their beliefs like that.'

'Why not?'

'Because it's unnecessary. You wouldn't argue with a child like that, would you? There's no point. You could run circles around a child just like you can run circles around them. What's the point?'

'I'm doing them a service. I'm disabusing them of their half-baked ideas.'

'No you're not. You're bullying them.'

I was always outraged by this suggestion.

'Me? Bully them? You must be joking. It's they who are feebly attempting to bully me. I don't go round trying to convince others that God doesn't exist. I don't go round trying to convince people that they shouldn't go to church. Why should they have the right to do unto others what I cannot do unto them?'

'That's not the point. They *think* that they are doing you a good turn.'

'Well, they're not. They aren't doing anyone a good turn.'

'That's not the point. It's what they think they're doing that counts here.'

'Well, I'm sure Adolf Hitler thought that he was doing good in the world. Unless your "doing good" can stand up in the face of rational argument then it's not doing good at all. Is it?'

Anna would grudgingly concede; however, she was always more than a trifle moody for the rest of the day after such a discussion. I never understood her inclination to defend these half-wits.

★

I was particularly intolerant of God that day, the reason being that I still had recollections of my most recent drink at the Union with Dave. You see, after we had discussed the pointlessness of existence and Dave had finished scanning for talent it was time for another round. Dave excused himself and while purchasing our beverages had become involved in what must have been – by comparison – a rather facile conversation with a young woman who I understood (by her dress) to be an *aficionado* of Britpop. Dave had given me some tutoring in the identification of sub-culture exemplars. During his absence I thought nothing of exploring the contents of his carrier bag, which included a textbook on medical genetics. I removed the weighty volume and began to flick through its contents. It was not so much a textbook as a catalogue of horrors. A bestiary of genetic aberrations and accidents. I had not realized that the tree of medical science boasted the cruel and unspeakable branch of teratology – the study of monsters – but it does. The chapter contained the most extraordinary photographs of dead babies. Dead, because their deformities were so grotesque, so obscene, that their life expectancy was naturally reduced to a matter of hours, days, or at worst, weeks. Huge bulbous heads, cleaved in two. Fused limbs. Multiple sets of genitalia. Facial features misaligned, misarranged or displaced, like some awful exercise in the possibilities of abstraction. It was as though these infants had served as the original models for Picasso or, alternatively, were the hideous product of genetic experimentation. Which of course they were, in a way. Natural experimentation. The random mutations that often serve to enrich the gene pool go wrong more often than they go right. However, it is rare that such progeny survive the full term of pregnancy and then manage to negotiate a birth canal. It is rare that these audacious parodies of the human form give vent to a cry that serves at once as a beginning and an end. It is rare that their bloody forms need to be urgently folded into generous swathes of swaddling and hurried out of the mother's sight. And it is rare that they confront us with the senseless, profligate cruelty of a mechanistic universe on whose moving parts we fail to see the signature or inscription of a higher sentience. This universe cannot embrace theology and teratology with equanimity.

By the time Dave returned, I had reached inborn errors of metabolism. The page fell open on a close-up of a tiny hand with stunted, truncated fingers. Each had a ragged end, as though the hand had been mauled in an industrial accident.

'What the fuck's that?' I said.

'Oh that. That's the hand of someone with Lesch-Nyhan syndrome,' he replied, nonchalantly, before looking wistfully back at the bar. 'I could have scored there, but I can't be bothered.'

I remained captivated by the truncated hand.

'What is it? Lesch-Nyhan?'

'Do you really want to know?'

'Yes.'

'It's an X-linked recessive disturbance of the purine metabolism. If you *must* know. It's caused by a deficiency of one of the enzymes that recycles purines. Simple as that.'

'But why does it do this to hands?'

'It doesn't. It affects the nervous system. The patient has bitten the end of his fingers off.'

'What?'

'Yeah, serious shit, eh? At the age of about two Lesch-Nyhans start biting the ends of their fingers off. Nervous or what? They start eating their own lips and try to eat the inside of their mouths. They have to be restrained in splints, otherwise they'd fucking eat themselves completely. Some have all their teeth removed to stop them doing too much damage.'

'But doesn't it hurt?'

'Of course it fucking hurts. While they're doing all this shit they're usually screaming in pain. They beg for help.'

'And an enzyme deficiency does that?'

'Yeah. One pissy enzyme.'

'Can it be treated?'

'No chance.'

68

I wonder, could a Jehovah's Witness honestly look a Lesch-Nyhan child in the face, listen to the scream emanating from its tattered maw, see the splintering bones projecting from the end of each finger and say, There's a point to this. I'll be fucked if I can see any.

I felt that I knew Dave. That I knew him well. I felt that I knew him and all his manifestations. Dave the lad, Dave the scientist. Cocky Dave, raving Dave. Dave on the pull, Dave on the piss. Deep Dave, shallow Dave. Or Dave, just being quintessentially Dave. We had got to the point where I was not expecting to be surprised by another Dave. But there was another one and I was unsettled by his appearance.

The question, as I recall, was an innocent one. Dave and I were walking down Green Lanes together. I was meeting Anna at Turnpike Lane Tube station and I had assumed that Dave would be walking all the way with me; however, we got as far as Bounds Green Road, and he suddenly stopped.

'I've got to get a bus,' he said.

'Oh yes. Who is it tonight then?' I asked.

The question, which was by no means a taxing one, seemed to confuse him.

'Sorry?'

'Which one of your paramours are you seeing tonight then? With whom are you to share an assignation?'

I enunciated the words with pedantic emphasis, meaning to be humorous by employing an antiquated style of speech. But it didn't work.

In response, Dave looked somewhat embarrassed. Rather coy, in fact. However, it was clear that he was not just embarrassed by my useless joke. There was more to it. He thought for a few moments, before saying, 'Oh, no. Not tonight. No. I'm going to see my brother, actually.'

'Who?' I was unable to disguise my shock. I almost barked the word.

'My brother.'

'I didn't know you had a brother.'

The news was quite disconcerting. Dave had never mentioned a brother before. A sister, yes. A sister who taught English in Paris. But not a brother.

'Look, I can't talk right now,' said Dave. 'There's my bus. Love to Anna.'

He ran off, and I stood on the corner for a moment, nonplussed. A brother? In London? When I reached Turnpike Lane Anna was already waiting. I forgot to say hello. I walked straight up to her and said, 'Did you know that Dave's got a brother?' The question was blurted out, and sounded like a demand.

'Hello, Tom,' she replied, gently squeezing my arm and pressing her cold, dry lips on mine. 'No, I didn't.'

'Hi,' I said, belatedly attempting to rectify my social blunder. Anna always made me feel worse than was necessary when I did things like that. 'Yes.' (I thought that I might as well continue with my chosen theme anyway.) 'He just said that he was catching a bus. He was going to see his brother. He hasn't mentioned a brother before.'

'He has a sister, doesn't he?'

'Yes. The teacher.'

'In France or something.'

'That's right. But no brother.'

'Oh, well.' There was nothing more to say on the subject really.

Anna was eager to get something to eat. We stopped off at a cheap-looking burger bar and then made our way to the cinema. The audience made so much noise in the first twenty minutes of the film we decided to give it a miss. We went home fuming. I know that it is probably politically incorrect, but people with low intelligence make me sick. Really sick.

Fortunately, we didn't have to wait long for the bus. It was empty, and we sat in the front seat downstairs. We were thus afforded panoramic views of urban desolation. Although the cheap displays were lit in the shop windows that lined Green Lanes, there was no one around. It was as though Haringey, unbeknown to us, had received a four-minute warning.

Anna and I were jolted and bounced through the night; the bus driver had apparently determined to make use of the empty road by initiating an impromptu attempt at demolishing the land-speed record (irrespective of the obvious limitations of his double-decked vehicle). At one point we both left our seats entirely. Took off, as it were, and for a moment in time must have hovered in the air, holding hands, like lovers in a surrealist painting.

When the road surface permitted us to remain on our seats, we were able to talk. Anna said, 'Someone call Ted telephoned. At about five-thirty. He wants you to call him back. He didn't leave a message. He was really odd.'

'Oh, yeah. That must have been Tad.'

'Tad? Who's Tad?'

I decided that I should be truthful (recalling my conversation with Dave on the veranda). Well, when I say truthful, I mean truthful enough.

'He's a businessman.'

'A businessman. He didn't sound like a businessman.'

'Why, what did he say?'

'Nothing much. He asked to speak to you. Well, he asked to speak to *Tommo* actually. When I told him you were out he asked me when *the main man* would be back. He sounded like he was on something. He was manic.'

'Yeah. That sounds like Tad.'

'Who is he?'

'A businessman.'

Anna was clearly unconvinced.

'Really. He calls me every now and again at the university. He owns a software company.'

'What does he want with you?'

'Oh, nothing much. Sometimes the software develops problems and they ask me to take a look at it. I de-bug. It's quite an informal arrangement. It's worth doing though. If I can see what the problem is, they're prepared to pay me. I'll give him a call tomorrow.'

71

Anna accepted my explanation, which was, indeed, generally true. I didn't really feel that I had to tell her what type of software Tad dealt in. It wasn't necessary. But I was certain that if she did know, she would object. I subsequently felt quite guilty.

There is something odd about the lighting on London buses. It is lighting that has no enthusiasm for the concept of illumination. It is slow-light. Failed-light. Light under duress. I'm sure that if Einstein had any experience of London buses he would have had to rethink relativity. The light was also the colour of my guilt. A gangrenous, yellow effluvium. A sickly residue that stained the atmosphere. I was glad to get off that bus. Glad to breathe in the chill night air.

As we walked down Green Lanes, I began to think about the quality of the light on the bus. Was it the same as usual, or was it different in some way? And if so, why was it so strange? I couldn't help wondering whether or not I had just experienced a visual disturbance. Working for Tad was all well and good, it solved the cash-flow problem, but how long should I do it for? Was it wise to continue? There had to be some risk attached. And then of course, there was Anna. I hadn't been honest. Not really. Did I want to go on like this? Lying? Dave might be able to cope with factual 'economy', but it made me feel bad.

'Home,' said Anna.

I almost jumped, even though she said the word softly. I had been completely preoccupied. Engrossed in my thoughts. Our walk from the bus stop to the flat had seemed to take no time at all. Anna twisted the key and opened the door. She then reached into the darkness and hit the light switch. Thankfully, the light appeared to be normal.

'What are you looking at?' Anna asked.

Rather stupidly I had begun to look at the space around the lightbulb.

'The lightbulb?'

'Why?'

'We never have spare ones when they go. I think I'll buy some tomorrow.'

4

The Paddington Basin

Anna and I enjoyed taking long walks. After a whole week spent hunched in front of a computer screen it was good to get out (even though the air was thick with soot, lead and varieties of trace elements). Every weekend Anna and I would act like subterranean creatures, ejected from our dismal burrow. We would stand outside our house in Wood Green and blink in disbelief at the miracle of sunlight. Irrespective of how many banks of raincloud were stacked on the horizon, we were determined to take our constitutional.

About that time, there had been a series of posters displayed in the Tube advertising places of interest in London. The idea behind the poster campaign was to inspire apathetic Londoners to explore their city using the Underground system. One of these posters showed a tree-lined canal and a host of colourful barges. The reader was invited to visit Little Venice, near Warwick Avenue.

I had never been to Little Venice. Nor had Anna. It seemed, therefore, a suitably picturesque destination. We soon found the small expanse of water that is supposed to be Little Venice's most attractive feature. It was once called Browning's Pool, on account of the famous poet's penchant for swimming in it. I was not overly impressed. The beautiful Nash terrace on one side of the water faced a 1960s architectural nightmare on the other, and close by, one could see the A40(M) climbing into the sky like a road that had torn free of gravity's influence.

We soon got bored of the main attraction and decided to explore Maida Vale. In Warrington Crescent we chanced upon a curiosity that made our journey wholly worth while. It was a small hotel, called the Colonnade. On the outside wall was a blue circular plaque. It informed us that we were standing outside not only the birthplace of Alan Turing but also a former home of Sigmund Freud.

'I don't think it's genuine,' said Anna, as she scrutinized the sign.

'No. It doesn't look like a proper one. But I'm sure they can't just make these things up.'

'Why not?'

'Well, there must be laws about it. Trade Descriptions Act or something.'

We continued to look at the blue plaque, like acolytes of some obscure religious sect.

'If it is true, then that's an amazing coincidence. That Freud and Turing should be connected with the same building,' Anna said.

'Who do you think was the most important, Turing or Freud?'

'Can't be answered.'

'All right, who *do you* think was the most important?'

'That's a very male question.'

'That's a very female answer. Why can't you just answer the question?'

'Because it's pointless. They can't be compared. They did different things in different ways.'

I dispensed with further discussion by obliging Anna with the correct answer.

'Turing.'

She was not annoyed. In fact she smiled.

'A hotel,' I continued. 'Difficult to believe really. He won the war for us, then changed virtually every aspect of modern life! This is where he was born and what do they do? Turn it into a hotel. How do they celebrate his genius? A dodgy-looking blue plaque that he has to share with someone else (albeit another genius). This should be a museum, a centre of learning, a monument, not a fucking hotel!' I was struck yet again by the intolerable cruelty of science.

If I had the slightest confidence in God I would have said a prayer for Alan Turing; but I don't, so I didn't. Being an atheist is a problem at such times. Instead of communing with the divinity and asking him to grant eternal peace to his most gifted and blessed son, I simply said to myself *Cheers, Alan,* which seemed hopelessly inadequate.

After a few more minutes of silent veneration, we decided to walk to Bayswater. Unfortunately we misread the *A–Z* and found ourselves walking down a busy road that ran directly under the A40(M). There was hardly any pavement to speak of. I'm sure we weren't supposed to be there. Over a small wall there appeared a vast empty plane. I later found out that this no man's land was part of the Paddington basin (originally marking the connecting point of the Grand Junction and Union canals). The abyss of grass, concrete, abandoned hulks, boarded-up Portakabins and disused railway lines was distinguished on my *A–Z* by absolutely nothing. An empty block of white, bordered by the A40(M), Westbourne Terrace and Bishops' Bridge Road. It was as if, as the motorway and surrounding areas were built up, the ground here had been entirely cut off. It had been made inaccessible and remote. Then forgotten.

As the cars and lorries thundered by, I pointed this out to Anna.

'Look, it doesn't exist!'

'What is it?'

'I don't know.'

'Strange place. I don't like it.'

We marched on under the flyover until we found ourselves at Royal Oak. By that time we were quite battered and tired. We gave up on Bayswater, and went Underground instead. When we re-emerged in Wood Green a freak gust of wind whipped up so much grit from the street it nearly flayed the flesh from our faces. We were home again.

The next time I saw Dave I was somewhat unsure of myself. I wanted to ask him about his brother but was rather reluctant to address the subject directly. Clearly, Dave had not been eager to discuss his sibling.

I had known him for many months and he had not mentioned him once. Indeed, it was obvious, at the time he had disclosed his existence, that Dave was in two minds. Caught by surprise, the balance of his indecision had been weighted, ever so slightly, in favour of disclosure rather than secrecy. I had discussed the matter with Anna again, and she had advised me not to pry. She had also admonished me, albeit gently, for taking what she described as an excessive interest in Dave's private affairs.

To tell the truth – and here I must be brutally honest with myself – I was more than a little peeved at the existence of Dave's brother. You see, Dave had few, if any, male friends. I was, to the best of my knowledge, his most intimate male acquaintance; a position that I coveted. The idea of another individual sharing Dave's confidence and, moreover, a blood relative, made me feel marginalized, excluded. I was jealous of this 'brother', whoever he was.

I had spent some considerable time rehearsing in my mind conversational ploys that would steer our talk in the general direction of fraternity, which, in the final event, proved to be unnecessary and a complete waste of time.

It was a King's day. And we met, as usual, on the veranda for luncheon. London was also, as usual, reliably grim. Nevertheless, we took a perverse pleasure in dining al fresco. We sat with our collars up, enjoying the bracing wind that came off the Thames with sustained vigour.

To my enormous delight, Dave mentioned his brother almost immediately. 'I don't think I've mentioned my brother before, have I?'

'No. Not before the other night.'

Again, I could see that Dave was uncomfortable.

'I don't really see him very much. You see, he's quite ill.'

I suddenly felt like a complete shit.

'Oh, I'm sorry, Dave. What's wrong with him?'

'Well, when I say ill, what I really mean is that he's mentally ill. Has been since he was a child. Although things got worse as he got older. His teens really.'

76

I didn't know what to say.

Dave chose to continue. 'I go to see him every now and again. Not as much as I should, of course. He's quite independent though. He lives on his own in Hendon.'

'Hendon,' I repeated. Quite pointlessly.

'Yes, Hendon. There's a sort of drop-in centre there. For people with problems. I usually see him when he goes there. It's a kind of social club. More fun for me that way. Actually, I've scored there a couple of times.'

The look on my face must have communicated my thoughts exactly.

'No, you schmuck, not with lunatics! They have voluntary workers helping out. Most of them are girlies. Dead keen, usually. Mostly psychology students doing voluntary work. Well, I don't need to tell you how *they* grip the road, do I?'

I was flattered and annoyed at the same time.

'What does your brother do when you're pulling?'

'Look, I don't start coming on strong in the middle of Scrabble, for fuck's sake!'

'Sorry.'

Dave grinned. The atmosphere lightened.

'Why didn't you mention your brother before?'

'Well, it's not the kind of subject that goes anywhere, is it? I mean, this won't go anywhere. Now that you know about him, what else is there to say?'

'I don't know.'

'Exactly.'

Dave was about to change the direction of our conversation but I felt unsatisfied. I did want to know more. I did think there was more to say. I wanted to know who Dave, 'brother' Dave, really was. All that I was being served were samples from the traditional Davian menu.

'What' – I stumbled for the right words – 'I mean, is it a disease or . . .'

77

'What's he got, you mean?'

'Yes.'

'OCD.'

'What?'

'Sorry, obsessive compulsive disorder. Though very badly.'

'What is it?'

'It's a kind of phobia, but more complicated. He's terrified of dirt and washes all the time. He can lock himself in the bathroom for hours. Washing and washing. He's got other problems too. It's all part of the OCD. He checks things. The oven, light switches. Always thinks that he's left things on.'

'Can't it be treated?'

'Oh, he's had all the standard treatments. Drugs, psychotherapy, more drugs. None of them have made much difference. He's been told that brain surgery is a final option, but he's not interested. Who can blame him, eh?'

We both remained silent for a few moments.

'Oh, I almost forgot.' Dave reached into a Tesco plastic bag and pulled out a small bottle. 'Here's your mercury. I'll get you some more soon. Incidentally, the lab tech was very grateful for your kind gift.'

'Oh, that's quite all right.'

'I'll collect your final order later in the week.'

'Thank you.'

I wanted to ask him more about his brother but I decided to take Anna's advice in the end. I wasn't going to press him.

'How's it going then, your camera project?'

'All right really. This will be very useful, thank you.' I picked up the small bottle. Mercury never ceases to amaze me. When you lift a bottle of mercury and shake it it gives your nervous system conflicting messages. You can feel it behaving like water or milk but its weight violates all expectations.

'Can I see it, when you've finished? The camera?'

'Of course. But only when it's finished. I want to get it just right.'

78

'You're a perfectionist. Do you realize that?'

'Yes, I suppose I am.'

In the 1960s the American neuroscientist Paul MacLean suggested that every cranium houses not one brain, but three. A reptilian brain, a paleomammalian brain and a neomammalian brain. The first two recapitulate aspects of our evolutionary history. For example, the reptilian brain is a stranger to emotion (because it reflects a stage in our history as a species that predates the development of emotion). The reptilian brain stores ancient nerve circuits that, when activated, will produce reptilian behaviour. Cold, automatic, unfeeling and unthinking. The paleomammalian brain reflects an evolutionary stage of development during which the major emotions were established. Fear, anger and attachment. The neomammalian brain, or cortex, is our third and most advanced brain. Its neuronal complexes mediate thinking and interpreting complex perceptual experiences. The cortex – or civilization – is only a few millimetres thick. We are far more lizard, far more blind rage, dependency and terror, than Socrates or Descartes. Far more Freud than Turing.

Although I was fully aware that my preoccupation with Anna's sexual history was irrational, I brought to bear on this problem the critical faculties of an iguana and the emotional sensitivity of a water buffalo. Of course, I knew what was happening. I am not stupid. I know my evolutionary sociobiology as well the next man. Rather better in fact, I imagine.

When it comes to reproductive psychology, discerning whether or not you can trust your mate is singularly important. Treachery cannot be countenanced. To be deceived, in Darwinian or evolutionary terms, is a catastrophe of monstrous proportion; however, there are many forms of treachery. The treachery that threatens my genes is considerably different to the treachery that threatens my partner's genes. Whereas she is programmed to fear a withdrawal of parental investment, I am programmed to fear that my investment is misplaced. I could waste my entire life ensuring the survival of another man's genes. Apart from employing a prophylactic measure, such as a chastity belt, there is no way a man can be totally certain of his paternity. Women of course have no such uncertainty.

Evolution has provided men with an insurance policy against the unthinkable. It is called male sexual jealousy. I'm wired to be jealous. I have no say in the matter. When it comes to sexual jealousy, I am all iguana and water buffalo. Cold blood and anger. When it comes to jealousy I can't see reason. I didn't ask to be like this. I just am.

This, then, was my excuse. My excuse for rummaging through Anna's possessions. Ransacking her drawers and despoiling each private recess. My fingers *copped a feel* of each nook and cranny, as if I were some kind of furniture fetishist. I looked through everything. But I couldn't find a single item, scrap of paper, photograph or phone number that would tell me what I wanted to know. Perhaps, like me, she had had no other sexual experiences. This seemed very unlikely indeed. I began to yearn for the age before tampons and female emancipation, when a preserved hymen and a tell-tale spot of blood would settle doubts about prior ingress.

I had not got very far before I began to feel quite ashamed. On the surface of my brain the neurotransmitters were brewing up rationality in a desperate attempt to contain the chaos below. It wasn't that I wanted Anna to be *virgo intacta*. Not really. I just wanted a little detail. Less uncertainty.

I still counted myself lucky to be sleeping with anyone at all. Hadn't I exceeded all my former expectations? Wasn't it enough to be living with a real, live woman? Before meeting Anna I had thought that the only interactive sexual experiences I might one day enjoy were those made available by donning a VR visor and an auto-suck. Did it really matter that Anna may have had one or two boyfriends in the past? My cortex said no, of course not, but pulses of dissatisfaction throbbed through the rest of my nervous system.

In a white shoe-box, at the back of the drawer in which Anna kept sundry items of underwear, I found a few old photographs. Most were creased and faded. Presumably the people who were caught, for ever, pouring tea or smiling in the face of an invigorating sea breeze were Anna's relatives. Their hair stood on end, the clouds were lowering and the spareness of the spread suggested an age of austerity, but they all appeared to be happy. Among these photographs was one that filled me with melancholy. A rather beautiful, petite little girl of about seven, with long blonde hair, tied with a red bow. Her dress was white and pink and seemed to fluoresce. It had an almost hallucinatory quality. She was standing next to a tall man with a kind, forgiving face. He was holding her tiny hand in his, ignorant of his imminent death.

Sometimes emotions are too complicated to analyse. Why did this picture make me feel sad? There were many reasons. I felt sorry for the little girl, Anna, who would soon lose her much-loved father.

I felt sad, knowing that this exquisite little creature, comprised of yellows and reds, would become the rather plain woman I lived with. A woman of greys and browns. Life would give her a dull patina, killing her natural shine. Her personality would take on the dark sonorities of her beloved cello.

I felt sorry for the man. So obviously a clever, good man, who would die in a hospital bed, hardly conscious on account of generous doses of morphine, administered to release him from – no doubt – excruciating, inhuman levels of pain. The cancer in his testicles was probably already quite advanced when the picture was taken. Life is full of intolerable, ridiculous ironies. The same organ that had produced the psychedelic little girl was also the same organ that would kill him.

Finally, I felt sorry for me. Sorry that I would never meet this man. Sorry that he would never be a surrogate father to me. He was, apparently, a physics lecturer. Only at the local college, but that would have been sufficient to create a mutual bond. He would have been proud of my achievements. He would have recognized my gifts. He would have wanted Anna to marry somebody just like me.

I could have done with a father-in-law like him. A family.

Nowadays, I hardly see my parents. I haven't spoken to my brother in eight years. I don't even know which country he's in.

There is a school of thought, I understand, which proposes that similar people seek each other out. They are, as it were, fatally attracted to each other. This would certainly be the case with respect to myself and Anna. We were always happy to gloss over critical information about origins and history. We knew the bald facts about each other, of course, but not a great deal more. It is as though we shared an unspoken pact to censor detailed discussion of the past (and needless to say, this tacit agreement did little to encourage a swift resolution of the boyfriend problem).

I knew that Anna's father died when she was about eight, but I had no real grasp of how the bereavement had affected her. She knew about my rather remote, elderly parents, but she never asked me about them. She knew nothing of my mother's staid ways, my father's preoccupation with the neighbours, their joint refusal to allow me any form of personal freedom. In a way, Anna and I were like two trauma victims. I once read that people who have experienced terrible things suppress anything that might remind them of their ordeal. They block out memories.

I suppose, if Anna and I had really wanted our relationship to work, then we would have spent more time talking about things that mattered. The fact is, we didn't.

I put the photographs back into the white box and replaced the lid. The flat felt like a mortuary. Damp and cold.

Unfortunately, I was unable to shake off my sense of melancholy, so I distracted myself in the shed by assembling the first-stage modulator of Locke's apparatus. As luck would have it, I had found a number of useful components in my hoard, but there were many other parts that I needed to find. Some of these I could steal from the university. Others, Dave would be happy to 'borrow' or 'purchase' on my behalf. There were, however, one or two items that could only be obtained by corresponding with collectors or by visiting dealers. I had already renewed my subscription to the *Science, Medi-*

cine & Engineering Antiquary (a quarterly publication) and was looking forward to scouring the columns for a much-needed Maxwell chain mechanism. The zinc bearings I could probably find without difficulty, but the governor I would have to make entirely from parts pirated from other devices.

By that time I had had ample opportunity to examine Locke's equations and formulae. I had also written a programme that simulated the condenser and modulator functions in a virtual space–time continuum. The simulation resolved itself by forming a temporal anomaly. In 'real' time, the anomaly would have lasted for approximately twelve seconds. It was clear from the constants that only retrospective anomalies were possible. Moreover, the depth or 'reach' of an anomaly was exactly correlated with energy consumption. Even though Locke's equations were shockingly elegant, his apparatus could not open an anomaly with a retrospective reach of beyond one month. Of course, a nuclear governor would possibly open an anomaly that might reach back to the Jurassic age. One might capture an image of a megalosaurus, making its stately way across tropical Hampstead. I shuddered as I thought of what might be achieved if an even greater power were harnessed. What kind of an anomaly might a vacuum governor open? Theoretically, one might produce an anomaly of near-infinite reach. What would one see through it, if one dared look? The hand of God possibly, reaching out to light the touch-paper of creation? Some chance!

The world would be completely changed by Locke's apparatus. History would, no doubt, require a major overhaul. What was once considered truth would be falsified, and apocryphal tales would surrender their kernels of authenticity. What treasures might the *New Britannica* hold? An analysis of the famous loaves and fishes sleight of hand, as performed by Jesus, the Nazarene conjurer? A soft-focus still of doting Anne Hathaway, leaning over the Bard's shoulder, correcting his first, rather inept draft of Hamlet's famous soliloquy? How the colossi would tumble and fall.

We would be forced to face our peculiarities as a species. Forced to face the Freudian incompatibilities of higher and lower selves. Yes, we would be able to capture images of Beethoven completing the Ninth Symphony; but we would also capture images of him masturbating. Yes, we would have images of Da Vinci sketching the *Last Supper*, but we would also have images of him with an apprentice's penis in his mouth. How would we ever be able to claim Mozart's divinity again, with pictures in the Vienna Archive of the young genius sniffing a healthy, dark, steaming stool, easing its way out of Constanze Mozart's rectum.

I can recall raising the concept of a time camera with Dave. It was an interesting exercise.

'Do you think there would be legislation, if it were possible to take photographs of the past?' I asked him. 'Would we protect the rights of the dead? Their right to privacy, for example?'

'No way!' responded Dave immediately, relishing the thought of icons crashing to the ground. 'It would be too fucking interesting. We wouldn't be able to stop ourselves. Anyway, who the hell would stand up for, say – that old lesbian bird, you know the one, the mother of all lesbians . . .'

'Sappho?'

'Yeah, Sappho! Who the hell would stand up for Sappho if a twenty-third-century Hefner wanted a holographic centrefold of the old girl muff-diving? Who would care?'

'Some people might.'

'Yes, but they would be a tiny minority. The possibilities are just too wonderful. Imagine the markets that would open up. Hellenic porn, featuring Socrates wanking off one of his homo-tarts. Or Caligula's orgies . . . or . . . or . . .' He became inarticulate with joy.

'The fact is', he continued, 'it would be this kind of shit that would make the headlines. People wouldn't give a toss about Galileo or Newton – not unless they were caught tossing, that is.'

I tried to entice Dave's intellect out of the alcoholic pool in which it had become immersed. I posed another question. 'What about social change? All technological breakthroughs bring about huge social changes. How would society change?'

'Well,' said Dave, swiftly gathering momentum, 'eventually, these time cameras would become readily available to everyone, like Kodak Instamatics. Then, we would all be able to raid each others' histories. There would be no secrets. There would be no skeletons in the cupboard. The skeletons would move into the lounge. The dirty laundry would be piled high . . . We would all know that we are all as bad as each other. A hopeless bunch of shit-sniffing, genitally fixated hypocrites and, frankly, I think the world would be a much better place for it. We would all have to grow up. We would all have to stop thinking that we were anything more than . . . apes and monkeys.'

As usual, Dave was right. There could be no secrets. As a result of this discussion, I was forced to consider what would happen if Locke's apparatus were turned against me. Could I ever claim that Locke's apparatus was my own invention? No. Of course not. I would be a figure of immense importance. It is inevitable that the apparatus would be used to catalogue my own personal history. My birth, my death. They – the biographers of the future – would discover me, in the DMS Watson, finding the Cavendish *Proceedings*. It was a depressing thought. I was destined to be John the Baptist, and a very inauspicious John the Baptist at that. I was destined to be the messenger. Oh, well, not such a bad thing, really. I would be the second-most-important person in the history of the world. I couldn't complain. I could have done a lot worse.

5

A Trip to Bournemouth

I suppose it must have been in the summer that I was introduced to
Anna's mother. I met her once – only once, but that was bad enough.
In all honesty, I really don't know why I accepted the invitation. I
didn't want to meet her and, at that time, I suspected that Anna didn't
want me to meet her either.

Anna spoke to her mother intermittently on the telephone. Their
gabbling seemed fairly harmless. I would listen of course (while
pretending to do something else). As you do. I would sit, close by,
turning the pages of my book at regular intervals, trying to catch the
drift of their conversation. My interest was inevitably aroused when
I became the principal topic of discussion. Anna always gave me a
staggeringly impressive report. I was doing *awfully* clever things. The
ploy was quite diaphanous, and I didn't believe for one minute that
the old woman was fooled. I suppose Anna's implicit logic went
something like: you married a clever man, so therefore you must
approve of clever men. Tom is clever, *ergo*, you should approve of
Tom. It was all so obvious. You could see the joins. I would imagine
Anna's mother making appropriately encouraging noises down the
wire, while at the same time assuming a *Look, I wasn't born yesterday*
expression.

There was no doubt in my mind that Anna was preparing the
ground for an imminent introduction, and she was trying very hard
to cultivate a positive mind-set in her mother. Although I should
have been appreciative, it seemed to me that Anna was betraying a
clear lack of faith in my winning personal qualities: if Mother's

attention could be trained on my Nobel-standard intellect, it might just escape her notice that I was a social quadraplegic. It hurt, to hear Anna doing the *Brilliant Tom* routine, it really did.

Very occasionally, I would pick up the telephone and exchange a few pleasantries with Anna's mother.

'Hello, is that Tom?'

'Yes, it is.'

'It's Jean, Anna's mother.'

'Oh, hello, Jean. How are you?'

'Very well, thank you. And you?'

'Fine, fine . . .'

Then my mind would go blank and I wouldn't be able to think of anything else to say. Fortunately, Anna's mother would save the moment with a solid, 'How is your work going?'

'Very well.'

'Good.'

But that was usually as far as we could take it. I would have to bring our horribly stilted commerce to an abrupt close by asking, 'Would you like to speak to Anna?', and an affirmative response would deliver me from my uncomfortable predicament.

'Well, 'bye then.'

'Goodbye.'

And so it went.

Talking to Anna's mother made me nervous. I suppose I wanted her approval. Wanted her to think well of me. God only knows why, but I did. So, when we spoke, I inevitably became tongue-tied, and what modest facility I have for the invention of small talk was promptly forfeited.

By August, Anna had not seen her mother for months. As a result of this unforgivable abrogation of filial duty, her telephone conversations with her mother had become somewhat strained. Anna's excuses were becoming increasingly threadbare. Yes, she was still *so* busy. No, she just *couldn't* get away. Yes, she would try to make some time *very* soon. And so on. Needless to say, the fact that she had been living with me for three months made the situation even more embarrassing.

Eventually, under duress, Anna capitulated. Her advance on me was wary, yet assured.

'Tom, I was speaking to Mum this afternoon. I said that I'd go down sometime . . . soon.'

'When?'

'The weekend after next.'

'Oh, right.'

'She said that you could come too. She really wants to meet you.'

'Oh, right.'

'I know it's a pain but . . .'

'You want me to come then?'

'If you don't mind.'

'No. I don't mind. I suppose I should meet your mother. Of course I'll come.'

Perhaps I have been uncharitable to Anna. Perhaps she wasn't trying to conceal me at all. Perhaps she simply wanted things to work out, and was reluctant to risk incurring Mum's displeasure. To do so would be a needless complication. Now, when I reflect on Anna's subsequent behaviour, I am more inclined to endorse this latter view; however, back then, my insecurities made it difficult to see things clearly. Whatever, the date was set for my introduction, and the dreaded weekend on the coast came towards me like an inescapable head-on collision that would brook no survivors.

I knew that the experience was going to be traumatic, from the very beginning. It would break away a layer of Anna's protective cladding, and I would be forced to peer inside. I knew that there would be shadowy figures, discernible in the moted shafts of light. Figures that I wanted (and did not want) to know about. It was remarkable how the most trivial conversation would provide sackloads of grist to the mill of my jealousy.

Needless to say, I was totally ignorant of the required protocol. My knowledge of visiting a prospective mother-in-law was entirely dependent on one or two half-recalled scenes from an American sitcom, an offensive (though quite funny) routine I once heard delivered by a stand-up comedian from Manchester, and a few contemporary novels. I was, let us agree, ill prepared (to say the least). And ridiculous things started to bother me. How should I address Anna's mother? Mrs Crawford? Jean? *Mum?* (for Christ's sake). Or should I opt for the noncommittal fall-back position of elision? It was this sort of worry that made me consult Anna about the correct way to proceed, and I immediately discovered the enormous potential at hand for the severe aggravation of my Darwinian difficulty with sexual jealousy.

'What should I call your mother?'

'Jean.'

'Not Mrs Crawford?'

'No.'

'Are you sure?'

'Don't be silly. You'll sound like someone from the Famous Five books.'

'Oh. I just thought . . . Well, you know how some people are.'

'Look, I can tell you for sure, it's best if you call her Jean.'

And that little, harmless sentence was enough. The use of *for sure* had done it. Those two words snarled and tangled in my neural net. Somehow the mental machinery couldn't shake them off and into the sluice chute. No matter how many times the wheels turned, they were still there, inside my head. Then the questions would start: *How come you're so sure? Have you taken boyfriends home before? How many? Did you sleep with them? Well, did you?* Relentless questions. Of course, none of these questions were ever articulated. I simply sat, listening to Radio Darwin, apparently broadcasting on all channels. There was nothing else to tune in to. So, I had a fairly good idea what I was letting myself in for from the moment the arrangement was confirmed.

The traffic on the way down to Bournemouth was absolutely diabolical, and the night was hot and sticky. It took us nearly two hours to get out of London and there were traffic jams every twenty minutes for the rest of the journey. Anna had chosen to do the driving. She said it was less stressful that way. I didn't argue. I am quite happy to admit that my tolerance of traffic jams is shockingly low. As soon as I see a trail of red tail-lights ahead, I routinely break out in a sweat and groan like I'm having a colostomy bag fitted without anaesthetic. It's such a dreadful waste of time.

Even if you only spend half an hour a week in a traffic jam (which is a gross underestimate if you happen to live in London), then that becomes twenty-six hours over a year, which represents the loss of two whole months during the course of a lifetime. I don't know why human rights activists bother trying to free Third-World political prisoners, they would do just as well to focus their attention on the outrageous violations of human rights that occur on the M25. I have calculated that some commuters spend a total of up to two years' intermittent captivity (in every ten) in a Ford Escort, through no fault of their own and having committed no crime. Why not deal with this important issue now? It is far closer to home and should not be overlooked!

After spending the greater part of Friday night crawling only half the distance to Bournemouth, even Anna got pissed off. She had to stop the car at a service station and call her mother; just to let her know that we were going to be late. Very late.

The road cleared a little as our journey neared its end. Anna was listening to her Walkman, and gently humming along to what I believe was the Dvořák cello concerto. The lights of passing cars would intermittently illuminate Anna's face. They had a vaguely stroboscopic effect. I could see Anna's expression changing, flash by flash, moment by displaced moment. A rapid parsing of Anna's existential line. Each sudden illumination marked a subtle change of emotion, as a phrase hooked her heart-strings and yanked them high and low. It was so strange how music affected her. How music *turned her on*. That may seem a curious way of describing her response to music, but it is remarkably apposite. Once again, I enjoyed one of those moments, where, for me, at that particular instant, she appeared very beautiful.

Anna noticed me staring, and wriggled her head out from beneath the headphones. 'What?' she said.

'Nothing,' I replied.

'Not nervous, are you?'

'No.' I seemed to be lying every time I opened my mouth.

Anna's mother was waiting by the door as we came down the small garden path. She had obviously been keeping a vigil by the window.

'Hi, Mum,' said Anna. And with those words, she was oddly diminished. Girlish.

The woman at the door hugged her while inspecting me over Anna's shoulder. I seized the inopportune moment with unerring accuracy and said, 'Hello, Jean.'

She didn't hear me amid the general fluster, and it wasn't until she released Anna from her hungry embrace that I tried again, a little louder the second time around. 'Hello, Jean.'

'Tom, I'm so pleased you could come.'

I held out my hand, assuming that a kiss would be too presumptuous. She clasped my hand and drew me toward her, pressing her cheek against mine and making the *mwa* sound. I wasn't reading the situation well.

She ushered us down the corridor and into the lounge, where I stood, awaiting further instruction. Anna flopped down on a settee, tugging my arm to make me sit.

'Would you like some tea, coffee . . . a glass of wine?'

'Wine, please, Mum.'

' . . . and you, Tom?'

'Err . . . wine's fine.'

'Red or white?' she continued.

'White,' said Anna.

'And Tom?'

'Err . . . White's fine.'

Jean disappeared for a few moments and came back with a bottle in a bucket of ice. 'I was going to take you both out tonight as a treat, but it's too late now. I've managed to put something together though. Not very much, I'm afraid, but I'm sure it'll do if you're hungry. You're not a vegetarian or anything, are you, Tom?'

'No, Jean,' I said – far too loudly, in the same manner as one might deny being a racist or a paedophile – then I laughed for no reason at all. Jean merely smiled serenely, tolerating my gaucheness with admirable poise.

Anna and her mother fell into their easy chat. It was quite interesting really, hearing the other half of the conversation for the first time. They tried to include me, every so often, but I'm afraid I wasn't able to make much of their social generosity. My contributions were limited to 'Indeed', 'Yes', 'No', and an involuntary impersonation of an epileptic after Jean said something mildly humorous.

After about twenty minutes a microwave bell summoned us to the kitchen. Jean insisted that I sit at the table while Anna helped her serve a pretty impressive-looking pasta dish, with a side salad that could easily have doubled as an aerial view of a rain forest. I didn't recognize anything in it at all. Eventually, the lights were dimmed, and we sat around a single candle carrying off a very passable simulation of a normal family. Unfortunately, Jean decided that it was time to get to know me properly.

'I understand that your supervisor is something of a character, Tom.'

'Yes, he is,' I replied.

'Do you get on?'

'Well, yes and no. You know. We do and we don't. Like, he's Hungarian. It sort of depends.'

If my single redeeming feature is my intellect, then I was surrendering redemption like I was big league – almost up there with Judas, Hitler, and the other boys who thought that they would 'pass' on redemption. Drastic reparative action was required. Perhaps the wine – sloshing around in my empty stomach – helped. I gave a spontaneous, detailed description of Béla, his history, his flaws and his achievements. I then gave a reasonable account of my work and attempted to describe its value within the broader universe of mathematical sciences. I was quite surprised to find that Jean was not unfamiliar with terms such as 'chaos', or names such as Hofstadter. Indeed, she seemed genuinely interested and well informed. Once or twice I glanced at Anna, whose expression induced me to continue. Nevertheless, in spite of recovering some credibility, it was impossible to feel any more relaxed than I might have felt had Jean been attempting to dislodge a Smartie from under my foreskin with a sharp pin. I was being closely examined. I felt like I had been staked out for dissection.

It is one of the most intriguing features of the human brain that, when an individual finds him or herself in a situation demanding absolute propriety, unacceptable and intrusive thoughts begin to bob up and down in the stream of consciousness. Who hasn't had an irrational impulse to jump in front of an oncoming Tube train or lean that bit too far out of a fifth-floor window? Who hasn't experienced that terrible moment of doubt when, during a wedding ceremony, the minister invites the congregation to voice any legitimate objections to the union? Every time I am overcome with the most powerful urge to call out. Once, the urge was so strong I almost had to excuse myself. I understand that I am far from unique in this respect. It should not have taken me by surprise, then, to find that my description of how chaos theory might one day help us produce better weather forecasts was punctuated by an accompanying internal narrative that was distracting to say the least.

Under the penetrating spotlight of Jean's gaze I began to feel the strain of maintaining decency and correctness. In such situations it is as though the brain can't tolerate the stress of civilization and etiquette any longer. It all gets too much, and the more primitive, natural tendencies begin to interrupt mental life. The first disconcerting thought that flitted around at the perimeter of my awareness was that, in spite of her age, lined face and general 'mumsiness', Jean was quite fanciable. There were curious, subtle recapitulations of Anna in her countenance. Oblique references to Anna's lips and eyes. And, in the time between starting and finishing a single word, I experienced thoughts something like: *I wonder what it would be like to snog Jean? Jesus, wouldn't it be really terrible if you tried to feel up Jean under the table right now? Oh, Christ, what if you somehow lost control for a moment? How could you excuse such behaviour? I mean, there'd be no excusing it. She'd just never believe it was an accident, whatever you said!* So, as you can imagine, it was extremely difficult for me to remain coherent, and all the time I felt as though I were on the brink of committing a *faux pas* of truly dazzling magnitude. A kind of Taj Mahal of *faux pas*.

Fortunately, the pressure eased a little when we began to discuss Jean's work. She was a teacher at a local school, and seemed to be very enthusiastic about her vocation. I was also somewhat surprised by Anna's interest in the future of the school, which had apparently been threatened with closure several times. Being a rather small institution (and catering for brighter kids from ordinary backgrounds) it was apparently considered to be somewhat élitist and unnecessary. A merger with a larger secondary modern had been mooted for years.

'Would you come and play for the children again, darling?'

'Oh, Mum, I can't. You know how busy I am.'

'But they enjoyed it so much, when you played before.'

'I know, and I really enjoyed it, but I can't. Anyway, my technique's going to pieces. I never get enough time to practise any more. Some of them are probably better than me now.'

'Oh, don't say that, darling. You really mustn't neglect the cello. It's such a gift. You'll regret it if you do.'

And so it went on like this for a while. I had acquitted myself honourably and things were moving along smoothly; perhaps I had become complacent. I really was beginning to feel like a *regular guy* visiting family. Sipping my coffee, and sucking on the odd after-dinner mint. Then Jean said, 'Anna, have you heard anything from Rupert?'

Rupert?

'No.'

'It's just, I ran into Mrs Pierce the other day. He's doing terribly well apparently.'

'Oh?'

'Yes. Well, you remember he was studying law?'

'Of course.'

'He achieved the best mark in his year at bar school and was subsequently taken on as a sort of protégé by a very distinguished QC. Sir Terrence Trent-Derby, or something like that. Mrs Pierce is absolutely delighted, obviously. She asked after you . . .'

Rupert? So what the fuck is Rupert to you then?

'Oh, that was nice,' said Anna. 'I'm surprised she still remembers me.'

'Of course she remembers you!'

There was an uncomfortable hiatus. Anna clearly did not want to continue discussing Rupert Pierce, and I could see that Jean wasn't entirely sure how to proceed. Yes, there was definitely something up. Anna lifted her hand to her mouth and stifled a yawn. I thought it rather contrived.

'Oh, you must be tired, darling, how selfish of me to prattle on so.'

'I'm sorry, Mum.'

'Well, I've had a long day too.'

The statement was a clear acknowledgement that it was time for bed, yet it occurred to me that the issue of sleeping arrangements had not been discussed at all. Again, I felt all at sea. Destabilized. I wondered whether we were going to sleep together or separately? What was the correct form here?

We finished our coffees in the lounge and, unexpectedly, Jean offered to show Anna – not me and Anna – her room. They both left, and I sat in the lounge, relieved to be alone for a few moments. I could hear some movement upstairs, and the sound of muffled voices. A few moments later Jean popped her head in and said:

'I'm going to bed now, Tom, I'll see you in the morning.'

'Good-night,' I replied, ' . . . and thanks for dinner, supper.'

95

I thought it best to cover myself with both terms, just in case. As she began walking up the stairs she added, 'Help yourself to whatever you can find in the kitchen if you're up early.'

'Thanks.'

'Good-night.'

'Good-night.'

For a moment I thought it was intended that I should just stay in the lounge for the evening. Was this the convention, then? I wondered. Did boyfriends sleep – fully clothed, seated in a sofa until day-break – as a matter of course? Was it some kind of symbolic act of penitence, or self-denial, in recompense for having enjoyed unrestricted access to Anna's body for the rest of the year. My speculative reverie on social mores was interrupted by Anna's arrival.

'Well, are you ready for bed?'

'Where am I sleeping?'

'With me of course.'

'Oh, right.'

I followed her up two flights of stairs and was led into our bedroom. It was quite small, with two single beds on either side of the room. The whole operation had been quite painless. Indeed, it struck me as rather slick. Well-practised, as it were. Had it all been done before? I looked at Anna, who was slipping out of her clothes.

'So? How did I do?'

She smiled. 'All right.'

'I passed?'

'Yes, I think you did. You seemed a little unsure of yourself at first, but I think all that stuff about chaos theory went down well.'

'Good. I wasn't sure whether I was overdoing it.'

'No. It was fine.'

Anna got into bed naked, and after I had taken off my clothes I made my way to the other bed.

'No, Tom. Get in with me for a little while. I want to cuddle.'

'OK.'

So, I got into bed with her. It was cramped, but not uncomfortable.

Anna reached out and turned off the bedside light. We lay there, in the darkness, enjoying the closeness. I could smell the familiar fragrance of her hair and was reassured by the gentle rhythm of her breathing.

'Love you,' she said.

I stroked her back and she murmured with pleasure. Perhaps she, too, had found the evening testing. In the redeeming darkness, I could feel the uncoupling of muscles, previously knotted and fused by tension. After a few minutes of quiet recovery Anna shifted her head and slid her body down, beneath the duvet. I felt her cheek on my chest, and then my stomach, where it came to rest. She began to kiss my flaccid penis. First the extremity, then the underside. Gentle, languid kisses, that left circles of moistness, warmed by her breath. Slowly, my penis began to stir. In spite of these detonations of pleasure, I can't say that I felt at ease. It felt really odd, Anna, sucking my cock with her mother so close. Strangely disconcerting. I couldn't help wondering, just then, what thoughts might be passing through Jean's mind. Would she be thinking about us? Would she be wondering whether her daughter was, just at that moment, taking her lover into her mouth, or perhaps engaged in some other act of intimacy? Do parents think such things? I didn't see why not (they must do). Under the circumstances, I believed it to be very likely. Families!

I began awkwardly to move my hips backwards and forwards. The mattress creaked and groaned before its tortured springs suddenly exploded, releasing a twenty-thousand-decibel sequence of *poing*, *doing* and *ping* noises. I immediately became rigid with embarrassment.

'What?' Anna mumbled.

I lifted the duvet and spoke into the steamy aperture. 'The mattress. It's making a racket.'

'No, it's not.'

I had learned not to argue when Anna's voice was pitched at a certain register. Anna's voice was pitched at *that* register. I let the duvet fall, and we continued to exploit the latent percussive qualities of our mattress. I was getting stiff, but my heart wasn't really in it.

I imagined Jean, eyes widening in the darkness, appalled at our insensitivity. Anna began to use a hand to help me out. She gripped my shaft and began to work me more vigorously. It was at that point that my mind changed gear, as though somewhere, deep within myself, the tectonic plates of my personal psychology had shifted along a fault-line. It suddenly became quite exciting. I began to think, *yeah*, Jean, I'm mouth-fucking your daughter, and you can't do anything about it. I couldn't care less whether you approve or not. I couldn't give a fuck. There was a certain pleasure to be had, listening to the springs cracking and whining. Brazenly announcing our activity.

It was really odd, as though fellatio had become a way of getting my own back. A way of claiming compensation for having had to try so hard to win Jean's approval.

My cock was getting really stiff. More so than usual. Extra hard. The weird thing was that Anna seemed to be *getting off* on it too. It really worried me. I have come to accept my own oddity as a matter of course, but when people I consider to be normal start behaving oddly it just isn't on.

I reached down beneath the duvet and placed a hand behind Anna's head. I pushed it down on my cock and started to thrust vigorously. Although I am ashamed to admit it, the violence was an aphrodisiac. The sheer brutality of each heartless, mechanical jerk made me feel more excited. By this time the bed was sounding like the battle of the Somme, but I was far too aroused to stop. I just thought, *Yeah, Jean, yeah!* And as I did so, I ejaculated. I could feel my cock pulsing, shooting spunk down Anna's throat. Every muscle in my body went rigid as I pushed my hips forward to gain a deeper ingress. I held the position for a few moments before a merciful release let me slump back. Anna kept my cock in her mouth, and I could feel her swallowing. She gripped the base of my penis between her finger and thumb and pulled upwards, squeezing out any reluctant issue like toothpaste from an old tube. She then gently sucked on my exhausted member, like a child with a comforter. It was too sensitive, and I made a stupid *Ooh, ooh* sound and pulled back sharply. Anna resurfaced and snuggled up close. 'That turned you on,' she whispered.

I wondered why she had done it. Was it some curious remnant of adolescence? An irrepressible urge to be naughty, disobedient? Or was it a reward for good behaviour? As I pondered Anna's obscure motives I couldn't help asking myself a further question: *Did she do that to Rupert too?*

Jean went shopping on Saturday morning, and Anna and I went for a drive. We took the ferry across the harbour and walked on a rather splendid stretch of beach called Studland. The sky was clear and the sea a deep and satisfying blue. Surprisingly, there weren't that many people around, and I began to feel quite relaxed. In my subjective universe, Rupert had returned to being the name of a bear, and nothing more. This happened every now and again. For no apparent reason, my mental apparatus would regain its equilibrium. I would be able to say to myself something like: *Rupert was probably just a friend of the family. You know, boy next door and all that crap. Mrs Pierce's son. Anyway, with a name like Rupert he's almost certainly gay, so what's the fucking problem?* And miraculously, my tortured emotions and anguished thoughts would sink below the awareness threshold and leave me feeling relatively normal. Of course, it was only temporary, and I knew it wouldn't be long before I felt messed up again, but that didn't stop me from enjoying the sense of manumission. Of being unburdened or set free.

Anna and I walked into the dunes, and sat, looking out to sea. There is something so pleasing about the way the flat horizon divides water from air. The proportions are so satisfying. The advance and retreat of the waves seemed to erase any unnecessary mental activity, and I was overcome by a wonderful sense of calm. Anna linked her arm with mine and rested her head on my shoulder.

'It's your subject,' she said.

'Yes. I suppose it is.'

'Do you think of it like that? Do you see it as numbers, systems, values?'

'Of course not. Anyway, what I do isn't applicable to the sea!'

'What does it make you think then?'

'Nothing. That's what's so good about it. It switches my head off.'

'Me too.'

Anna kissed my cheek. 'When I look at something like this,' she said, waving her hand in an arc to define our prospect, 'London feels so very far away. It's almost as though it doesn't exist. When I get out of London, it starts to feel unreal.'

'Well, it does exist, I can assure you,' I replied, 'and we've got to go back tomorrow.'

Anna sighed. 'Do you like London, Tom?'

'I don't know.'

'But you're a Londoner. Surely you must have formed an opinion by now.'

'That's exactly why I can't say. It's like asking a fish, What do you think of water, then?'

'But you've lived in Cambridge. You have somewhere else to compare it with.'

'Not really. I was unhappy when I was living in Cambridge. So I can't judge. When I think of Cambridge I just think of really awful parties, and friends who weren't really friends. Just people to hang out with. Other maths students.'

Anna breathed in deeply, to underscore the freshness of the air. 'I don't think I like London. I can't do *that* in London without coughing immediately afterwards. The place is toxic.'

'It's not that bad.'

'It is. I can't breathe properly when the weather's hot. There's so much pollution. It's like there's a steel ring around my chest.'

'Well, maybe you're becoming asthmatic or something. You should go and get it checked out.'

'No, I'm not asthmatic. It's just London.' Her voice was curiously charged with emotion.

'You make it sound personal. As though London's out to get you!'

Anna's face suddenly changed. She acquired a peculiar, harassed look. 'Do you ever get feelings about places, Tom? Really strong feelings?'

'Yes.'

'Well, I think I have strong feelings about London.'

'What are you saying?'

'I don't know. It's hard to explain. But London has never felt like home to me. I've never felt really comfortable in London.'

'But that's because we don't have much money, and we're working hard. If we lived in a big house in Hampstead and had good jobs, maybe you'd feel different about it. I didn't like Cambridge, because I had a bad time in Cambridge. There's nothing wrong with Cambridge *per se*. You feel bad about London because our quality of life is crap. That's all.'

'Maybe.' She sounded unconvinced. 'Maybe, but I don't think so. I feel it in my bones. A strong feeling.'

That was too much. I wasn't prepared to let that one go.

'What on earth are you talking about? In your bones!'

Anna grinned. She had anticipated my response. 'Yeah, you're right. I haven't really thought this one through.'

I picked up a stone and cast it in the direction of the sea. It fell miserably short and landed with a dull thud in the sand.

'Missed,' Anna said.

'Yeah, well, the target's so small. What did you expect?'

Anna picked up a stone of her own and threw it (emitting a sharp effortful grunt as she let go) but, thankfully, it came to earth even further short of the sea than my own abortive attempt. Her physical inferiority helped to shore up my sense of masculinity.

'Tom, do you think we should leave London, when we've got our Ph.D.s? Live somewhere like this? Not here necessarily, but somewhere like it. Somewhere where it's possible to just empty your head. Be.'

'You sound like a hippie.'

'I know.'

The idea of moving into the country had never really occurred to me. It just wasn't an issue.

Anna continued. 'If a job came up, or you had the chance? Would you move?'

'I might do. Yeah, why not. But it would be difficult for both of us to get jobs. At the same university. Junior lectureships in mathematics and psychology . . . What are the chances of both becoming available at the same time in a provincial?'

'Not very high. But, still. If we really wanted it to happen . . .'

'It's possible, I suppose.'

And so we talked of our future together. Our future as a couple. Our future as two regular university lecturers, preparing our courses, supervising our students and undertaking original research. Making friends, and maybe even throwing the odd small party. Long walks at the weekend, by the sea or through the woods. Watching the leaves change colour with the seasons. Books we might one day write. A real fire, a wood-burning stove, earthenware pots. Money to spend on nice things. We were almost there. I could smell the pot-pourri in the ceramic bowl that Anna would inevitably buy at the local craft fair. And as we elaborated our fantasy, I suddenly began to think to myself: *Locke's apparatus. Locke's apparatus.* For a few moments it seemed unreal. Ridiculous almost. Using electricity to burn a hole in time! Photographing the past! The Cavendish Society! But suddenly, I felt a pain behind my eyes. I must have winced.

'Are you OK?'

'Yeah. It's nothing. One of my headaches coming on, I think.'

And as the pain increased, the cottage crumbled to dust. The sea became waves and I saw how each wave could be summarized in a mathematical expression. I saw at once the fraction that would describe the proportions of sky and water. I calculated the iterative sequence that determined the regular pattern on a shell by my foot. I noted that the wild flower that I had plucked from its stem had five petals: like all flowers, its number of petals formed part of the Fibonacci series. And the name Rupert bothered me.

We arrived back at Jean's in time for lunch. I was able to make the odd contribution, but didn't say very much. Eventually Anna and her mother just carried on without me. Perhaps it was because I had begun to merge with the wallpaper that they were able to continue in a less mannered way. Indeed, they became so relaxed that they were able to raise the vexatious topic of Huntley.

'You should try to see him more, Anna,' urged Jean, in a voice that was uncharacteristically overwrought.

'I would if I could, but I can't.'

'I know you're busy, but . . .'

Anna cut in. 'It's not *only* that. I am very busy, but even if I wasn't it would still be pointless. You know what he's like. Even if he got himself together enough to own a phone, the chances of him actually sticking to an arrangement are virtually nil.'

Jean's face became pained. She sighed. A deep, heavy sigh of profound resignation.

'Look, Mum,' continued Anna, 'we've done everything. Tried everything. And there's only so much you can do. I know it's difficult, but it's up to him now.'

There then followed an uncomfortable silence, during which I felt utterly misplaced. Like an intruder almost. This sensation became worse when Jean turned her gaze towards me. Her lips curled upwards, but they failed to part. Moreover, her eyes had become glassy. It was an expression of such complexity one might delve into its deeper meanings for a lifetime. I still think of that smile sometimes. It's a kind of personal *Mona Lisa*. It spoke of embarrassment, pity, haplessness and grief. It made me feel like a child. Thankfully, Jean released us.

'This isn't fair on you, Tom. I'm sure you don't want to hear about our troubles.'

'Oh, it's quite all right. If there's anything I can do to help . . .'

'It's very kind of you to offer. But I fear that Anna is right. There isn't a great deal one can do for Huntley. For the moment at least.' The atmosphere suddenly cleared. 'Well,' continued Jean, 'what would you two like to do this afternoon?'

'I'd like to go for another walk. How about you, Tom?' asked Anna.

'Fine,' I replied.

We had decided to drive out to Lulworth. I had no idea what pleasures awaited me there, but I was promised spectacular views of the sea and interesting rock formations. On our way out of Bournemouth, Jean wanted to drop something off at a friend's house. I can't for the life of me remember what it was. A book, a cake-tin or something like that. I really can't remember. The plan was, as I recall, for Jean to jump out of the car and then back in again. No introductions were planned.

We parked outside a tall, rather austere-looking Edwardian pile. Jean hopped out, rang the bell and was shortly engaged in a very animated conversation with a man of about her own age.

'Who's he?' I asked Anna.

'I don't know,' was her unenlightened reply.

I was beginning to get a little impatient and was glad that Anna seemed to be showing signs of irritation too.

'Oh, come on,' she said out loud.

Then, the inevitable happened. Jean started to beckon us out from the car.

'Oh, no,' said Anna.

At first we feigned stupidity but quickly realized that this was a strategy without much potential. Reluctantly, we got out of the car with our gold-standard false smiles fixed in place. As we approached, Jean called out, 'Anna, Tom. Let me introduce you to Duncan. Duncan Gilmour. He wanted to meet you both.'

'So,' said Duncan, looking right through me. 'You're Anna. I've heard so much about you, I really had to say hello.'

'Pleased to meet you,' said Anna.

Duncan Gilmour beamed at her, and I couldn't help noticing that his eyes seemed to *take in* Anna's face, her breasts and her crotch, in that order, before finally swivelling up to catch my expression of undisguised horror. He shook my hand vigorously as he articulated a hearty 'Tom!'

'Look, Jean,' he said. 'Do come in. Just for a cup of tea.'

Jean's face acquired a slightly strained expression and she began to emit a curious wavering sound.

'Oh, please do,' pleaded Gilmour.

Suddenly Jean succumbed. 'Would you mind?' she asked us both.

'No, of course not,' we chorused together.

'Marvellous,' cried Gilmour, waving us in like an eighteenth-century dandy. I walked very close behind Anna, as I felt almost certain that the extravagance of his gestures was cultivated to increase the likelihood of a chance physical contact. He closed the door, and sighed with satisfaction.

Jean showed us into Gilmour's lounge, where we sat waiting. She immediately joined Gilmour in the kitchen, where we could hear them preparing tea and chatting.

Anna looked at me. 'Sorry.'

'It's OK.'

I looked around the room, and my attention was immediately captured by a large glass case in the corner. I got up and walked over to it. There, neatly laid out in rows, was a collection of what I thought must be antique medical instruments. And beneath these, in a small wooden box lined with red velvet, was a copper-plated Caxton sphere. A component of Locke's apparatus. I couldn't help saying aloud: 'Christ!'

'What is it?' asked Anna.

'This thing here,' I said. 'It's quite rare.'

'Are you sure?'

'Yes. Quite sure.'

'I wonder if Mr Gilmour knows.'

'Look, don't say anything about it.'

'Why not?'

'Just don't, OK?'

'But why not?'

'Just don't.'

I had begun to breathe quite heavily. Anna looked perplexed. However, before she could say anything else, Jean came in with a tray of biscuits and cakes. 'I was just saying to Duncan how much the children enjoyed your concert . . .'

Gilmour followed her in. 'Yes, I'd love to hear you play. I adore the cello.'

They arranged the tea things on a coffee table, and I suddenly felt quite disorientated. I looked at Jean and Gilmour, fussing around, then back at the Caxton sphere. Two separate worlds had suddenly collided. Like matter and antimatter. The effect was devastating.

'Tom. Come and sit down,' said Anna.

I couldn't move. I simply looked into the glass case.

'Ah, I thought that lot might interest you,' said Jean. But her voice sounded distant.

I could hear Gilmour laughing. It seemed to reverberate, as though he were laughing in an echo chamber. 'Quite gruesome some of those things.'

'Tom collects scientific antiques,' said Anna, by way of an explanation for my sudden transportation.

'Does he now?' Gilmour came over to me. 'Let me show you, Tom.' He turned a small key, and opened the glass case. As he did so I almost swooned. The sense of history was palpable. 'They're mostly surgical instruments. My great-grandfather was a GP, and in his day, the local doctor performed most of the routine operations. Take a look at this.' Gilmour reached in and took out what looked like a large pair of scissors with a fork attached. He held it up to my face and said, 'Open wide.'

I opened my mouth. Like an idiot.

'Let's have a look at your tonsils. Oh, yes, they'll have to come out.' He jabbed the fork forward saying 'skewer' and then released two blades that snapped together loudly, saying ' . . . and guillotine.'

'Oh, how ghastly,' said Jean.

'Yes, and all without anaesthetic,' continued Gilmour.

'What was your great-grandfather's name?' I interrupted.

'Henry, I think.'

'No, his surname.'

'Gilmour. Yes, Henry Gilmour.'

'Do you know much about him?'

'Not a great deal, no.'

'Did he leave any papers?'

'Not personal papers, no. He did write a small treatise on hysteria, I believe.'

'Do you have a copy?'

Gilmour rested a hand on my shoulder and laughed again. 'I say, you are keen.'

'Tom!' said Anna. 'Not now.' Her voice had become quite tense, but I couldn't stop myself.

'Do you have a copy?'

'No, I'm afraid not.'

'Do you know if he was a member of any scientific society?'

'I don't know.'

'Does the "Cavendish Society" mean anything to you?'

'No, I'm afraid not.'

'Tom!' said Anna. The tone of admonishment had become unmistakable.

'It's quite all right,' said Gilmour. 'It's very rare that I have such an appreciative guest.'

'Do you know what that is?' I continued, pointing at the Caxton sphere.

'Well, not really. I had always assumed that it was some sort of quack cure for rheumatism or something. Do you?'

'I'm not sure. May I take a closer look?'

'Be my guest.'

I reached in and lifted the Caxton sphere from its bed of velvet. It was very tarnished, yet I could still see my distorted reflection on its surface. My nose and lips bulged out, giving me the appearance of an ape. Gilmour returned to the table to officiate over tea, and the hubbub of trivial conversation receded. I turned the sphere in my hand, transfixed by its beauty. My communion was interrupted by Anna.

'Tom, your tea is getting cold.'

'OK.'

I reluctantly replaced the sphere in its box, and sat beside Anna.

'So, any idea what it is?' asked Gilmour.

'Not really. I think you're probably right. A quack remedy. Though it's an attractive piece.'

'I wouldn't call it attractive exactly.'

'Perhaps not.'

The subject returned to music, and Gilmour proved to be something of an expert. Remarkably, he was very knowledgeable about the cello repertoire and was able to discourse with some eloquence on *the Kodály* while examining the slight bulge that marked the confluence of Anna's thighs. I couldn't believe that Anna and Jean were oblivious to this. He was hardly being subtle. Yet, they didn't seem the least bit perturbed by his blatant lechery.

'Tell me,' continued Gilmour, 'have you heard the Gavin Bryers' cello concerto?'

'Yes,' replied Anna.

'What do you think?'

'I like it very much.'

'Me, too. It's such a wonderfully romantic work. Such lyricism. And the orchestration is so sensual.'

He was almost salivating.

'Yes,' agreed Anna, 'it is well orchestrated. Particularly the percussion.'

'Oh, indeed, so musical. So very musical.' Gilmour gesticulated like an Italian. Almost every statement had to be emphasized with a flamboyant wave of the hand. '. . . and the richness of Lloyd-Webber's tone.'

'Yeah. It depresses me.'

'Well, it would do. Although, of course, he does have a rather better instrument, I imagine.'

He then laughed again. A kind of *ho-ho, ha-ha*, stagy laugh. I expected him to reach out and squeeze Anna's leg at any moment. His lechery thinly disguised by *bonhomie* and an avuncular manner.

I think I would have been quite annoyed if I hadn't been distracted by the Caxton sphere. I kept on looking over at the cabinet, wondering how I might make some discreet offer. The situation was, of course, hopeless, and I was sufficiently in possession of my faculties to recognize this. I had already behaved badly and was expecting an ugly scene with Anna later in the day.

Fortunately, after Jean had drained her third cup of tea, she said, 'Good heavens, look at the time. We must be on our way.'

I sprang up, too eagerly.

When we reached the door Gilmour grasped Anna's arm and said, 'So pleased to have met you. When you come down next, do bring your cello.'

Oh, yeah, I thought.

On our way to Lulworth, Anna asked Jean about Duncan Gilmour. Apparently, he didn't work. Indeed, he had never worked. He was a man of independent means. A shrewd ancestor had invested wisely in textiles. Over three or four generations the money had been gradually squandered. Nevertheless, there was still enough left to keep him in the style to which he had become accustomed. Jean had met him at a meeting of a local pressure group. A *Stop this!* and *Stop that!* kind of group. They had become quite good friends. I could hear the subtext of Anna's enquiries quite clearly. So could Jean, because she suddenly felt compelled to clarify the issue: 'No. It's not like that at all, dear.'

After a temporary lull in the conversation Jean said to me, 'Duncan's collection seemed to take your fancy.'

'Yes, it did.'

'I didn't realize you were so interested in medicine.'

'I'm interested in all kinds of scientific antiques. That includes medical antiques, of course.'

'Do you have a large collection?'

'Yes, he does,' Anna cut in.

Jean smiled.

I knew that what I had resolved to say was entirely inappropriate. But again, I couldn't stop myself. 'If Duncan ever wants to sell off any of those instruments . . .'

I felt Anna jab my ribs hard. *Oh, shit.*

'I can't see that ever happening, Tom,' said Jean, before I could embarrass myself any further. 'They have enormous sentimental value.'

'Yes,' I said, 'of course.'

When we got to Lulworth there were spectacular views of the sea and interesting rock formations. As promised.

It wasn't until we were in bed that evening that Anna had the opportunity to raise the topic of my behaviour.

'That really wasn't on, you know. What you did at Duncan's today.'

'Oh, it wasn't that bad, for Christ's sake. I just got a bit carried away.'

'Carried away? Is that what you call it?'

'Yes.'

'First you tell me not to tell Duncan that he owns a rare antique. Then you pretended that – whatever it was – isn't actually worth very much. Then you try to get my mum to negotiate a sale. What on earth did you think you were doing? Think about it!'

I did. I stopped, and thought about it. Long and hard. And, out of nowhere, came a great tidal wave of shame and remorse. Genuine shame and remorse. It took me completely by surprise. I was quite overcome.

'I'm sorry, Anna,' I said in a feeble, rather tremulous little voice. 'You're right. I behaved like a complete dickhead. I'm really sorry.'

My eyes began to burn and my tongue felt thick in my mouth.

'But why? Why did you behave like that?'

'I don't know. Maybe I was upset.'

'Upset? What was there to be upset about.'

'Well. Didn't you see the way he was looking at you?'

'What?'

Her voice was sharp and mystified.

'Oh, fuck. I don't know what I'm saying. I've really fucked up, haven't I?'

My voice began to waver. Anna placed a hand on my cheek. I drew back quickly, hopelessly trying to conceal the fact that I had begun to cry.

'Tom,' she whispered.

I sniffed, reached out for a paper tissue, and blew my nose.

'Tom?'

I regained a modicum of composure with considerable effort. Took a deep breath and said, 'Anna. Don't leave me. I know I've fucked up this weekend. I know I've been crap with your mother, but . . .'

'Oh, Tom.' She pulled me close to her, and began to rock me from side to side. 'It's all right. Really, it doesn't matter.'

'But it does. I don't know what gets into me sometimes.'

We lay together, locked in each other's arms. I don't know why, but crying had helped. I felt somehow calmer. A little like how I had felt on Studland beach, before I started to think again of Locke's apparatus.

'I'm sorry, Anna, I really am.'

'It's OK.'

'Do you ever think of leaving me?'

'No. Of course not.'

'But I don't understand why you stay with me.'

'Why do you think?'

'I don't know.'

Anna sighed. 'Because I love you.'

Again, I felt like crying, but I was able to control myself.

'But what does that mean?'

'What sort of a question is that?'

'A genuine one. I don't know what it means. Does it have a justification, can you' – I paused for a moment, wondering whether I should actually say what I was thinking, but went ahead anyway – 'argue it? Can you argue your case, explain it?'

'It doesn't need to be argued, Tom.'

'Everything needs to be argued. Otherwise it's invalid.'

Anna kissed my head, and laughed.

'That's why I love you. Because you say things like that.'

'I'm serious. I want to know.'

'I love you because you're interesting. Knowledgeable. Seem to be able to think quicker than anyone else I have ever met. I love you because you are generous. Because you're always the first to buy a round of drinks when we go down the pub with Dave. I love you because I find you attractive. I love you because you do my stats. I love you because you're not a chauvinist. I love your rationality. It makes me mad sometimes, but I love it. OK, is that enough, or do you want me to go on?'

'It's not just an emotion then?'

'No. It's not just an emotion. And even if it was just an emotion, it would still be worth while.'

I felt very peaceful. Her reassuring words eased away my pain. I felt like she was owed an explanation.

'I'm really sorry about what happened at Gilmour's. I really did get carried away. Now that I think about it, I'm not even sure his *objet d'art* was a Caxton sphere.'

I was telling the truth. I had really begun to doubt myself.

'I'm not making any excuses for my behaviour. What I did was wrong. But, even if I had got him to part with it, he wouldn't have been losing very much.'

'OK. Let's just forget it, shall we?'

'Yes. Thanks.'

Again there was a pause.

'You don't think I've fucked up too badly then, with your mum?'

'No, not at all. She probably thinks you're a nice young man.'

'That's all right then.'

'Go to sleep now. London tomorrow.'

'Yes. London.'

The morning was quite subdued. Jean prepared a large breakfast and Anna and I felt obliged to eat it. We sat, munching toast, long after our appointed time of departure. Jean asked me if I had much to do when I got back to London. The answer was, of course, *Yes*. I was referring to my academic work, but I was also considering the Locke machine. Did I have to pursue it? Was it absolutely necessary?

'What do you intend to do, Tom, after your Ph.D?' Jean asked. Perhaps she was considering Anna's prospects.

'I could do a number of things. I could work in IT. I'm fairly competent on a computer.'

'He's being modest,' said Anna, 'he's more than competent. Businesses headhunt him.'

I blushed. I know I did.

' . . . or . . . or I could continue working in academia,' I hurried on. 'I do enjoy my work. I do enjoy pure maths. I think that would be my preference. To remain an academic.'

'And where do you think you will work, eventually?'

I saw my opportunity to earn a few brownie points here.

'Well. That depends on what Anna's doing. I think Anna would like to move out of London.'

This went down very well indeed. Jean had barely concealed her desire for Anna to come back home. My potential acquiescence to such a scheme was most welcome.

We finally left at about eleven. Jean kissed me goodbye. Although she was obviously a kindly disposed soul, I can't say that I was reluctant to leave. My two nights in Bournemouth had required monumental effort. Playing the part of *the boyfriend* was a role I found mentally exhausting. On the doorstep, Jean hugged her daughter – her only child really – and said, 'Don't leave it for so long next time.'

'I'll try not to,' replied Anna.

As we drove away I waved at Jean and smiled. She was clearly saddened by our departure. I saw a thin, rather well-groomed woman, vanishing into the distance.

Our journey back to London was uneventful. Anna and I chatted, quite naturally. The evening before had brought us much closer. I even felt sufficient courage to ask her a question that, under different circumstances, could have been quite impossible.

'Who's Rupert?' I asked, somewhat casually.

'Who?' replied Anna.

'Rupert. Your mother mentioned him. The barrister.'

'Oh, *that* Rupert. He was a friend of the family. You know, boy next door. If only his mother knew.'

'What?' I asked. My heart in my throat.

'By the time he was fourteen he'd been laid by half the old queens in Christchurch.'

6

Sex and Character

When people asked me about my financial situation, my default setting was to respond, *I'm broke*, but really, I was always better off than most students. A logical mind is a much sought-after commodity. I have a very saleable cortex. One of the immense benefits of a mathematical training is that you learn to think in a certain way. Systematically. The kind of way that is very useful if you wish to write a computer program. A great deal of the fluid-movement modelling I undertook as part of my Ph.D. involved writing specialized software. To a very high standard, might I add.

I was fortunate, insofar as I had made the acquaintance of one or two individuals of questionable reputation who not only recognized my gifts but were willing to pay me for them. No, I wasn't a payroll hacker, although I could have been, of course. I have been approached by innumerable company men at software exhibitions. Dear me, I was spotted as a potential recruit at the Data-Soft Next Generation 'con' at the Bloomsbury Hotel when I was only thirteen. But it wasn't to be. I may be many things, but I am not stupid. There are risks and there are risks. Most risks involving friendly men who show no discernible signs of homosexuality are not worth taking. Besides, the fact of the matter is, I liked modelling the motion of fluids. As people say nowadays, it's *my thing*. I could have been a payroll hacker, but that certainly wasn't, still isn't, *my thing*. Not at all.

Nevertheless, penury was testing, so I adopted a compromise position. I did nothing that would be considered illegal; however, ultimately, I was almost certainly in the employ of criminals. Somewhere, many links removed up the food-chain, were men who I had no desire to meet. Fortunately, they had no desire to meet me either. To them, I was an individual of little consequence. An intellectual menial. The arrangement, therefore, was most practicable. I quite enjoyed being a freelance programmer, although it could be somewhat distracting.

Not all of the Locke parts were cheap. Indeed, one of them, the gimbals (which housed the principal chronometer), would cost more than all of the other parts put together. It was a precision piece, requiring much delicate work. I began to wonder whether I would eventually be forced to seek the services of a maritime watchmaker – a prospect that filled me with some trepidation. The acquisition of significant capital, albeit intermittently, had become something of a necessity.

My freelance work was rather straightforward. I would be given a program, usually for a game, and be asked to *polish it up*. By the time the software got to me it was usually in pretty good shape. Sometimes, I would only have to insert one or two commands. More rarely, I would be given a program with a major glitch. Sorting those out could be time-consuming, but the money was good. Cash in hand.

The office, or what I euphemistically called the office, was located just off the Camberwell New Road. I had received a call the day before, requesting my services there. The call happily coincided with the recent onset of a minor financial crisis. I was, therefore, kindly disposed to the message on my answering-machine, in spite of its brevity:

'Hey, Tom, it's Tad. Can you get your butt down here tomorrow? After four is cool.'

There then followed a loud, percussive sound, which was no doubt the receiver being slammed down with considerable force.

Anna had not got to this one before me. Even if she had, I would have been honest. I would have said that I was going to do some more freelancing. On the other hand, I would not have told her anything about the work itself. I was still pretty unsure whether I would ever tell her anything about that.

Tad is short for Tadweusz. Tadweusz Wodiezko. He is something of a character. His parents were Polish immigrants who came to England from Katowice in the 1950s; however, there is nothing Polish about Tad. He is very much at home on the Camberwell New Road. He has become a creature of south London. If things had been different, only slightly different, Tad might have been a millionaire. But he wasn't. Instead, he was one of that strange company of disaffected, though intelligent individuals who exist in the outer circle of cyber-crime. A circle for whom the flow of digital informa-tion down wires has replaced the mail train and the safety-deposit box. A circle for whom lifting a single zero from a bank transaction between New York and Geneva might mean a penthouse in Bangkok by next Tuesday. Tad was never really 'in' on the big scams. But I guess he managed to grab the occasional 'bit part' in a few of the more ambitious productions. He never planned it this way. Indeed, when he started his first business enterprises he was completely 'legit'. A youngish entrepreneur who seemed to have a strong grip on the handle of information technology. A man who could see how the entertainments industry might be transformed, beyond recogni-tion, within only a decade or two. However, things went badly wrong, because of one project. The *Virtual London* Project (or ViLP).

Virtual London was – and still is – the only VR game ever to become criminalized before general release. It was subsequently banned. Quite impressive, when you think about it. Like most computer games, it could be played on several levels, although the action on each level took place in 'London'. The first level was a kind of cops-and-robbers chase through the city. The villains, so I was told, were standard East End stereotypes. If you scored a certain number of points on level one, you graduated to level two. This level was essentially the same as level one, although the characters were a little larger than life – in a way, Dickensian. At the third level the 'London' one entered became distinctly odd. Westminster became more Gothic, the weather became more apocalyptic, the villains more surreal. Apparently, the Soho sub-routine at level three contained some of the most erotic material ever to be realized within a VR visor. The character named Rosa Drab would offer punters services that were scarcely imaginable; this alone would have ensured its notoriety. However, the sex was, surprisingly, the least offensive feature of *Virtual London*. It was the violence that was the problem. *Virtual London* was a blood bath, an essay in mutilation.

The final level, level ten (a level incidently that was never actually reached by any player without using the 'cheat' facility), was allegedly a paradisal London set in an alternative universe, a future in which the Christian reconquest of Moorish Europe was unsuccessful. London was transformed into an *Arabian Nights*-style dreamworld of scented fountains, golden domes, minarets and palaces that, in comparison, made the Alhambra look like a chicken-shed.

The difficulty with *Virtual London* was that it proved to be too good. The unsuspecting player was gradually weaned off reality. As the game made its insidious progress, the mental machinery was gently lifted out of its cradle and set adrift on a hallucinogenic sea. *Virtual London* had the power to unhinge minds.

Certain members of the production team started to get VR sickness. Headaches, nausea and visual disturbances. At first these visual disturbances were relatively mild – fleeting shadows at the periphery of vision, flashes, and sooty motes in the air. Opthalmic investigations failed to reveal any abnormalities. However, the condition worsened. The visual disturbances grew more marked, becoming fully fledged hallucinations, particularly just before sleep. Figures were seen by the bedside, and duvets seemed to accommodate the supine bodies of unwelcome guests. And then, the confusion set in. Members of the ViLP team started seeing characters from *Virtual London* in Regent Street or Piccadilly Circus. Something terrible was going to happen but nobody blew the whistle. There was too much capital riding on the commercial success of the game. Moreover, fundraising had already started for the next project, *Virtual Sarajevo*.

When the first murder happened, it was explained away as a freak occurrence. One of the programmers skewered an innocent bystander through the neck with his umbrella while returning from his local pub after a bout of late-night drinking. He claimed to have no recollection of the event and was at a loss to explain the bloodstains on his clothes. He could, however, remember playing *Virtual London* earlier in the same day, and decommissioning the character Dancing Queen by impaling him on the Beef-Eater's staff. Two days later, another member of the team performed a similar murder. While inquiries were being made a third person – this time a policeman – was killed by yet another member of the team. The whole operation folded within a week.

Tad lost on all of his investments. Tad was ruined. Tad resorted to cyber-crime.

Sometimes, as I walked up Camberwell New Road toward the office, I would worry a little. Tad had spent many a happy hour road-testing *Virtual London*. One could never be quite sure that the sheet metal of his mind was punch-riveted to reality at the appropriate loci. I always watched him very carefully. Too carefully. He suspected, of course.

'Look, Tom, you fuck-arsed jerk, I am not – you reading this? – I am *not* about to kill you.'

'Sorry,' I would say demurely.

'Well, stop looking at me like that!'

'I am sorry. Really, Tad.'

'Jesus. Every time I put my hand in this drawer you tense up like a chick about to take it up the arse. What do you think I got in here? D'you wanna take a look? Wanna see my collection of eighteen-inch murder weapons?'

'No, Tad, it's quite all right. I believe you.'

He would then reach into his drawer and take out something like a floppy disk, which he would throw on to the desk in front of me. 'Fuck, Tom, you better get out of here. I'm armed with half a dozen floppies and thirty-two sticky labels. This is serious shit, Tom!'

The joke always made him laugh.

'Jesus, Tom. How many times do I have to tell you? The guys who went AWOL were typical university jerks. Like you, yeah. Spec-eyed wank merchants. They had no experience of getting out of their heads. They got VR sickness, for Christ's sake. I had so much acid in the seventies that this virtual shit was like Thorpe Park to me!'

I believed him. Without doubt, Tad had been around.

Wodiezko Recreational Consultants (WRC-International) was based above an off-licence. You gained access to Tad's office by an almost vertical flight of stairs that went from the street directly to his room. I got the tube to the Oval at three-thirty. I did not know that I would never make the journey again. That afternoon was to be my very last visit to WRC-International. I remember, he welcomed me in with the cry, 'Yey, Tommo!'

That day, the Boisterous dial was set on maximum.

'Hello, Tad, how are you?'

'Fucking great, man. Fucking great. It's your lucky day, Tom. Your lucky day.'

'Why everything twice, Tad? Why everything twice?'

I really couldn't resist it.

He gave a huge, cacophonous guffaw. 'Don't be cheeky now!' he said, giving me a mock slow-motion punch on the side of the face. 'No. Seriously, Tom. This *is* your lucky day. I've got something in from Amsterdam that I want you to take a look at. It's got a glitch. It kind of fragments after five minutes. If you can sort it out by this evening, it'll be worth two hundred quid. OK?'

'And if I can't?'

'I'll give you fifty for trying your best. Now, tell me that ain't fair.'

'That's not fair.'

'Well, tough shit. Do you want to give it a go or don't you?'

'I'll give it a go.'

Tad booted up and gave me the visor while singing, 'That deaf, dumb and blind kid, sure plays a mean pinball.' He then looked at me intensely, and sang, 'Tommy, can you see me?'

I responded by giving him a blank expression.

I could hear him chuckling away as I fixed my head in the apparatus. It was the usual stuff. Typical WRC. I found myself in a room that looked like a Turkish brothel. A curtain at the far end of the room parted and in walked a very large black woman with three breasts and two vaginas (one in the correct place, the other like a post-box, beneath her belly button). The soundtrack was rather frenzied, and the woman began to dance. To be honest, the graphics were of a rather poor quality. I wasn't terribly impressed. Nevertheless, I thought that it might have been the work of one of the *Virtual London* team. It might even be a corrupted cut from one of the Soho entertainments. Before long the image began to flicker. Intermittent flashes. Sheets of jagged colours.

'Yes,' I said. 'I see what you mean.' I took off the visor.

Tad was rolling a joint. 'OK, boy genius. Go, go, go!'

I didn't leave Tad's office until ten o'clock. The walk down to the Oval was rather unsettling. There were few people on the street; however, those who were enjoying a late stroll had cultivated a threatening attitude. As I passed them, my neck would tingle. It was as though I was stepping through a field of static. The violence was palpable. Needless to say, I ensured that I never made eye contact. I had spent so much time looking through the visor, my eyes hurt. By the time the Tube station was in sight, my visual field had begun to break up like a corrupted VR game. This had happened once or twice before after visiting Tad's office. It usually went pretty quickly. But that night, it kept on happening. I started to get panicky. Indeed, I had to stop and lean against a wall for a few minutes. I shook my head and took a few deep breaths. Gradually I calmed down and my visual field stabilized, but something was wrong. I still didn't feel right. I began to reflect on the propriety of what I had been doing. What was it all for? A modest financial supplement! And that night, it was very modest indeed. I had left Tad's office with only £50 in my pocket. The program was a mess. A total mess. All that concentration! My head started to throb. This couldn't go on. I had tried to pretend otherwise, but the truth was becoming more and more difficult to ignore. Maybe I was spending too much time in *Virtual London*? I continued my walk towards the Oval station, having made a resolution that I hoped I would be able to keep.

There were times when Anna surprised me. I think if someone can surprise you while you are living with them, then you don't really know them. I remember, a friend of hers (from University College), Laura, was having a party. A birthday party, as I recall. Anna wasn't really the party-going type; however, she felt obliged to go. Most of the other UC psychology post-grads were going, so her attendance was something of a necessity.

I had invited Dave along. It was *that* kind of party. Anna's invitation said 'Bring a crowd.' I hate going to parties on my own. Yes, Anna would be with me, but she would want to talk to her friends and then I would be stuck with some psychologist who I didn't really want to talk to. So I thought recruiting Dave would be most helpful. In the final event, this proved to be a somewhat misconceived scheme.

When Dave arrived Anna was still getting ready. We waited in the kitchen. When she appeared I was dumbstruck. She was wearing a skirt. I had never seen Anna in a skirt before. A long black skirt and – these I had no idea she possessed – black boots. She was also wearing a thin black jumper which emphasized her breasts. But what really fazed me was the make-up. The works. Whatever it is that women do, she had done it. She looked absolutely amazing.

'Are you ready then?' she said.

I couldn't reply. I had never had cause to comment on her dress before.

Fortunately, Dave was able to intervene. 'Well . . .' he said. 'You look great.'

'Thanks.' Anna smiled. A radiant, self-assured smile.

'Yes,' I followed. 'Really great.'

She came over to me and interlocked her fingers with mine.

To tell the truth, it upset me. Instead of feeling proud of her I felt ashamed of myself. After half an hour in the bathroom Anna had transformed herself completely. There's more that you can do to yourself if you're a woman. You have more tricks at your disposal. I couldn't compete. I felt devastated. She wasn't my Anna. She was anybody's Anna. But not mine.

'Well,' said Dave, 'shall we stop off at the Nightingale?'

'Oh, I don't know about that,' replied Anna. 'It's getting late.'

'Why, what time is it?'

'It's nine, and we were supposed to arrive at eight-thirty.'

'What's the problem then?'

'We're already late.'

'No, we're not. No one, but no one arrives at parties on time. Look, this is elementary stuff here. I can't believe that you two haven't learned this yet. Where have you been? It's just not done. I've never arrived at a party on the *day* it started. I would consider it rude.'

Anna placed a finger on her lips and evaluated our position.

'You don't want to seem too uncool!' urged Dave.

Anna gave him one of her *Boys!* expressions and said, quite pointedly, 'Dave, how old are you?'

'OK, OK,' he replied, 'but we could be helping your friend to arrange the twiglet bowls for at least an hour if we split now.'

'All right. How about a compromise? We'll go to the Nightingale for about forty-five minutes, and then go.'

'Fine,' said Dave. 'Rolling up at about eleven will be less difficult for me. What about you, Tom?'

I was still looking at Anna's clearly defined lips. They were so much fuller, when painted. A curious fact that I had once read many years before came into my mind: lipstick was originally used by Roman prostitutes, to indicate that they were willing to perform fellatio.

'Tom?' asked Dave again.

'Err . . .'

'Is that an Err?'

Anna laughed.

'Sorry, Dave. I don't care. You know . . . whatever.'

'The Nightingale, then.'

We spent over an hour down the pub, during which Dave seemed to be psyching himself up for action. He was even more outrageous than usual, and regaled us with a compressed (and euphemistic) history of his various exploits at parties. I was very tense that night, made worse by the fact that Anna seemed to be quite relaxed. Much more so than usual. Eventually, much later than intended, we got into the Skoda and Anna set the controls for Crouch End (what is it with some London place names? Crouch End, for Christ's sake).

The party house was fairly small. Situated in a side-street off Crouch End Broadway. We couldn't park near by and had to walk some distance. As we approached I could hear the dull thud of loud music. The door was open, and a few people were standing on the doorstep, smoking.

'Hi,' they said.

'Hi,' we replied.

Inside, the atmosphere was thick with smoke. The corridor was lined with people and we passed a front room which had been emptied of furniture. About half a dozen people were dancing. Mostly women. Anna weaved her way ahead of us into quite a large kitchen at the back of the house.

A woman in a skin-tight red dress, with tortoiseshell horn-rimmed glasses and longish dark hair suddenly screamed as though she had been stabbed through the heart. 'Anna! You made it! You look wonderful.'

This was Laura.

'Happy birthday,' said Anna.

Some rather superficial introductions followed before Laura darted off to attend to some more arrivals. Dave placed our bottles on the kitchen table and searched for some glasses. There were none available so he simply took some cans from a six-pack and handed them over.

A tall, thin man in jeans and a T-shirt pushed through and said, 'Anna!'

'John!'

John leaned down and gave Anna a kiss on the cheek. It made me feel uncomfortable.

'John, this is Tom. And Dave.'

'Hi. Hi.'

Dave and I just nodded.

'John's from the department,' said Anna, by way of an explanation. They began to make some small talk, which I was drawn into. It was predictably dull. Inevitably, the conversation began to lean towards psychology. John was doing some tedious research into attentional biases in anxiety disorders. It all seemed rather obvious to me: that anxious people should be more sensitive to threat-related information than non-anxious people. However, for Anna's sake, I feigned interest. To be fair, John did ask me about my work, but I lost him after about two sentences.

While I was acting interested, Laura interrupted Anna and dragged her off. I felt suddenly alone. I turned around to find Dave, but he was nowhere to be seen.

John continued to tell me more about his research, and I found it almost impossible to extricate myself. Eventually, I was inspired and asked if he knew where the toilet was. He pointed upstairs. I said thanks and wrestled my way out, back into the hall. Immediately to my left was a small, darkish back room. Anna was standing next to a man who must have been about thirty or thirty-five. Her can of lager had been replaced by a glass of white wine, and I noticed that she was laughing. I wanted to go in, but felt foolish with John still able to see me, so I continued down the corridor and turned to walk up the stairs. Typically, the stairs were littered with individuals, and I was the cause of considerable annoyance; several people had to stand so that I could pass. I felt so stupid – making my way up to the toilet when I didn't really want to go.

When I got to the toilet there was a queue outside.

'Hello,' said a rather plump girl in a leather miniskirt and lacy tights. 'Come for a piss?'

'It would seem so,' I replied.

'From the uni?' she asked.

'Yes,' I replied.

'Thought so,' she said.

Clearly, my appearance had given me away.

'Come on, come on!' she said to the toilet door. She then put her hands over her crotch, let her knees fall together and swung from side to side like a child attempting to stem an imminent flow of urine. I looked on in mystification.

'So what do you do then? At the uni?'

'I'm a Ph.D. student.'

'Yeah, but what?'

'What subject?'

'Yeah. No. Don't tell me. Let me guess.' She paused for a few moments. 'History.'

'No.'

'Is it something sciency?'

'Yes.'

'Physics.'

'Close.'

She looked at the door and said again, 'Come on, come on.' She seemed to have forgotten that she was in the middle of a conversation.

'I think I'll come back later,' I said, though why I felt I needed to justify my actions is beyond rational understanding. As I gingerly picked and probed my path down the upper stairs, I saw Dave at the other end of the landing. He had one hand against the wall, cornering a very petite oriental woman. They were deep in conversation. She was looking up, into Dave's eyes, as though he were revealing to her the secrets of the universe, instead of the utter bullshit that was his stock-in-trade. His success with women was truly alarming.

When I got half-way down the staircase I could see into the back

126

room again. Anna was still standing there, talking to her older man. And at that moment *something inside me snapped*. I felt it give. I slumped down and sat on an empty stair, and looked through the bannisters. I pressed my head against the grimy painted wood, and in a moment, I was back in Cambridge. Those hopeless, lonely years came flooding back. Those terrible, terrible years of sexual frustration and emptiness. Anna ceased to be Anna. She joined the ranks of juvenile sirens who populated my memory. Those slender, elusive creatures, who would torment me from afar. Anna looked so sophisticated. The way she held her glass, the way she stood – even the fall of her hair. And when the man offered her a cigarette, and she took it, she became completely unknown territory. My Anna didn't smoke! There was something in that simple social transaction, the way she leaned forward to catch the flame of his lighter, that tipped me over an internal precipice and down into darkness. There was something so compliant about it. So reciprocal. My stomach knotted and turned. I felt anger welling up inside me. The same anger that I had known so well in Cambridge.

In a peculiar way, it was like an old friend. I was surrounded by fools, idiots. The injustice of my predicament had been preserved, like an insect in amber. These imbeciles had, in their presence, a man who would break the fundamental laws that govern the universe, with the power of his intellect alone. Yet, they were oblivious. Anna was oblivious.

At that moment someone put on 'Brown Sugar', and this seemed to represent something of a clarion call. Inert bodies were revitalized, and a tribal mass gathered in the front room. One moron, at the bottom of the staircase, carried by the tidal sweep of the moment, rose to his feet and began to gesticulate frantically like a burning spastic. His partner, so pale and emaciated that her presence was more an emanation than a physical reality, stood beside him, swaying to the beat. I noticed Anna, below, carried in the swell (and accompanied) into the throbbing mass.

I stood and went back up the stairs. The toilet door was open. I couldn't see Dave anywhere. I knew that he would have retired behind one of the other closed doors with his new friend. All terribly predictable. In fact, as predictable as me, ending up sitting on a toilet, behind a locked door, trying to fight down feelings of despair and anger. After a while, somebody tried the door handle and I realized I would have to leave my unlikely sanctuary. I splashed cold water on my face. It issued out of a diminutive tap, into a claustrophobic sink. I shook my head and dried my face in my handkerchief. The visage I caught in the mirror was not a happy one.

Outside, I was accosted by John again. He began a conversation which I felt obliged to continue. Well, if I am entirely honest, it was something of a relief. It would have been embarrassing if I had spent the whole evening talking to no one. I had already begun to wonder what on earth I could do next. Again, we talked for quite a long time. My guess was that he was not feeling terribly comfortable either, and we had therefore found each other to cling to, in order to avoid feeling like social inadequates. When he began to talk about *Star Trek* I knew that I had found my level.

On reflection, I am surprised that I was able to keep the conversation going. I wasn't really listening. I was simply obsessing about Anna, and the man who she had spent so much time talking to. When the slow music came on, I imagined them dancing together, his hands on her hips. Her head, resting on his shoulder. His breath, on her neck. And while this was going on inside my head, I was saying things like, 'Of course, the new work on photon entanglement does suggest that teleportation may one day be possible.'

My conversation with John was brought to a close by the emergence of Dave.

'Hello, Tom.' For some reason, Dave's appearance seemed to unhinge John who, apropos of nothing, said, 'Be seeing you then,' and ran off down the stairs.

'How you doing?' asked Dave.

'OK.'

'You look bored stupid.'

'I am really. What were you doing in there?'

'Snogging.'

'With that Chinese . . .'

'Malaysian.'

' . . . girl?'

'Yep. Fucking ace!'

'What's she doing now?'

'Adjusting her make-up.'

'Oh.'

'Then I'm walking her home. Lives in Finsbury Park.'

'Oh, I see. You won't be needing a lift, then.'

'No. I don't even want a lift, thanks.'

'What does she do?'

'Hand relief, blow-jobs, the light-bulb trick, I suppose.'

I didn't laugh.

'All right,' he continued, 'she's a trainee accountant. Magic, eh?'

Dave looked at me closely.

'Are you all right, Tom?'

'Yeah.' How many times have I said, *Yeah*, to that question? How many times have I said that things were *OK, great, fine*, when they were blatantly not!

'You look a bit pissed off, that's all.'

'No, I'm just jealous.' The statement had several meanings. I let it hang there for a while before continuing. 'I've been talking about *Star Trek*.'

'Never mind, old son. You're going home with Anna. She looks fucking great tonight! You've got nothing to complain about.'

The snog-room door opened, and Dave's oriental friend came out. She was staggeringly attractive on closer inspection. Dave introduced me to 'Doris' (this was surely a Davism) although she didn't so much as flinch when he said the name. Perhaps she was drunk. Dave then said that he would give me a call *in due course*, and off they both went.

I followed them down the stairs and Dave turned and winked as he left. I walked back into the kitchen, where I found Anna talking with Laura, another man I didn't recognize, and John. Anna smiled when she saw me. But what did that mean?

In the car going back, Anna said, 'What happened to Dave?'

'He went off with a Malaysian woman.'

'I didn't see a Malaysian woman.'

'You didn't see Dave either. That's because they were snogging all night in a room upstairs.'

'Typical. He's incorrigible, isn't he?'

When we reached Turnpike Lane she said, 'Who did you talk to?'

'Oh, only John, really. I did have a talk with a woman . . . but she wasn't very coherent.'

'Which one? What did she look like?'

'Fat. She was wearing a leather miniskirt.'

'Oh, her. Yes, she did seem pretty drunk. He's nice, isn't he, John?'

'Yes. He seemed like a nice bloke.'

But all the time, I wanted to know who the older man was. I wanted to know what happened. *Did they dance together? What happened?*

'I thought I saw you smoking,' I said.

'You did. Well, one or two won't hurt.'

'But why?'

'Why?'

'Why were you smoking?'

'Because I felt like it.'

'I didn't know you smoked.'

'I don't.'

'But you were, you just said so.'

'That's not smoking, is it? I was just . . . joining in. That's all right, isn't it?'

'Yes. Just seemed odd. To see you smoking. I was surprised.'

The pressure inside me was building. Like the pressure you get when you choose the slower-moving of two queues in the supermarket. I had to ask the question. 'Who was that man you were talking to? The older bloke.'

'Tony.'

'Who's he?'

'A friend of Laura's.'

'What does he do?'

'He's a producer. He produces records. We were talking about music.'

'What was he like?'

'Interesting.'

Interesting! She had me sitting next to her and she had the audacity to say that *he* was interesting. I bit into my lower lip until it really hurt for the remainder of our journey, looking at Anna, and wondering.

Although I concealed the Locke paper from Dave, I did, once or twice, show him the odd new acquisition. I remember, when I obtained a copy of Weininger's *Sex and Character*, I recognized its potential immediately. It was published in 1903. Sadly – or perhaps not so sadly – the author committed suicide at the age of twenty-four. Nevertheless, his masterpiece (so the English-translation foreword informed me) was, in its day, the talk of Vienna. Weininger had some curious ideas about sex. He wanted to develop a metaphysics of sexuality.

After laughing our way through most of the introductory chapters, Dave become rather stuck on a particular passage. Weininger suggested that there were essentially two types of women, the absolute prostitute and the absolute mother. He believed that the mother type existed for a sole purpose, the preservation of the human race. Weininger posited that her only aim was to have a child, that she would become a mother by any man, and that she was – and here we found much amusement – *courageous and thrifty*. The language was splendid. The prostitute type, however, is only interested in sexual intercourse. According to Weininger, she is *cowardly and lavish* –

although what he meant by 'lavish' was by no means clear from the text.

After laughing for a while, Dave suddenly stopped. 'You know, it's not that stupid, is it? Not really.'

'It's ridiculous.'

'Yeah, I know it sounds ridiculous. But is it? I mean, if you're going to attempt some character typology of women, then doing so on the basis of their sexuality is as good as any other way. And when I think about it, I think women do fall broadly into those two categories.'

'That might be regarded as sexist in politically correct circles.'

'Then, in my defence, I would beg to call Charles Darwin. What are women here for? To fuck and to raise kids. That's it, really. They're not here to become doctors, lawyers or company directors. They're not here to publish academic articles or go to the moon. They're here to fuck and to raise kids. That's what the man said. In the same way that we – young Thomas – are here to fuck indiscriminately. So, dear old Otto wasn't being that stupid, when you think about it.'

I sipped my drink.

'So what's Anna then? What category would you put her into?'

I felt rather uncomfortable.

'She's a prostitute.' I said this without hesitation. As I said it, my stomach turned. It was as though, inadvertently, I had faced some terrible reality. Dave laughed aloud. He thought I was joking. I began to laugh with him, to save the situation; however, I remained unsettled. By that time I had become almost phobic of discussing Anna with Dave. So, I quickly changed the subject.

'What happened with Doris?'

'Who?'

'The Malaysian girl?'

A flicker of recognition suddenly ignited. 'Oh, Patricia.'

I did not seek a further explanation. I had become entirely familiar with the implicit logic of Dave's sense of humour. He smiled to himself for a while before adding, 'No, nothing.'

'Nothing?'

'Nothing happened. Dead loss, really. I was expecting the works, but there you go. Turned out to be a bit of a Christian. According to her reading of Christianity, it's OK to let a bloke snog you all night and occasionally rub your arse, but it's not OK to have sex after. Well, not on a first date, anyway. Where do they get these ideas from? Is there something I missed in the Bible? Is there some passage in there that explains when God thinks it's OK for women to give head? Because this has happened several times before. Just as I'm about to get down to the real business, the woman under inspection will profess some religious belief and defer proceedings. Yet, I'll be buggered if I know where they get their schedule from. Is it in there? Somewhere in Corinthians or something? Chapter three, verse eight . . . And lo, it is so, that the swapping of tongues is no offence in the eye of God on the first date, but damned is she who goeth on to giveth head (for she must waiteth for the third date).'

I decided that, at least on one level, I would take Dave's conversation seriously.

'I think it's quite easy to understand. I'm no psychologist, but I would suggest that *the schedule* is an attempt at resolving conflict. The conflict between the natural desire to have sex – the Darwinian imperative – and the unrealistic expectations of religion. A sort of pseudomorality emerges, as a compromise position. It has no real justification, and makes no sense from a secular or religious point of view. Which is why it annoys you so much.'

'Yeah,' replied Dave, I think, a little disappointed that I had taken his expostulations so seriously.

'Hey, talking of religion. I heard some absolutely fucking amazing gossip today,' said Dave, drawing his chair closer to the table.

'Oh?'

'Have I mentioned Keith Ward?'

'Yes.'

'One of the senior lecturers in the department, yeah? Anyway, he hasn't been in for months, and there were rumours going around that something was wrong. He was ill maybe. Well, it turns out that Ward found God. But not in a quiet, contemplative, mystical way. You know, the way physicists usually go, in the end. No way. Ward finds God in a kind of in-your-face, evangelical, David Koresh-madman kind of way. He was arrested for trying to burn down an abortion clinic last week. And, the poor fuck has been locked up.'

'What happened?'

'Well, this is it. It's really amazing stuff.'

Dave paused, and took a sip of his drink. He was, after all, an accomplished story-teller, and it was essential that I be made to wait for a few seconds more. Dave returned his glass to the table.

'He had been awarded a very substantial grant. Really prestigious. Sequencing a part of the genome. The junk above PGM-1.'

'PGM-1?' I asked (sometimes Dave forgot that I wasn't a biochemist).

'The Phosphoglucomutase-1 gene.'

'Right.'

'So, there he was, sequencing all this DNA above PGM-1, when he reckoned that he noticed peculiarities in the sequence. After examining these, he came to the conclusion that certain base sequences corresponded with letters in the alphabet. So, you might get cytosine, guanine, adenine, thymine, adenine, thymine.' As he said these words he drew the letters CGATAT on the table with a finger dipped in lager. 'So, that sequence might represent the letter A. GCTAAT, say' – he paused and drew the second letter string – 'might represent B, and so on.'

I had become quite engrossed in his tale, against my better judgement. Dave still had the power to haul me in, and keep me there.

'Well, after analysing all of these sequences and cracking the code, Ward found something written in the junk above PGM-1. Actually written in the DNA.'

'What? A message?'

'Sort of.'

'What was it?'

134

Again, Dave paused for effect, before saying, 'The first few lines of a Beatles number. "Yellow Submarine." You know the one.'

Unfortunately I couldn't stop him before he started to sing. 'We all live ... da-da, da-da, da-da, da ... yellow submarine, yellow submarine.'

A rather cretinous chap sitting at the next table turned and grinned inanely at Dave. For one terrible moment I thought that Dave was about inadvertently to initiate an episode of community singing.

'Yes, Dave, I do know the song.'

'All right, all right. Just checking. So, what are the chances of that? Eh? What are the chances of the lyrics of "Yellow Submarine" turning up above PGM-1?'

'Remote.'

'Right! Ten to the power of fuck, yeah?'

'Fuck squared, at least.'

'At least!'

'And they were all there? The complete song?'

'I don't think so, a couple of lines, I think. Nevertheless, it's there. It really is. Defying both probability and credibility. And my sources are reliable, I can assure you.'

'And this discovery turned Ward to God?'

'Yep. I guess he thought, this is so unlikely it must mean something. And, in the end, he decided that it meant that God existed. Well, he started to talk about this to his team, and everybody said, *Yes, Keith, this is pretty weird shit but, you know, we're scientists, and the most parsimonious explanation for an anomaly like this is chance, not the existence of God!* And apparently, he said, *No way.* He went off, did some calculations, and came back saying that even if the universe were ten times its actual age, that would not be enough time for this to have happened by chance. There had to be another explanation. And God was the best alternative hypothesis. And then he started looking at the lyrics of "Yellow Submarine" really closely, and seeing some stupid eco-message in them. You know, all working together, blue skies, sea of green . . .'

135

'And they let him stay in the department?'

'Well, yes, he was still doing good work. It was just that he had developed all these crazy ideas. Anyway, things came to a head when the lab was visited by the US half of the team. These guys were pretty sharp. So everybody had to be on best behaviour. The Prof. had told Keith just to go through the data and mention *the anomaly* as a joke. It was, after all, very funny. But when Keith got up to speak, he sort of ditched the human-genome spiel and explained how he had discovered evidence for the existence of God, and a method for establishing peace on earth by the year 2010. It was all very embarrassing, and Keith was subsequently relieved of his duties. Soon after that, he started traipsing around abo-houses, threatening to burn them down. Apparently he was arrested soon after, with one of his disciples! Fucking amazing, eh?'

I didn't know what to say. Dave's story set up curious resonances in my mind that I couldn't quite understand.

'Yes. Quite extraordinary.'

I began to wonder how my own work with the Locke apparatus might be received. With similar scepticism, no doubt. Even so, there was a difference between myself and the unfortunate Dr Ward: I would have evidence on my side. Lots of it. Moreover, Dr Ward had clearly become mentally unstable. No one would dare suggest that I was.

Dave picked up the Weininger book and flicked though it again. 'So he killed himself in the end, did he?'

'Yes.'

'How old was he?'

'Twenty-four.'

'Christ! Our age!'

'Yes. Our age.'

'There but for the grace of God, eh?' said Dave.

I didn't really understand what he meant by this. Nor was I prepared to ask him.

7

The Schwenck Problem

I would sometimes look through Anna's psychology books for diversion and amusement. They were, on the whole, about quite respectable topics such as memory and attention. She was, to her credit, an experimental psychologist, and her work was largely undertaken in the laboratory. Fortunately, she had not been seduced by her undergraduate psychopathology lectures into areas which might be described as 'clinical'. Nevertheless, her bookshelves still entertained a range of titles that made reference to psychiatry and psychiatric conditions.

I can remember, she was once working through a pile of books that were stacked on the kitchen table. I sat down beside her and passed an idle moment scanning the contents of one or two volumes that she had discarded. By chance, I discovered an interesting description of something called de Clerambault's syndrome. Afflicted individuals often become obsessed with a celebrity with whom they fall hopelessly in love.

'Do you know anything about this?' I asked Anna, pointing to the relevant section. I wasn't altogether sure of how to pronounce the name.

'De Clerambault's? Not really. Something to do with stalkers, I think. Why?'

'It says here that individuals with this problem often fall in love with celebrities. They also think that the celebrity in question is in love with them. They're not like fans, as such. They actually fall in love. Passionately.'

'So?'

'Do you think it's possible to develop de Clerambault's syndrome and fall in love with something inanimate?'

'An object?'

'Well. Yes.'

'I suppose so. I suppose it's possible to form an abnormal attachment to anything. Although that would be more like fetishism, really. Why?'

'Just asking.'

Anna went back to her text without further questioning. She was obviously looking for something and was happy not to get involved in a detailed discussion about an obscure psychiatric condition. Of course, I wasn't 'just asking'. I never 'just ask'. If I ask a question, it is almost invariably because I am looking for an answer.

The fact of the matter was that while reading about de Clerambault's, I was reminded of my father. He too, seemed to have a crush on a celebrity, except the celebrity in question was inanimate. A train, to be precise. The *Flying Scotsman*. To say that my father was a trainspotter would be to do him a grave injustice. He never went trainspotting. Nor did he ever use Elastoplast to repair his glasses. Not that there is anything wrong with trainspotting. I have never really understood why individuals with an interest in the rail transport system should be specifically selected for public contempt. Why is it trendy or fashionable to be fixated on a pop group but deeply unfashionable to be fixated on a train? It is a distinction I am unable to make on rational grounds. Whatever, the fact of the matter is, my father shared – with a sizeable proportion of like-minded contemporaries – a passion for the steam age. He would often describe 'the romance of steam', a sentiment that I could understand. Where I feel my father parted company with the common herd was with respect to the specificity of his interest and the manner in which he pursued it.

In retrospect, I do not think it an overstatement to say that he loved the *Flying Scotsman*. He called it 'Scottie'. Not 'the Scottie', but 'Scottie', as you might refer to a person. Scottie had broken the speed record, not the driver or the engineer who designed 'him', but Scottie 'himself'. My father did have a more general interest (if you can call it that) in steam locomotives, but this too seemed to have been curiously narrowed by his passion. Thus, other engines were mentioned (for example the *Pride of Argyle* and *Pumping Angus*), but all were linked by a distinct Caledonian theme.

As well as the tartan-framed picture of Scottie on the mantelpiece, my father possessed an old vinyl recording of famous steam engines, one of which was Scottie. I was quite fascinated with his ritual, particularly when I was very young. He would take the record out of its sleeve, clean it with a special fluid (and yellow cloth), and place the shiny black disc on the turntable. He would then, with painful care, release the deck arm above one particular track. If, by mistake, the stylus landed on the track itself, he would become quite annoyed. It seemed essential that he hear the track from the very beginning, preceded by a few moments of reverential silence. Well, I say silence, but I can still recollect the hiss and quiet 'thump' of the vinyl as it revolved on the turntable.

My father would sit in his chair, the record sleeve balanced on his knees, close his eyes and be transported as the station sounds filled the room. Then, almost immediately, Scottie's powerful mechanical pulse would begin and accelerate. His steam-breath exhalations would spice the air with oil and coal dust, displacing the trappings of everyday existence from the recesses of my father's mind. The pistons would work, in-and-out, pushing and pulling, to turn the great wheels, thrusting the *Scotsman's* huge metal bulk forward, faster and faster. And as the volume and momentum increased, my father's chest would rise and fall in sympathy. His expression would take on a curious cast, a cast that, when I observed it as a child, made me somewhat uneasy. My father was strangely changed. Now, when I conjure this image to mind, I cannot help but conclude that my father was aroused. Excited. He never communed with Scottie when my mother was present. And, when I was older, he always asked me to busy myself elsewhere in the house before placing the record on the turntable.

But I knew what he was doing. The roar of the locomotive was clearly audible as it rose through the floorboards and into my bedroom. Some years later, my father purchased headphones. Thus, he eventually managed to keep his sordid activity entirely clandestine.

To contemplate one's parents' sexuality is almost impossible. There seems to be some curious automatic censor in the mind that forbids it. However, I am curiously drawn to inspect these recollections, in the same way that one is drawn to view any outrage or atrocity; it is difficult to turn away.

My father must have had conventional tastes at one time. There is some evidence to support this. Like most fathers, mine had a shed. This served not only as a storehouse for his meagre and symbolic supply of tools, but as a sanctuary into which he would, occasionally, retreat. The shed was always locked; however, I knew where the key was.

I must have been about thirteen at the time. Just prior to undertaking an experiment that utilized several combustible materials, I considered it prudent to relocate my laboratory to a safer environment. That is to say, somewhere more resistant to the consequences of an incendiary accident. I thought I was being very adult and responsible. Indeed, I anticipated praise for my considerate behaviour.

My mother and father were out of the house and (eager to complete my investigation) I could not wait to request their permission to use the shed. The shed itself was quite small and unremarkable. An old chest of drawers served as a worktop. Of course, I could not resist opening them. The first two drawers contained old tools, several of which were rusting. The bottom drawer, however, contained a number of old newspapers. My attraction to old documentation must have been burgeoning, even then, because my curiosity got the better of me. As I opened an old copy of the *Telegraph* magazine, another magazine fell out of it and on to the floor. A scantily clad cover-girl promised to reveal all inside. She wore a basque, stockings and suspenders. I was, of course, fascinated, and immediately viewed the contents. The magazine – *Viva* – was published in 1972.

I imagine that my father must have spent months psyching himself up to purchase his wank mag. The fact that it was bought before I was born suggested that he was disinclined to throw it away. It must have cost him dearly to enter an anonymous newsagent's and reach for the top shelf. I am sure it was something that he could only ever summon the courage to do once in his lifetime. After I had examined the vaguely frightening photographs of female genitalia in sufficient detail to arrest my appetite for knowledge I returned the magazine to its place of concealment.

I subsequently completed my experiment, which was a success.

When I told my father that I had used the shed, he was livid. He told me that I had done a *very bad thing* and that I must never – and he repeated it several times – *never*, use the shed without his prior permission. I was sent to bed without my supper. I cried, wretched and hungry, into a pillow.

Two days later, my father was somewhat sheepish. He explained that he had lost his temper with me because I had done something very wrong. I had been 'behind his back'. Nevertheless, in principle, he did not object to me using the shed if it was essential for my experiments.

I returned to the shed the following day. When I searched for the vintage copy of *Viva*, it was nowhere to be found. It must have been a great personal sacrifice, to dispose of his only (and hard come by) pornographic magazine. Such are the sacrifices that a father must make.

I wonder, did he fill the resulting gap in his life with Scottie? If so, then I am perhaps responsible – albeit indirectly – for his creative and idiosyncratic choice of sex object, a thought I am uneasy with. However, in the end, do I really care? In the end, doesn't all this represent further proof supporting my argument that families are damaging and best avoided? I would swap my father for a test tube any day.

In spite of the fact that I was spending so little time on my Ph.D., supervisions with Béla weren't going badly at all. Things had *picked up*. This wasn't because I had suddenly started working. Not at all. In fact, I was working less than ever before on my thesis. It was just that, during the course of modelling anomalies in the space–time continuum, I had seen an application *vis-à-vis* my own work. I had taken the smallest crumb from Locke's banquet and offered it to Béla as my own. He hailed it as a major breakthrough.

'Tom, this is excellent,' he said, dispelling the frown that had become a near permanent feature of his Neanderthal mug for the past six months. 'I think we have done well here.'

I noted the use of 'we'.

Mathematicians peak younger than athletes. Therefore, ageing maths professors must lay an immediate and equal claim to the achievements of their protégés if they are to have any credibility at all on the world stage. In Béla's mind, he was already presenting my findings at an expenses-paid conference in Aspen or Venice.

'Tom,' he said, placing a bear-like paw on my shoulder, 'we must celebrate.'

He opened a bottle of Sainsbury's wine (probably not worth more than £2.98) and poured it out with a theatrical gesture and a facial expression that suggested he was offering me freshly collected nectar from Elysian fields. I tried to look grateful. We both sipped the coarse liquid, which was so dry it almost made me cough.

After a while, Béla looked at me quizzically. 'Tomash . . . You have done well here, and I am very happy. But, for many months now, you have not been so sharp. No?'

'That's very true, Béla, I haven't been performing very well.'

'And why is that? Why *is that* you should not perform well?'

'I don't know. Things just haven't been coming together.'

He stopped for a moment, fixed me with a lunatic stare and shouted: 'Woman!'

At first I thought he was accusing me of being a transsexual, so unexpected was his exclamation.

'Woman!' he hollered again, thumping the table between us so

142

that the chess pieces jumped to attention. 'You have been going with a woman. No?'

'Yes, I have a girlfriend, if that's what you mean.'

Béla inhaled, and his chest expanded. He then let out an explosive blast of air while articulating the syllable, *Pfah!!* 'Woman and mathematics. They don't mix, not at your age. You will have plenty of time for woman, when your brain stops working. Plenty of time, you will see. Too much time! And when you do, you will regret it. That you have spent so much time with woman, now.' He grunted, and fell into a sullen silence.

'Yes,' I said, unsure how to react. 'I'm sure you're right'.

'Yes,' he returned, extending the word as though trying to break the world yes-extension record.

The rest of the supervision was relatively calm after this extraordinary outburst. When we talked about the new work Béla's spirits lifted again, and all was well. When I left he raised his glass to me.

'Thanks for the advice,' I said, with transparent insincerity.

'Yes,' he said again. Although what he meant by this, I have absolutely no idea.

I had stopped having coffee in Russell Square since my encounter with the ancient mariner. Consequently, I went directly to the Tube station. The sky was, again, overcast, and it was threatening to rain. When I walked out at Wood Green the street was wet and the air smelt strange, like damp charcoal. The pavement was covered in litter, and sudden blasts of wind were lifting paper cups and discarded newspaper into the air. I decided I wouldn't walk home, so I ran for a bus. It was crowded and I had to stand upstairs. The air was fetid with stale breath and the clothes of my fellow occupants had begun to reek. Why does the rain do this in London? I had to hold a handkerchief over my nose, as the putrid stench was beginning to make me nauseous. The traffic crawled up Green Lanes at a pace that barely qualified as movement. By the time I got home it was fully dark. When I walked into the kitchen I found Dave and Anna seated either side of the table. They both looked at me, and I looked at them. Their expressions were curiously neutral. This blank moment seemed to last for an unfeasible length of time, and I began to hear a curious, electrical humming in my ears. Then, as if suddenly released from the spell of temporal stasis, Anna and Dave's features became animated.

'Tom,' said Dave, smiling.

'Hello, Dave.'

'Hi. Do you want a coffee?' Anna chipped in.

'Please.'

'I was in the shopping centre and thought I'd call in. See if you and Anna felt like a drink?'

'Great.' The word was articulated without much enthusiasm. I wished that I had put more effort into it.

'So what have you been up to?'

'Supervision.'

'How did it go?'

'Fine. I think I've redeemed myself.'

I told them about Béla's reaction to my latest work. I also described his peculiar outburst, which caused some amusement. It also triggered a conversation about the iniquities of the Ph.D. system. Postgraduates love to tell each other horror stories about friends of friends – the particle physicist whose supervisor refused to allow him to submit after early completion so that he could squeeze a few more publications out of him; the viva voce examination that went horribly wrong in the first ten minutes; and so on.

We went down to the Nightingale, where we sat for the rest of the evening. Dave lit a cigarette and exhaled slowly. 'It's difficult being a mathematician, isn't it?'

'What do you mean?'

'It's a lonely business.'

'All Ph.D. students are lonely,' said Anna, in wistful, contemplative mode.

'No, I didn't mean it like that,' continued Dave. 'What I meant was, it must get frustrating, not being able to really explain what

144

you're doing. You see, when I talk about organic chemistry, I think people have a fair idea of what I'm talking about. The big concepts, like DNA, aren't that difficult to get your head around. If you say it's like a set of instructions, that about sums it up. When Anna talks about cognition, we know what she's on about because we're actually doing 'cognition' as she speaks. But you, Tom, when you tell us about vectors in n-dimensional space, I'm not at all sure that we really grasp what you're describing.'

'I don't know, you seem to be able to get a handle on it . . . sometimes.'

'Don't you get pissed off with everybody? For not understanding what you do? At the end of the day, although Béla's a complete pain in the arse, he's probably one of only half a dozen people on the planet who really understands what you're on about. Really understands, that is.'

'I suppose so.'

'Maybe that explains why maths supervisors are always sticking their oar into their students' lives. The relationship is more unique. They get over-involved.'

'Perhaps.'

Anna nodded, reached out and rested her hand on my thigh. I must say, they both seemed inordinately solicitous. They seemed to want me to feel understood, or supported. Ostensibly, we spent a very pleasant evening together; however, I felt very uncomfortable.

Dave said goodbye outside the Nightingale at about ten o'clock and walked off into the night, his leather jacket flapping in the wind. Anna and I walked home, slowly, exchanging only a few words.

When I got into bed I began to ruminate. Why had Dave just *dropped in*? He always called first. How long had he been sitting with Anna? There were four cigarettes in the ashtray. That would mean at least an hour. Or did Anna smoke one of his cigarettes? Did she *join in*, again? Why didn't I hear them speaking when I first walked in? They must have heard me open the door, and then stopped. And why was it that they were so still? There was something unnatural about that pause. I began to bite my tongue in an effort to bring myself back to earth, a hook of pain that might catch my consciousness before it lost all purchase on reality. Dave would hardly be interested in Anna, for God's sake! She just wasn't *his* sort. But there again, she had made herself very alluring when she had dressed up for Laura's party. She could look really sexy, if she wanted. What was I thinking! The idea was preposterous. And as for Anna, well, she liked Dave. She had even said that she could understand why other women found him attractive; however, she thought that he was a complete chauvinist. Besides, Anna and I were happy together. Most of the time, anyway, so I thought. I tossed and turned the whole night. This would have to stop.

The following week Anna and I had arranged to meet up at the Students' Union. We intended to catch some French film at the Renoir. It was called *L'objet* or *L'outil* (or some other exercise in lexical economy so typical of our Gallic cousins). I must say, continental cinema has never been a significant interest of mine. A medium in which the lighting of cigarettes appears to be the most important leitmotif arouses certain doubts. I imagine that, if you extracted the numerous shots of cigarettes being lit, put out or tossed nonchalantly into the Seine and put them together, they would constitute the greater part of most French films. Indeed, the fashionable connoisseur of continental cinema often fails to realize that the average French film lasts, in fact, for only twenty minutes. The rest, of course, is tobacco.

Anna loves French films. Indeed, she seems to be keen on them for all the reasons that I dislike them. She says they are atmospheric. However, watching a Gauloise becoming ash through a haze of smoke (for ten minutes) before a man in a long coat says '*C'est fini*' and leaves the room is boring. Yes, the correct word is 'boring', or 'dull'. Not 'atmospheric'. Nevertheless, I was happy, now and again, to sit in the dark with Anna, watching images of tobacco.

It never failed to amaze me how easily and deeply moved Anna was by these films. She invariably cried. Indeed, she often left the cinema looking quite unwell, her eyelids raw and her nose running. She would sniff her way to Russell Square Tube gripping my hand.

'Did you enjoy it?' I would ask (somewhat bemused).

'Oh, yes,' she would reply. 'Did you?'

'Yeah . . .' (and I fear I spoke with little conviction). 'Yeah. This one was . . . all right.'

Anna would say nothing for a short while, attempting to preserve the film's impression. Then, after a meditative silence, she would say, 'She loved him, didn't she?'

'Yes, I suppose she did,' I would respond.

' . . . and that was why. That was why she had to leave him.'

I never had the slightest grasp of these paradoxical statements. They went way over my head. Nevertheless, I would say something like, 'She had no choice, not really,' and it always seemed appropriate. Anna would hug me close on the Tube and would want to make love when we got home. This effect was so reliable I once suggested that we go to see a French film specifically for this purpose. And it worked.

I was to meet Anna at the Union. At about six o'clock. Dave had said that he might join us for a few drinks. We had invited him to come along to the film, but he said that he would *give it a miss*. He had some 'work' to do. *Oh, yeah?* I thought.

Unfortunately, at five-thirty I was stuck in supervision with Béla. Well, I say supervision, but it was really nothing of the sort. Béla was far too distracted. He couldn't have supervised a zebra crossing. Indeed, he was in an extremely agitated state. He had received a fax through from Grzyzgy. Apparently, a young associate professor from Chicago, William Itō, was visiting Harvard and had presented a new solution to the Schwenck problem. This was enough to ensure that Béla's mind was fully derailed for at least twenty-four hours.

What came to be known as the Schwenck problem was originally described by Adolf Schwenck, a remarkably talented civil engineer (and amateur mathematician) working in pre-war Dresden. Sadly, he was killed in the notorious fire-bombing; however, not without first bequeathing his problem to the world. Stated very simply, Schwenck suggested that, given a pre-specified set of fifty-seven complex-polygon tiles, any arrangement of these on a two-dimensional dodeca-hedral surface would fail to cover the surface completely. There would always be an area that would not be covered, whatever arrangement was tried. This area, or the value for that area, became known as Schwenck's P.

Schwenck's original article appeared in a minor journal and prompted little, if any interest. After the war, however, a commentary appeared in *Mathematica Hungarica*, written by István Vrost, suggesting that Schwenck might have been wrong. That is to say, perhaps it was possible to cover the dodecahedral surface entirely (with the fifty-seven polygons), leaving no P value. Notwithstanding this, Vrost clearly believed that 'the problem', as it then stood, was not worthy of his interest. His article pointed in the direction of a solution, but he had no intention of pursuing the task of finding that solution himself. In the early 1950s he discussed the Schwenck problem with the juvenile but precocious Béla, who with youthful enthusiasm resolved to crack and bury Schwenck.

One year later 'A refutation of Schwenck' appeared in *Tessellation and Mapping* (an international journal that is alas now no longer published). Béla had not only discovered a solution to the Schwenck problem, he also managed to furnish the scientific community with a series of proofs demonstrating that his solution was *the only* solution possible. Béla's proofs (the Bartók proofs – his parents had a failure of imagination when he was christened) were subsequently accommo-dated in the arcane literature on 'complex tessellation', where they remained, unchallenged. That is, until Grzyzgy's fax arrived with news of William Itō's presentation. Béla was confused and bemused in equal measure. I must say, I was rather taken aback myself. Not because I had nurtured any great belief in the power of Béla's juvenile proofs; rather, I was taken aback by the idea that anybody should be bothered to look at them. I was staggered that there were people in the US working in departments with sufficient capital to fund assistant professors who wanted to take another look at the Schwenck problem (and its solution). I wanted to get away, but Béla was having none of it. He waved the fax at me.

'Who is this? This Itō? Yōtō? Whatever? You have heard of him?'

'No.'

'It is not possible, that he has another solution. Not possible!' Béla knelt on the floor and rummaged through the bottom drawer of his most ancient-looking filing cabinet. Under his breath I could hear him cursing: 'bastard Chinaman.' He retrieved a document – an old translation of 'A refutation of Schwenck' – and thrust it in my direction. 'Tom. I want your opinion on this. I want you to take a good look and see if you can find any . . .' he paused for a moment before saying ' . . . inconsistencies.'

The word was clearly chosen in preference to 'mistakes'.

I was always amazed how, when it really mattered, Béla's English improved tenfold. I had always suspected that his over-the-top Hungarianness was an affectation.

'Béla,' I said calmly, 'surely, the most sensible thing to do right now is ask Itō for a copy of his proofs. I mean, he hasn't published yet.'

Béla jammed his fist in his mouth and bit on the knuckles. He adopted a rigid expression of absolute terror, which he held for an interminable amount of time. He then took his fist out of his mouth and shook it at the sky. 'God forbid that he should publish.' Béla went and sat down behind his desk. He grabbed another chair and pulled it next to him. He drummed on the empty chair seat with both fists. 'Come, Tomash. Be sitting here.'

I thought of Anna and Dave, enjoying a quiet drink, and resigned myself to being very late. I wasn't going to get away. I got up, like a condemned man, and sat next to the master.

'Let us begin,' he said ominously.

I didn't get out of Béla's office until six forty-five. I ran down to the Union. Dave and Anna were sitting at a small table, tucked away in a corner. Anna was looking at Dave intensely, nodding, while he was gesticulating and talking in an animated way. I began to get that electrical humming again. A crackling over my skull. I banged my head with the side of my hand, as though trying to realign a misplaced component. Fortunately, the sound stopped dead.

I know that this will sound stupid but I hoped that Anna would see me, standing there. That she would notice me, waiting by the door. I didn't move, I just stood there. But Anna didn't notice me at all. After catching my breath, I walked briskly over to their table.

'I'm really sorry,' I said, 'it was Béla. I just couldn't get away. He wouldn't let me go.'

'That's all right,' said Dave.

'What do you want to drink?' I asked.

Anna began shaking her head at me and tapping her watch.

'What time does it start, then?'

'Another twenty minutes. We've got to go,' replied Anna.

The film, as I recall, was fairly typical of the genre. Why do so many French films feature two men (who are bosom companions) and one, rather elusive woman? And why is it that she – Mélisande, Martine, Mimi (or some such moniker) – always lives in a spectacularly beautiful flat in the centre of Paris, even though she works in a shoeshop? And why is it that the last scene always involves this curious, ephemeral creature closing the door on her flat and walking briskly into the night? These questions are, for me, revived after every trip to the Renoir.

Anna, true to form, left the cinema crying.

The journey home was a nightmare. The Tube was full of football supporters. I have no knowledge of football. I had no idea who they supported, where they came from, or where they were going. All I knew was that their chants and grimacing made me feel uncomfortable in the extreme. When we got off the Tube at Wood Green, we did so with considerable relief.

It was quite late when Anna and I got into bed. She rested her head on my chest and wrapped an arm around my waist. Neither of us spoke for some time.

Then she said, 'I spoke to Dave about his brother this evening.'

'Oh, yes.'

'I wanted to say something. I felt that I should.'

'What did you say?'

'That I was sorry to hear about it. I told Dave a little about the trouble we've had with Hunt. I suppose every family has problems.'

'Yes.'

I stroked her hair, and let my hand slip down to her breasts. My penis began to stiffen. Anna shifted uncomfortably.

'He's a curious chap, isn't he, Dave?'

I really didn't want to talk about Dave, but Anna clearly did.

'How do you mean, "curious"?'

'Well, he's so full of bravado. Yet, he's very sensitive too. He says things sometimes that you just don't expect.'

I became a little uneasy and prayed that Dave had been discreet. 'What do you mean?' I asked tentatively.

'Well, he was telling me about his brother, in a kind of dismissive, cavalier way. He was talking about loonies and geeks and being generally offensive. I was sitting there hoping that you were going to arrive soon. I was thinking to myself, if he carries on like this I'm going to have to say something.'

'He doesn't mean anything by it. It's just his way.'

'Yes, I realize that now.'

'Why, what changed your mind?'

There was a gravid pause.

'Well, he was describing his experiences at school, with Timothy – did you know that was his name, his brother?'

'No, I didn't ask.'

'He's two or three years older than Dave. He was always quite obsessional but his contamination fears became very serious when he was about thirteen. Apparently, the other kids realized that he had problems, and they would bully him. Really badly.'

'In what way?'

'They used to put dirt in his hair, drag him into the lavatories when the teachers weren't looking. That sort of thing.'

'Oh.'

'It doesn't sound much, but if you fear contamination more than anything else in the world, it must have been hell . . . and Dave said he had to watch it, for about a year. He said it was the most painful period of his life. Having to watch his brother being tormented. He said that he couldn't do a thing to stop them. He was younger, and smaller. He said that once or twice he tried to intervene, but he just got beaten up as a result. Timothy pleaded with him not to get involved.'

There was another period of silence. I could hear a train in the distance.

'Why are children so cruel?' Anna asked.

'You're the psychologist.'

'Dave said that when Timothy had been tormented, he would go home, lock himself in the bathroom, and stay there for most of the evening. Sometimes he would wash so much, for so long, that his hands bled. Timothy would come out of the bathroom with his hands in bandages. It's difficult to believe, isn't it? That anyone could be that scared of dirt?'

'Yes.'

' . . . but what really surprised me was what Dave said next. He said that he would sometimes sit outside the bathroom, listening to the running water, and he would begin to cry. You see, he felt that he was to blame. He hadn't been able to do anything. It's really sad, isn't it?'

'Yes.'

'You just don't think of Dave like that, do you?'

'No.'

I felt rather peculiar. Rather odd. Hearing about Dave in this way made me feel off balance.

I began to rub Anna's breasts. She responded by turning over and facing the wall.

'No, Tom, not tonight. I don't really feel like it.'

This had never happened before. Not after a French film.

I turned the light off but couldn't get to sleep. So, I got up and read through Béla's bloody Schwenck paper. I couldn't see any problems with it. I messed with some of the proofs on the computer for a while, but it all seemed watertight to me. William Itō was either very stupid, or very clever. Either way, I was pretty sure that he would be for ever a bastard Chinaman in Béla's eyes.

I saw Béla a few days later. To my enormous surprise, he did not mention the Schwenck problem. He was in a rather jolly mood, and only enquired about my own work. Eventually, I produced the Schwenck paper and returned it to him.

'Ah yes, thank you, Tom. Did you enjoy it?'

I really didn't know how to respond. So I played safe and said, 'Yes.'

Béla placed the paper back in his file and returned smiling. He was clearly not going to say anything. He sat down in his armchair, rubbed his upper thighs with both hands and said, 'Hey, Jo!' (Which I understand is Hungarian for 'good' rather than a sudden decision on Béla's part to quote from the Jimi Hendrix songbook.)

This really was too much.

'Béla?' I continued, with extreme caution.

'Yes, Tomash.'

'Have you heard any more from Grzyzgy, about Itō's second solution?'

'Yes, yes,' replied Béla, nodding furiously. 'I spoke to Gabor yesterday.'

'And . . .'

'There is a second solution.'

I should have said at this point, 'How interesting.' But it wasn't that interesting, so I didn't. However, I did venture to ask a potentially dangerous question.

'And . . . where is Itō going to publish this second solution?'

Béla looked at me and smiled. 'He is not going to publish the second solution. He has decided that the Schwenck problem is – what is it that you say, old cap?' He knew very well what the saying was, and he knew that I knew that he did. Nevertheless, he kept his eyebrows raised, enquiring, waiting for my correction.

'Old hat, Béla?'

'Ah, yes, old hat. Charming. Old hat.'

'I see.'

'The Schwenck problem is old hat. It is of no interest today. It would not be good for a man of Itō's obvious ability to publish in this area. He has made a very wise decision, if you are asking me.'

'I see.'

That seemed to be it. We spent the rest of the supervision on my work. However, when I got up to leave and opened the door, our eyes met, just before I stepped out.

'Tom,' said Béla, 'we have a saying in Hungary. If you get into a revolving door with a Hungarian behind you, when you get out, he will be in front of you.'

I had to smile.

A month later Itō was given a plum job at Harvard.

8

The Daguerrotype

When I had almost finished collecting the principal components of Locke's apparatus, I took them out of the suitcase under the bed and stacked them in the kitchen. It was then that Anna and I began having our altercations, with respect to the propriety of building a scientific antiquity in a relatively small living-space.

When is it going to be finished, Tom?

Please move this box, Tom.

Jesus, I can barely open the door, Tom.

It was like a domestic variant of water torture! One question followed by another. And she was never satisfied with my answers. Looking back now, I wonder if being honest would have made a difference. What if I had explained to Anna what I was really doing? What if I had sat her down and talked her through the Locke equations? Would she have been more supportive? More sympathetic? I doubt it. Indeed, I can picture quite clearly how things would have gone – her eyes narrowing, her brow furrowing. No, in this matter my 'discretion' was entirely appropriate.

Even though Anna was clearly unhappy with my intransigence, I was not prepared to compromise. I stood my ground. Subsequently, Anna insisted – with uncharacteristic assertiveness – that immediately after I had conducted my 'experiment', the components of my apparatus should be stored in the shed. *Of course*, I replied, *of course*. But the truce we secured was an uneasy one. I would catch Anna staring at my carefully stacked components with undisguised contempt. She even sighed loudly at such times to underscore her dissatisfaction. I thought this quite mean-spirited. Inexcusable, really. We had made an agreement and that was that. I would certainly be sticking to my side of the bargain!

In spite of Anna's moodiness I remained excited. It would take more than her disparaging glances to dampen my enthusiasm. After all, I was just about ready to begin work in earnest.

I placed the individual components on the bedroom floor and surveyed them: the governor, the first- and second-stage modulators, the compressor, the condenser and the field attenuator. It was deeply satisfying. I set to work on the gantry and, once the main framework was complete, began to attach and affix the components. When I looked at the empty frame, I was reminded of the dinosaur skeletons in the Natural History Museum. Indeed, there was something peculiarly organic about the structure taking shape before me. Flex and cable like veins and arteries. The governor, like a metal heart. When activated, it would pulse and beat with such ferocity, it would punch a hole through time. I was thrilled. This beautiful machine would exert such pressure on the fundamental forces that space would groan, bend and finally buckle under its hammer blows.

I was fortunate enough to find the address of a dealer, a Mr Friend, in the East End of London, who luckily had in his possession the minor parts I required to complete the apparatus: a Rochester cam and two pin-shuttles. I was in a breezy mood that day. The Tube journey to Stratford was long and tedious; nevertheless, the prospect of completing Locke's apparatus kept my spirits high. I was also rather amused when, as I negotiated Gerry Raffles Square, a left-hand-drive vehicle pulled up beside me and I was asked in broken English where Shakespeare's house was. I pointed in what I considered to be the direction of Stratford-upon-Avon and told them to keep going for about three hours. I don't think they understood. Nevertheless, they smiled at me, and I laughed at them, and we parted on the best of terms.

The Romford Road was on top form. Dismal, noisy, and jammed with tightly packed traffic. The lorries were all suffering from what can only be described as toxic flatulence, and the good people of Stratford looked (to me) as though they were drunk, mentally ill or attempting to force themselves back down the phylogenetic continuum. Usually, when placed in a hostile environment, I get very scared, but that afternoon I felt strangely above it all. So much so that when my first vagrant of the day approached with outstretched grubby paw and spit-covered beard I merely wished him good-day. When he rather predictably yelled after me, 'Fug ye, ye cun'', and shook his fist, I was completely unperturbed and called back 'Fug ye, yesel' in my best cod-trampese. He did not follow.

Mr Friend's basement flat was a rather grim affair, approached down a long and deep flight of concrete stairs, partially hidden behind a row a large dustbins. The noise of the passing lorries was shocking. I pressed the button, designated 'Friend' (in biro under yellowing Sellotape) but didn't hear anything. I decided not to try it again; if it was working, then repeated use would be perceived as a sign of impatience. Eventually, my resolve crumbled, and I kept my finger on the button for a minute to no avail. I then resorted to banging the door with my fist, which immediately summoned the coenobitic Friend.

Here was a strange specimen indeed. He was a small, wiry creature, with long, lank hair. Unfortunately, he exhibited a facial tic, which, like all facial tics (however modest), continued to surprise me, even though it appeared with predictable regularity.

'Are you the bloke who called?' he shouted, while his right cheek danced about on his face.

'Yes.'

'Come in.'

I was shown down a dark, damp corridor, and entered a large room. It stretched from the back of the house to the front, and every conceivable space was filled with oddments and artifacts.

'What was it again?' asked Friend.

'The Rochester cam and the two pin-shuttles.'

'Oh, yeah, that's it. Give us a mo.'

Friend moved a ladder from one side of the room to the other and raked over a shelf near the ceiling. He then climbed nimbly down with a black dustbin bag which he emptied on to the carpet.

'There you go.'

This was an invitation to inspect his wares. He observed me closely, his face convulsing as though being repeatedly galvanized by electrodes embedded in his gum.

I lifted the cam and held it up, rotating it. I repeated the procedure with the pin-shuttles.

'They're fine,' I said.

'Good. Must say, we've had 'em for ages. Not much call for gear like this.' Spasm. Spasm.

'No. Probably not. We agreed, £15.40 . . .'

'Did we?' Spasm.

'Yes.'

'Fair enough.' Wince.

I counted out the money, which Friend stuffed into the pocket of his jeans. I looked around at the crammed shelves and piled boxes.

'Are all these scientific antiques?'

'Nerr . . .' he replied, lighting a cigarette. 'We deal in general goods as well, domestic electrical appliances, some motor parts and quality vinyl.'

'Vinyl?'

'Records, vinyl,' he said again. He reached into a box and held up a battered album sleeve. 'See, *Tonto's Expanding Head Band*. Worth about twenty quid this. One of the first albums to be done entirely on a synthesizer.' Spasm. 'They were all Moogs then.'

'Well . . .' I replied, not knowing how to continue the conversation. 'Well, thank you for your help. I'll certainly be using your services again.'

'Hope so. Been difficult, of course, what with the recession and that. Hard times, but then again, can't complain, eh?' Spasm. 'Can't complain.'

He led me to the door, and said, 'Cheerio,' as the meat on the right side of his face attempted unassisted flight.

'Goodbye,' I said, although I doubt that he heard my reply as he opened the door.

I have a winter memory of Dave that is, on the face of it, rather trivial. Yet, it has proved tenacious. We were standing on the corner, outside Dillons on Gower Street. It was quite early, though dark, and raining heavily. We had been shopping. Occasionally Dave and I would meet up and peruse the latest popular-science publications. In order to conserve capital, we would purchase books in twos – one each – with a view to a subsequent exchange. I forget which titles we had procured that evening.

I was going to meet Anna again at the Renoir, to see one of her dreadful French films. Dave was going home. A rare evening of solitude. Quite suddenly, he became almost – I say almost because he never quite managed this without alcohol – melancholy.

'You know, Tom,' he said, 'I envy you.'

I almost laughed out loud.

'No, seriously,' he said. 'I think that you're really sorted now.'

'Sorted?'

'Yes, sorted! You've arrived.'

'I hardly think so.'

'No, you have. What else do you need from life? Your Ph.D. is going well, you're about to meet your girlfriend, and if someone stopped you and asked you what a Poincaré section was you'd be able to tell them. See, well sorted. Be seeing you.'

And off he went, toward Russell Square. Loping into the mist of glowing water droplets that diffused the neon glare.

Yes, I thought, some time later. I do have favourable circumstances. My tedious, though secure life must have, on rainy nights like these, provided Dave with a not unattractive prospect. From afar, a curious, cosy warmth must have emanated from the flat in Wood Green. He knew nothing of my torment, of course. My Darwinian jealousy problem. What did I see in his eyes that night? Anything? A flicker of envy? Not envy of my intellect, no. I knew that expression well. It wasn't that one. But something else? Envy of something else? I really don't know. To this day, I cannot say what I saw with any certainty. But I do know where it all led in the end. Of course. I would do.

It was a curious experience, completing Locke's apparatus. It took me by surprise. Somehow, I had miscalculated. I had imagined that I would spend many more afternoons, refining the device. Instead, I suddenly found myself looking at the completed structure. It really was quite impressive. Copper and steel, wood and glass. Coils and flex, bearings and porcelain rings. I sat on the bed and looked at it. The most remarkable invention ever. I expected it to make a sound, or to vibrate, even before being powered up. I expected to hear it, breathing, panting, ready to tear at the fabric of time and space. There was something dangerous about it. Like Blake's *Tyger.*

I made myself a cup of tea and then walked back to the bedroom. It was still there. Waiting. I should have been excited, but I suddenly felt uneasy. This was such a momentous occasion. Yet there was no trumpet fanfare to herald the dawning of a new age. No plaudits. Only the sound of a motor bike, rattling off towards White Hart Lane.

I looked around our *dingy* bedroom. The paint was yellowing and the old-fashioned wallpaper was washed out. It looked anaemic. The room felt tired, exhausted, broken. The landlord had been scrupulous in his efforts to provide second-hand furniture that evoked an air of stagnancy and decay. Our large old bed dominated the room. Its heavy, wooden headboard was like a tombstone, the mattress, a grave. The wardrobe, a hideous coffin, was pocked with woodworm, and small pyramids of dust could be found between its ugly, deformed feet. I have always hated that wardrobe. If you looked at it for long enough, you began to see faces in the grain. Horrible, evil faces. Our bedroom was desperate. If it is possible for a room to be ill, then our bedroom was a terminal case.

Anna and I never really cleaned the flat. She tried to keep it tidy, but we never cleaned it. Like most student accommodation, it was demoralizing. Moreover, the fact that we had no intention of staying on after qualifying meant that we had no affection for the place. A cobweb had been spun between the curtain rail and the wall. It would stay there, in all probability, until our departure.

It was here, then, in this drab little hole, that history would be made. In imagination, one always feels that past events of historic importance unravel in a cinematic way. I was waiting for the score to begin. A pulsating soundtrack of strings that would reach a crescendo as I powered up the apparatus. Incidental percussion, glittering against a wall of harp glissandi, to evoke the numinous. A crash of cymbals, and the weighty majestic blooming of sonorities as an orchestral gong is struck. Instead, there was nothing. Apart, that is, from the occasional motorbike and the yelling of a Greek neighbour, one house removed. Why should that day have been different to any other? I am sure that most breakthroughs in science occurred under similarly inauspicious circumstances. Under a comparable, leaden pall.

As I contemplated my next step, the doorbell rang. I was not expecting anyone. I walked to the front of the house and opened the door. A middle-aged black woman, with a younger companion (who I took to be her daughter) were standing there and smiling.

'Good morning . . . We were wondering if you would be interested in some good news?'

'What good news?'

'The good news of our blessed Lord, Jesus Christ, who came to save us.'

'Not now!' I said with anger, and slammed the door in their eager faces.

This was really too much.

I walked back to the bedroom. It was still there, waiting. Was there any point in delaying? Of course not. I knew that there was no point. What made me resist proceeding? Was it the fear of failure? The fear that all my dreams would evaporate within the next half-hour? No, I don't think it was. I have always been confident of my academic abilities. I had modelled the equations. There was nothing to worry about. Locke's apparatus would function properly, as planned, I had no doubt of that. My reticence seemed to have a more obscure origin. It was as though my unconscious mind had become prescient and (having gleaned an inkling of my fate) was attempting to restrain me. Nevertheless, I resolved to continue with the experiment, albeit in an atmosphere of disquiet and unease.

There was no point in repositioning the apparatus. It could be tested there as well as anywhere else. The bed was occupied nearly as often as it was empty. I would get a daguerreotype of the bed. I would see if I could catch myself, or Anna, lying in it.

I set the calibration dials and powered up the main compressor. It was impossible to calculate the exact reach of the anomaly. Unfortunately, Locke's instrumentation did not allow a precise estimate to be made. Nineteenth-century engineering admitted a not insignificant margin of error. What might be calculated to the nearest millisecond using a computer simulation could only be calculated to the nearest day in actuality.

I could not risk standing near the apparatus once the fields had been generated. There was always the possibility that something could go wrong. A modest accident would involve a stray electrical charge. I could get burned or even killed. A more exotic accident might involve being crushed by a gravitational ripple or being swallowed up by the expanding time portal. If I survived the fall, I might find myself quite literally living in the past. Displaced by twenty-four hours or so. The fact that I hadn't seen myself walking about the flat suggested that this particular outcome had not happened; however, my absence was no guarantee. The *many universes* account of reality could accommodate such an accident and the absence of my *doppelgänger* without incurring the slightest credibility fatigue. I had devised an automatic triggering mechanism to minimize the chances of a serious accident occurring. This meant that Locke's apparatus could be left to function, unsupervised. After my departure, fifteen minutes or so would elapse before the creation of a temporal anomaly. When the portal was at its widest the daguerreotype would be taken. The exposure time would naturally be long. The anomaly would eventually collapse, and the portal would close. After another fifteen minutes or so, the space–time continuum would be free of perturbations. I would be able to return to collect the plate.

There was nothing else to do. I pressed the start button, in the same way one might press the start button on a hoover or food-mixer. The condenser began to power up and I swiftly left the bedroom and closed the door. Of course, I could not concentrate. I paced around and made myself another cup of tea. I had no real intention of drinking it; however, the mechanical routine – water in kettle, teabag in mug, water in mug – offered some modest distraction. As I waited, watching the boiling water evaporate, the doorbell rang again. I was furious.

I got up and walked down the hall with every intention of ensuring that Jehovah's Witnesses would never trouble me again. I would not have the time to strangle their beliefs in the logical half-nelson; I would have to resort to less subtle means. The verbal abuse I was about to unleash would be of mythic stature. Biblical, no less. I pulled open the door and set my mouth wide. But a rather perplexed, wheezy noise came out instead.

'Tomash,' said Béla.

'Béla,' I said.

'I am here.'

'You are here.'

'Tom, do not repeat what I say. It is irritating, no?'

'Uh . . .'

'Well?'

'Béla, I'm so sorry. I forgot.'

I had. Ridiculous as it was, I had forgotten. He had explained to me the previous afternoon that he was going to a conference in Paris. He would be driving through north London and wanted a print-out of some of my new results. He had told me not to bother coming in.

I had agreed. This whole episode, which had previously vanished from my memory, suddenly resurfaced.

'Come in,' I said. 'It won't take a minute'.

I guided him into the lounge, where my computer was. I should have offered him something to drink, but I just couldn't. I wanted him out as soon as possible. He sat down in a rather tatty armchair.

'You have a nice flat, Tom.'

'Well, it's OK.'

My Toshiba came to life.

'You have been here for long?'

'Not very. Six months. Béla, I'm really sorry this isn't ready I . . .'

'Tom, it is no problem.'

There was an uncomfortable silence. Béla had not even taken his coat off. When the computer stopped booting up, another sound could be heard. A clunking, chugging sound, from the bedroom. Béla looked around, nervously.

I found the file, and started to print it up.

'Looking forward to Paris, Béla?'

'Yes, I am. I haven't been for some time now. It will be good to see Paris again.'

However, my crude attempt at diverting his attention was unsuccessful.

'What is that sound, Tom?'

'Builders, Béla. We have builders next door.'

'How can you work here with that going on?'

'Not very easily.'

The sound became more violent. The clanking noises became more rapid. I scooped up the print-out, and handed it to Béla.

'Here it is.'

'Thank you.'

He scrutinized the figures carefully. As he did so, the noise seemed absolutely cacophonous. I began to sweat. My head became hot and my forehead damp. A trickle of sweat ran down the side of my face. Suddenly, the noise cut out. Béla looked up. I don't think he realized that something had changed. He was too engrossed in the equations.

'Yes, this is fine, Tom. Thank you.'

He placed the print-out in his case, and stood to leave. 'I am sorry to have troubled you this afternoon.'

'No trouble at all, Béla.'

I saw him to the door.

'I will be back on Tuesday. Give me a call later in the week, I'll tell you how it went. I am sure Gabor Grzyzgy will have some valuable comments to make.'

'I bet.'

'Goodbye, Tom.'

'Bye, Béla.' I closed the door. My body slumped back against the wall. I sniffed the air. It smelt like the air smells just before a thunderstorm. I let myself slide to the floor. My head was throbbing and I felt very strange. Ill almost. It was time to collect the plate.

I stood in front of the bedroom door for a good ten minutes before slowly turning the handle. I don't know what I expected to happen. Of course, nothing did, apart from the escape of a weak draught of ionized air. Locke's apparatus was just as I had left it. Brooding. Dangerous. I gingerly approached the gantry and inspected the antique camera, which was, perhaps, slightly warm. Everything seemed to have worked smoothly. I removed the plate and retired to the cupboard under the stairs, which I had converted into an impromptu dark-room. I was using Daguerre's original procedure and materials, as specified by Locke. Why Locke had chosen to use an antiquated procedure (antiquated even in his time), I had no idea. Nevertheless, I was not prepared to deviate from the great man's suggestions. He had recommended a daguerreotype, and who was I to disagree?

After exposing the plate to the heated mercury fumes, I washed the plate in a salt solution. I must say, the whole thing was completely haphazard. I had no idea about exposure or soaking times and took what I fooled myself into believing might be a series of educated guesses; however, every great discovery depends, to a greater or lesser extent, on a liberal helping of good fortune. It was curious that I should have taken a historic picture of my bed. That this old, sagging monstrosity, was destined to feature in scientific textbooks for eternity. The earliest surviving daguerreotype, I believe, is of a few plaster casts and a wicker bottle. Not very auspicious; but Daguerre could hardly have waited for a grand state occasion to test his camera. He was eager to see if it worked. So, he took a picture of what happened to be in the room, at that time. Debris, discarded in the corner. It was fitting that I should have taken the first temporal photograph of my bed.

I edged out of the cupboard and stupidly banged my head on the door. My head was already hurting and the chemical fumes made me feel sick. My eyes had not adapted to the light in the hall and I had to close them. My heart was pounding. When I felt more comfortable I opened my eyes and, squinting, looked at the plate. At first, I thought that the procedure hadn't worked. The plate seemed blank, but, as my eyes became accustomed to the light I was able to discern a faint image. When I realized what I was looking at, I ran out into the garden and vomited.

9

Temple Church

I made for the North Circular road and then drove far too fast toward Finchley. Bishops Avenue welcomed me with its contrived splendour. There is always somebody in front of you on Bishops Avenue driving too slowly. They are driving too slowly because they are not really driving. They are actually looking out of their windows and estimating the cost of the houses. Large, flamboyant, provocative and vulgar. These buildings capture the attention of hapless drivers, like sirens. They keen and wail, setting up sympathetic vibrations in the heart-strings; and the drivers yearn and ache, ache and yearn, for wooden floors and chandeliers, marble shipped from Italy. Marquetry, gold and big, big TV. I hooted the car in front, but to no avail. His brain was enveloped in a cloud of vaporized caviar and envy.

When I finally reached the end of Bishops Avenue I veered left, unintentionally mounting the kerb, and sped off toward Kenwood. Fortunately, it was easy to park outside. I walked in, and sat on a bench, looking out over London across Hampstead Heath. A thick layer of putrid air encased the city. The taller structures, like Telecom Tower and the Nat West building seemed to poke their summits through a mucal deposit. An expectoration of inhuman magnitude.

I sat there, waiting for my heart rate to decrease. It didn't happen. I don't know how long I sat there, looking at London becoming overwhelmed by shadows, but it must have been a very long time. I seemed to enter a timeless trance-state. When I came to my senses, it was dark and dank. The lights of the city had begun to shine, blink, wink and sparkle. Not like stars, but like the tawdry, cheap lights in a shop-window at Christmas. My mouth still tasted of vomit, and my eyes were sore. I suppose I had been crying, but I had no recollection of tears. Just a burning sensation as though my eyes had been splashed with acid. I also became aware that I wanted to urinate.

When I got up, my limbs were stiff. My legs hurt when I moved, as though I had slept on the bench all night. I made my way over to the public lavatory, which was only a few hundred yards away. It stank of piss. I stood in front of a urinal, legs apart, and tempted my penis out through the gap in my boxer shorts. As I emptied my bladder, I was suddenly startled by a finger prodding my arse. I turned around quickly, urinating on my trousers in the process.

In front of me stood a tramp of about fifty. His face was bruised and he had a cut over his left eye. He looked as though he was about to expire. His breath rasped like a saw. Yet, even in this state, I could see the dull embers of sexual interest pulsing a soft red glow behind his eyes. He was standing between me and the exit, making me feel trapped.

'Fuck off!' I shouted.

I pushed him aside and, to my great surprise, he fell backwards without any resistance. As I ran out, I heard a dull smack as his head hit the ground. It called to mind an image of an over-ripe watermelon, splitting and spilling its pulp. I stopped running and listened. All that I could hear was my own heart, pounding in my ears. I took a deep breath, turned on my heels and walked back, slowly. The toilet was a dark, penumbral chamber. I could see the tramp, a bundle of rags on the floor, and hear the rattle and rasp of his tortured lungs. It had felt good, to feel him give way so easily. I had never successfully defended myself in my life. Even in my dreams the most pathetic adversaries would be magically transformed into *hardcases* at the merest hint of my retaliating. This scum had no right to abuse me in that disgusting way. My arse felt hot and bruised where his fingers had touched me. Like a radiation burn. He had no right to assault me. I ran at the bundle of rags and buried my foot in the shabby pile. The material gave and I made contact with something more substantial. A line of ribs perhaps, or an internal organ. He emitted a loud, anguished groan which tailed off into a wheezy, cancerous cough. I kicked again and again. 'Satisfied?' I shouted at him. 'Satisfied, are you?'

I kicked him one last time and ran out of the toilet, sobbing and blind with rage. A water buffalo or something less.

I sat for ages in traffic jams until I arrived in central London. I parked on Gower Street and walked to the department. My room, little more than a broom cupboard, would be private and quiet. I really needed to think.

I lifted my briefcase on to the desk and opened it. I took the plate out and stared at the image. It was not clear – by any means – but it was clear enough. The female figure, kneeling on the bed, and slumped forward, was Anna. Behind her was a male figure. He too was kneeling, although the upper half of his body was upright. His hands were gripping Anna's hips. He was entirely naked, save for a short biker's jacket. It wasn't me. It was Dave. I could not see his features very clearly, but it could not be anybody else. Given the parameters of the temporal anomaly, their assignation must have occurred at about three o'clock the previous day. My supervision time. They would have known, of course.

What was I to do? I had no idea. I felt confused and distraught. I seemed to swing between numbness and pain, a deep, deep pain that I had never known before. Waves of appalling grief passed through my mind and body with grim regularity, like an advancing tide of suffering. In the wake of each wave I would sob and cry. Then the numbness would come. I would be empty. Not a person, but a hollow vessel. A husk.

I had no experience of dealing with emotion. I was like a child, ill equipped to address the problems of a premature and unwanted adulthood. Why had Anna done this terrible thing to me? Dear, sweet Anna? Anna, who would squeeze my hand in the darkness,

169

hold me close and stroke my hair. Anna, who would play the cello and spend a quiet evening, reading her journals or a Penguin classic. How was it possible? Then I remembered her face, that day in Trent Park. Sweaty and hungry. An appetite so alien as to be beyond my understanding. I looked at the plate again. Yes, this was the true Anna. I had been deceived. I had been mistaken.

And Dave? How could he have betrayed me? He was my friend. My *only* friend. All those intimate conversations now took on a sinister turn. They were reconnaissance, nothing more. He was viewing the territory, albeit from a distance. How well he would have performed! Knowing (as if informed by some preternatural carnal sense) where to stroke, where to touch, where to kiss. He would have dispensed with the customary *fumble and grope*. Oh, yes. Dave would have plotted his course like an accomplished navigator. And why not? I had, with unguarded disclosures, drawn him a map of Anna's sexuality. Like an artless fool, I had detailed each cove, nook and harbour. Anna wouldn't have had to utter a single word to Dave; not a murmur even, to encourage a burrowing finger or a daring caress. He would have engineered a communion of souls. His love-making would have laid claim to perfection. How stupid, clumsy and inept I would have seemed by comparison. A chemistry-set adolescent in a brothel.

How long had they abused me like this? I wondered. From the beginning? From before the beginning? Who could say? Anyone party to so foul a deception was, to my mind, capable of anything.

I was totally exhausted and my head felt as though it was going to explode. A build-up of pressure that threatened to shatter my skull, spraying blood and brain tissue over the walls and ceiling. In a pathetic, primitive, fearful gesture, I placed my palms against my temples and spread my fingers over the crown of my head until they touched. I was holding my head together.

Perhaps I passed out. I really don't know; it was then that I had the dream.

I was walking by the Embankment. The sky was typically grey

and overcast. The Thames was the colour of gun-metal. It seemed to be flowing in slow motion. A lazy, rolling motion. I passed King's College, but there were no students around. In fact, the whole place seemed empty. There was, however, an odd, keening wind. I could feel drizzle on my face.

When I arrived at the Temple area, I walked up the stairs, toward the imposing Elizabethan bulk of Middle Temple Hall. The building looked derelict. Most of the windows were smashed. Its red bricks were streaked with grime and the roof appeared to be encrusted with bird droppings. Again, there was no sign of life. No hustle and bustle of lawyers on their way to court. Only the keening wind, and a terrible sense of desolation. I walked wearily past the hall and up a small flight of stairs into a small secluded space, hemmed in by further crumbling buildings. At its centre was a small fountain over which a leafless, lightning-blasted tree suspended branches of charred wood and ash. The fountain projected a weak jet of brown, viscous water into the air, which fell into a shallow, stagnant pool. An empty wooden bench was situated under the tree.

In the distance, I saw Richard Dawkins, walking briskly, before he disappeared between two buildings. When I looked again at the bench, it was occupied by the ancient mariner. He appeared more dishevelled, his hair a wild tangle of knotted threads. Yet his eyes were the same, clear and blue. Unblinking. I shivered as he began to speak.

'Lies,' he said, 'all lies.'

I was struck dumb. He raised the can of Tennent's to his lips. 'What's the matter? Lost your tongue?'

It was as though I had become paralysed.

'I heard you've been down Soho again.'

He threw his head back over his right shoulder, indicating that I should look behind him. A naked black woman leaned out from behind the tree. She stepped forward, her three pendulous breasts swinging together in synchrony.

I was suddenly filled with terror. I ran off, past the entrance to

Middle Temple Hall and into a complex maze of alleyways. I thought that I could hear the repetitive beat of the mariner's boots behind me, but when I looked over my shoulder the spaces between the abandoned buildings were empty.

A door opened behind me, and out stepped Duncan Gilmour.

'Tom! So good to see you,' he said, extending his hand. It was covered in a viscous sheath. I drew back. 'But where is Anna? Where is the girl?'

'I don't know.'

'Dear little Anna. I must say, I was altogether impressed by her tight little arse. And those delightful, petite breasts. So dainty. What a lucky fellow you are!'

'I don't know where she is.'

He stepped out from the doorway and began to approach me. I retreated, stepping backwards.

'Don't be coy now, we can discuss this man to man. Would you be so kind as to procure for me a small phial of her juice?'

He kissed the tips of his fingers like a gourmet.

'So sweet, no doubt. Such a cheeky bouquet. Oh, how glorious it would be, to languish in a sea of dark sonorities – a droplet of her essence on my tongue – while indulging in onanistic gratification.'

'Go away, you pervert.'

'Come now, not so tetchy, please. I would make it worth your while of course. Name your price. A Caxton sphere perhaps?'

I turned on my heels and ran. I made my way toward a shadowed area, beneath a roof supported by large columns. I paused to get my breath back, and rested my back against a pillar of stone. In front of me stood Mr Friend. The skin on half of his face had been removed, and I could see a raw, exposed muscle, jerking and pulsing. He placed his right hand into his mouth and bit off the ends of his fingers. His scream filled the air. When the silence returned he said, in a pathetic, desperate voice; 'Help me?'

'I can't.'

'Come on, mate. Please.' Twitch. Spasm.

'I can't, there's no cure.'

He sucked his lips into his mouth and repeatedly bit them, as if ravenous. He yelled, an awful, hopeless cry, as the blood trickled over his chin, and his lower lip detached itself. It swung below his face, suspended by a sinewy string of fibrous tissue.

'Please, mate. Do us a favour?'

'There's no cure.'

'Please . . .'

'I can't.'

'Well, fuck you, then.'

I ran off again, as another scream echoed through the air.

When I stopped running, I found myself in front of a church. The stone was mottled with lichen, and a lamp hung over the arched doorway. It emitted a sickly, greenish light. I turned and looked back across a bare concourse. I heard another of Mr Friend's cries and leaned on the damp wood. The door creaked open and I stepped into the semidarkness. My footsteps echoed. I found myself looking into a circular chamber, littered with statuary. Supine knights. The tombs of crusaders, laid to rest for eternity. Tombs of men who had fought a holy war, under a strange, unforgiving sun, blazing in another sky.

Then, all of a sudden, there was a curious sound. A cracking and rending of stone. One of the supine figures sat up. I looked at his impassive, noble face.

'Pray for us now and at the hour of our birth,' he said, in a clear, resonant tone.

I was not frightened. In fact, I was suddenly very calm.

'Who are you?' I asked.

'Trust me.'

'But who are you?'

There was a moment's silence, before he said, 'London,' and lay back, resuming his supine position.

These two syllables persisted in the air, like a whisper in a vast and empty gallery.

★

When I woke, it was something like two in the morning. The voice of London was still in my mind. The sonic equivalent of the retinal after-image acquired by looking at the sun. A curious sibilance that played at the edge of my awareness. I felt very strange. My emotion had gone. It was as though it had been drained out of me, in Temple church, where London had spoken to me through the effigy of a dead knight. My mammalian brain had gone. My limbic system had been cauterized.

What did it mean, to put my trust in London? How do you trust a city anyway?

I gave up trying to make sense of my dream and went to the toilet. The lights were off and I had to grope my way down the corridor before finding the switch. When I saw the stranger in the mirror I was unmoved. I should have been appalled, but I simply acknowledged that it was me. The boy genius was nowhere to be seen. This face would never appear on the lid of a chemistry set.

I left the building and walked back to the car. I am still surprised by how many people walk the streets at this time. Outside the London University Students' Union building I was stopped by a black man wearing sunglasses. He attracted my attention by making a noise like an air pump in a garage. He opened the palm of his hand to reveal a small white tablet.

'Tenner,' he said.

'Why are you wearing sunglasses? The sun isn't going to be up for hours yet.'

'You taking the piss?'

'No, I'm asking you a question. Why are you wearing sunglasses at this time?'

'What the fuck are you on? You want this shit or you just fucking me?'

'How much?'

'Tenner.'

'Fiver.'

'Fuck off, man!'

174

'Forty guilder then.'

He grabbed my jacket and pulled me up so that I had to stand on my toes. I really wasn't scared. A police siren wailed in the distance.

'Put me down.'

'Listen, I can't be doing with this shit, you stupid fuck.'

'Fiver, then.'

He put me down and held out his hand. I found a screwed-up ten-pound note and gave it to him. Amazingly, he then took out his wallet and produced a crisp five-pound note, which he popped into the top pocket of my shirt with the pill. He then turned and walked briskly away. I couldn't resist calling out, 'Take those sunglasses off. They make you look conspicuous. Like a racial stereotype, in fact.'

'Fuck you!' he called back.

I stood for a moment, inhaling the heavy, grime-laden air. I retrieved the pill and looked at it. It seemed profligate to waste good money. I put it into my mouth with a movement that resembled a mechanical arm in a car-assembly plant.

When I got back to the flat I was still in a curious state – as though parts of my body had been replaced with metal. I also felt full of energy. I felt I could punch my way through a wall, like Jeff Goldblum in Cronenberg's remake of *The Fly*. I remembered that Anna would be in bed. I didn't know what to do about Anna. I hadn't decided.

The door at the end of the corridor opened, and Anna stood looking at me. Her hair was mussed and she was staring at me in a strange way.

'Tom? What's happened?'

'Nothing.'

'Tom, you look terrible. What's happened?'

'I told you. Nothing.'

I walked to the bedroom, brushed past her and went in. When I saw the bed I suddenly felt a stab of emotion. But it disappeared as quickly.

'Where have you been?'

175

'Working.'

'Why didn't you leave a message?'

'I forgot.'

'What do you mean, "You forgot"?'

'I neglected to retrieve information from long-term memory.'

'Tom, this really isn't very funny. Have you been drinking with Dave or something?'

His name was like a blowtorch in my face. I winced.

'No.'

'Then what . . .'

'What what?'

'You can't just come in like this and . . .'

I looked at Locke's apparatus, which was still beside the wardrobe, its brass fixtures catching the light and its dark wood smelling of polish.

'Tom, I've had enough. I really have.'

'Had enough of what?'

'Everything.'

'*You* have had enough?' I said in disbelief.

'You don't let me know where you are. You come in at three in the morning and to top it all you leave all this in the bedroom!'

'All this?'

She gesticulated at the apparatus.

'This junk.'

'Junk?'

'You said it was an antique.'

'It is.'

'Tom, it's not.' She reached out to touch the first-stage modulator.

'Don't touch that!' I couldn't stop myself from shouting.

Anna's hand remained outstretched, her fingers an inch or two from the apparatus.

'You haven't tampered with it, have you?'

'No.'

'Are you sure?'

I took a step closer and examined the principal components. For some reason Anna's outstretched arm had remained frozen in the same position. I pushed her hand out of the way so I could scrutinize the connections. It looked OK, but I couldn't be certain.

'Never touch this, do you understand? Never!'

She looked at me and tears began to brim in her eyes. Little transparent bubbles that grew on her lower lid and then burst open, leaving silver trails on each cheek. 'Tom, it's not an antique. It's not anything.'

'I'll be the judge of that.'

We stood, either side of the apparatus, like two people from different worlds.

'Where were you when I was at my last supervision with Béla?'

'What?'

'Yesterday. Well, I suppose I should say the day before yesterday now. Where were you?'

Anna narrowed her eyes.

'I'd like the car keys, Tom.'

'Why?'

'Please. Give me the car keys, Tom.'

'Where are you going?'

'Please, give me the car keys.'

'Why?'

'Please, give me the car keys, Tom.'

'Please, open the pod-bay doors, Hal.'

'Tom, give me the keys.'

'No. Not until you tell me where you are going.'

She had begun to shake. I noticed that her nipples had become erect under her nightgown. There was a strange ripple of excitement that passed through my body.

Anna said nothing, opened the wardrobe and took out a jumper and some jeans. She did not take her nightgown off, but simply pulled her jeans up under it. She then let the nightgown fall to the floor. I only saw her bare back for a moment, before the jumper went on.

177

'What are you doing, Anna?'

She sat on the side of the bed and put on a pair of trainers.

'You're leaving me, then?'

She said nothing.

For a moment, our eyes met. She was crying and shaking violently at the same time.

'Oh, Tom,' she said. Quietly. In a whisper.

'You can't just leave, Anna.'

'Tom . . . I . . .'

'Where were you? The day before yesterday.'

'Please, Tom.'

She leaned forward to do up her laces. Her hair fell forward to reveal her bare, white neck. She was obviously off to Dave's now. Off for an evening of petting and screwing. The quality of the light changed. The world became grainy, like an over-enlarged photograph. For a moment – just a moment – my visual field began to break up.

I pulled the main compressor out of its housing and brought it down hard on the back of Anna's head. She slid off the bed and on to the floor. Her body was an angular mass of bones.

The room was quiet, yet it had that strange 'noisiness' that quiet rooms have. As though it was roaring. When a train passed in the distance it seemed somehow quieter.

I knelt beside Anna's body and placed my ear next to her mouth. She was breathing, though very faintly. I took a pillow from the bed and placed it over her face and pressed hard. I had no idea how long it would take to suffocate her. Not long, I thought, and I was right. After two or three minutes she was dead.

10

$$S = K \, log_{\mathrm{w}}$$

The backwaters of Wood Green are not very busy at three-thirty a.m. They are even less busy when the early hours coincide with a deluge. Water ran from every roof, porch and gutter, splashing on the pavement and flags below. I carried Anna over my shoulder and put her in the boot of the Skoda. There was no one around. It was that easy. Then, I drove off. I must have been soaked, but I have no recollection of it.

Reflecting on my behaviour at that time, I suppose my reasoning was suspect; nevertheless, my nascent plan was not entirely misconceived. I could not store Anna's body anywhere in the flat. That would be impossible. There was no basement or accessible loft. Even if I could store her, what end might this temporary solution serve? I did not have the wherewithal to construct an acid bath, nor did I have the patience to carefully monitor her dissolution. I did not have the stomach to cut her up into little pieces and, besides, I was sure that some tell-tale sign or residue would persist – a dormant informer – if I chose such a theatrical method of disposal.

People get killed all the time. People go missing all the time. Providing no evidence was left that might link me with Anna's murder, I could leave her, dump her, virtually anywhere.

The rain pelted down; a timpani roll on the roof. The wipers could barely clear the windscreen before another torrential downpour obliterated my view. I drove slowly, very slowly. I did not want to get stopped for speeding. That would be foolish.

Off I went, down the North Circular, through Hampstead, and

179

westward. In my mind's eye I saw my destination. The vast, appalling plane at Paddington. Hemmed in by cliffs of concrete, bridges and motorway. Cut off by disused railway lines and stagnant canals. *The basin.* That nightmare wasteland, spurned by the *A–Z*, denied existence by the Ordnance Survey. Too terrible an absence even to merit a shading or a name.

London is full of wastelands. A legacy of the Blitz, no doubt. It has almost become a tradition to leave certain areas untouched. Even in Soho, you can still find the odd bomb-site. It is as though there are two Londons, the London of shop-windows, gaudy lights and tightly packed pubs and bars, and the other London, the London of neglect and ruin. A London of crumbling concrete, graffiti, weeds and garbage. Both Londons are interleaved, constituting a complex mosaic. They slot together, and the fit is tight and snug. Yet they are two distinct capitals, boasting two distinct populations. I felt as though I were travelling to the nerve-centre of the other London. The Piccadilly Circus of dereliction.

The weather was my co-conspirator. It blasted the streets with torrents of water. Few people would brave this extraordinary flood. When I stopped outside the psychiatric unit of St Mary's hospital I switched off the headlights. The slip road leading down into the basin was like a river. Rapids of liquid neon, tumbling and roiling until swallowed by darkness. The splatter and spray produced by the downpour was volcanic.

I drove the car down the track and into the wide sweep of the waste. For a moment I thought I might become submerged. I switched on my lights again and drove forward. The basin was wonderful. An urban catastrophe. Ahead of me, the A40(M) flyover, barely visible through the rain. Car lights blazing a trail through a sky awash with sulphur. The far horizon, broken by metal girders. This was the end of the world. A prescient glimpse of post-apocalyptic London. The incessant pounding on the roof became for me the thunderous gallop of the four horsemen.

When I arrived in the heart of the basin I opened the car door. I was next to a deep trench, the bottom of which was full of rubble and empty cans. Twisted fragments of metal and the debris of cars. I got out, to be smacked in the face by a wave of water. It was like stepping into the sea. I waded and plashed my way to the back of the car while rain poured down the back of my neck. My hair hung like a sopping curtain over my forehead.

I opened the boot and pulled out Anna's body. Her dead weight hit the ground with a sodden thud. I couldn't really see her through my bespattered glasses. Without much further thought, I pushed her, rolled her – blindly – into the trench, and got back into the car.

I was home again by five in the morning. There were one or two other things I needed to do. I dismantled Locke's apparatus and stacked the parts in the kitchen. I would put them in the shed. The plate I kept in my briefcase. I stripped the bed, with the intention of taking the sheets and pillow cases to the laundry. Just in case. There was no real reason for doing this. I just felt safer that way.

I ran a hot bath and placed my clothes in the laundry bag. When I finished bathing I lay on the bed, naked. The rain was still going strong, beating and banging at the window-panes like an enraged assailant.

I am not sure that I slept. If I did, it was for so brief a period I did not notice. I seemed just to lie on the bed. At about midday I went and did the laundry. The rain had stopped, but the pavement and roads were still wet. On my return I made myself a cup of tea and sat in front of the television. There was nothing on that captured my interest and I flicked from station to station with increasing rapidity. After a few minutes I was changing the station every two seconds. Eventually I tired of this senseless activity and returned to lie on the bed.

I felt burnt out. Like there had been a detonation in my head. All that was left was a scorched cranium. The inside of my skull would be scored and streaked like a bombed-out bunker. I imagined wisps

181

of smoke issuing from the stump of brain stem. There was nothing left of me. I had become a lower life-form.

I had often wondered, before that moment, at the patience of insects. Their ability simply to wait. To be still and not want for diversion or entertainment. There was no longer any mystery in their gift of stillness. I, too, would be absolutely still. I, too, would be without movement. In truth, I cannot say that I was alive that day. I functioned, until my consciousness ebbed away. A final residue of awareness flickered, before extinction, silence and darkness.

The laws of physics do not seem to be bothered by plot. They work equally well on rewind or fast forward. The models of the material universe that we derive from the seminal texts function equally well with time running in either direction. Whoever we choose to base our models on, be it Newton, Einstein or Heisenberg, the universe is rather indifferent to the concept of serial priority. Beginning, middle, end. End, middle, beginning. Both are fine. Some of the greatest minds have come to the conclusion that our day-to-day sense of time moving forward is an illusion. They describe it as 'subjective time'. A derisory, belittling term.

There is an exception. This is the second law of thermodynamics. The law that points out that heat can only flow from a hot body to a cooler body. The law that, in a more general sense, points out that things have a tendency to go from order to chaos. The second law is a narrative law. Unlike the others, you can't run it backwards. It only works one way. Unlike the others, it seems to resonate with our sense of subjective time. It likes a story.

On the fifth of September, 1906, Ludwig Boltzmann, the man who worked out how to express mathematically the disorder at the heart of the second law, so elegantly, as $S = K \log_w$, was forcing himself to enjoy a seaside holiday in the Adriatic village of Duino, near Trieste. Frau Boltzmann had noticed that his suit was looking shabby. It needed to be cleaned. She thought, no doubt, that a gentleman of his standing should not be seen in a shabby suit. Ludwig was not happy. He wanted to go back to Vienna. In my mind, I have a distinct image of Boltzmann's bulky frame, pacing around the holiday home. He was irritated. Annoyed, that his wife should delay their return because his suit should be taken to the cleaners! However, Frau Boltzmann insisted.

She took the suit, and after visiting the cleaners both she and her daughter went for a swim. When they returned they found Ludwig suspended in the window casement. All his life he had been preoccupied with the direction of time; he had finally provided himself with a dramatic demonstration of its irreversibility. The second law of thermodynamics and its implications held Professor Boltzmann in an intractable state.

I had committed an irreversible act. The second law had me. No matter how I felt about it, or ever felt about it in the future, what was done was done. I was swinging with Boltzmann, as we all do. Did the jazzman who once said 'If it ain't got that swing, it don't mean a thing' ever realize the potential resonances of his catchphrase? No, of course not. The jazzmen of the swing era were never noted for their knowledge of thermodynamics and entropy.

The following day my emotions returned, and the first emotion I experienced was fear. When my eyes opened, the daylight caught me by surprise, like the merciless beam of a headlight turned upon a wild animal. My limbs were paralysed but vibrating, animated only by a near-imperceptible tremor. I had been unbelievably stupid. I had killed Anna and then I had dumped her body in a trench located next to one of London's busiest railway terminals. Was this a wise thing to do? I could remember thinking at the time that this method of disposal was as good as any other, but after a good night's sleep, this seemed remarkably sanguine. Doubts multiplied in my mind, with attendant images of arrest, trial and incarceration. I began to pace around the flat, thinking; however, my thoughts simply resolved themselves into a series of questions that had no answer. Should I call the police? Should I report her missing? How would this help?

183

Should I have taken her body far away? To Scotland, where I might have sunk her in the depths of a brackish loch?

Although I had taken sensible precautions, I knew nothing about forensic science. It was inevitable that Anna's body would be found. Probably within weeks, days even. What could a forensic scientist discover? Dissecting, probing, analysing. A forensic scientist might have techniques at his (or her) disposal that would unequivocally identify me as the killer. Had I unintentionally autographed her corpse?

My tremor became more agitated, until my teeth chattered and my body shook. My bowel loosened and I had to run to the toilet. A jet of diarrhoea spurted from my anus, filling the air with the stench of rot and decay. My stomach turned over.

'I don't believe it,' I said out loud. 'How could you be so stupid?'

It was then that I resolved to recover the body. I would return to the Paddington basin and, if there were no police cars, cordons or forensic scientists, retrieve Anna's body. There were so many places I could have dumped her: Scotland, Wales, at sea! Why had I chosen Paddington? For the first time it occurred to me that I might not be well. My mind might not be working as it should. I sighed and turned my intellect – with much effort – toward consideration of the immediate problem.

I decided that I would not drive. I would do my reconnaissance on foot. A disguise would also be helpful. I had not shaved and had acquired an unkempt, neglected look. In the shed, I had an old lab coat and a few items of clothing that I had worn while decorating. Emulating low-life would not be difficult.

I packed my tramp clothes in a plastic carrier bag, then went off to Wood Green Tube station. I bought a travel card and set off for Paddington. The carriages were relatively empty at first, although they began to fill up closer to central London. The journey seemed interminable. An endless burrowing through the earth.

When I emerged in Praed Street, I made for the hospital without delay. The psychiatric department was a large, box-shaped building.

Next to it a huge metal chimney disgorged vapours. I wondered if it was attached to an incinerator, necessary for the disposal of diseased or redundant human debris. A curious thought, human rubbish. I read the sign, which said Paterson Centre.

The psychiatric department of St Mary's seemed to get by without security. I walked up and down outside, assuming an air of nonchalance as I peered through the glass doors and into the foyer. Nobody challenged me. It was relatively quiet. The only people walking in and out appeared to be patients. I followed one of them through. The carpet was peppered with cigarette burns and the air smelt of urine. I vanished into the first toilet I could find and got changed in a cubicle. Getting out was just as easy. There were no attendants at the door. Indeed, the place seemed rather empty. As though the hospital had been closed. Nevertheless, this dereliction did nothing to discourage the patients from returning. Like ghosts, they haunted the featureless corridors, listening to the bad electricity (crackling in the wires) beneath strip lights that made vision an effort. When I left the hospital I felt a profound sense of relief, in spite of my unusual circumstances.

Acting the part of a drunk I walked down the road to the basin. Where it terminated, the road surface was marked with large white letters, spelling out the warning PRIVATE ROAD. There was also a sign. It had the words NO ENTRY on it, in bold red capitals. A further sign informed me that CCTV was in operation. Shit. I had seen none of this. I walked back for a while, then stopped. Unexpectedly, a black London taxi came up the track, out of the basin, and drove off toward Paddington. I waited, and shortly after, another taxi followed. I had no idea what they had been doing in the basin. Whatever, no one was stopping them. This seemed to be encouraging.

I walked back to the entry point and looked around. In spite of the hostile signs, I could see no evidence of surveillance. No cameras, no men in uniforms. I resolved to continue my quest. I passed two rusting metal gates, hanging off their hinges, and walked on. A stone bridge (another feature I had not noticed) passed over the road as it descended steeply downward, into the basin.

It was late afternoon, and the sky was darkening. The landscape was even more impressive than on the night of the deluge. The brutal horizon, the girders and concrete. The flyover, guiding its angry, roaring river of metal over this wasteland at high speed. I wondered how many people travelling on the A40(M) bothered to look to the left, so that they might register this marvel of desolation.

To my left was a Portakabin, with its windows boarded up. I noticed that the door had been broken in and wondered if there was anyone inside. There were some parked lorries that looked as though they were not abandoned, but it was difficult to tell. I had a dim recollection of where I might find the trench. As I walked on, I couldn't help reading the graffiti. The *tags* and statements, the curses and protests: *Fuck, Shit, Piss, Christian Goldman is Dead, Jesus never failed me yet, Babillon-Kool, FRG, Lezbians, AIDS Poofs die.* I had a curious urge to raise the tone of the place by carving $S = K \log_w$ into the wall of concrete. And how appropriate it would have been.

What kind of people, I wondered, came to the basin? To paint, to sit, to talk. That the basin had its own population was indisputable. There were too many signs. I could see small areas of scorched grass and stone where the denizens of this 'other' place convened, to warm their hands in front of makeshift fires. This was the longest journey of life, walking the basin. However, as I continued, I could not repress a sudden surge of optimism. It was, after all, empty. There were no flashing blue lights, no cordons, no crowds. Surely, if they had found something, they would still be around.

I wanted to turn back, at that point, but couldn't. There was no need for me to continue. I had all the information I required. It would be possible to return with the Skoda later. Nevertheless, I found myself drawn forward, toward the ditch. Like a zombie. The traffic was loud, over my head. The air smelt of petrol and exhaust fumes. The only atmosphere possible. Toxic and deadly.

My foot caught in a metal track, and I stumbled. I broke my fall

186

on a nettle and sucked at the dirty flesh, cursing. I spat out the bitterness and picked myself up. I could hardly believe what I was doing, but still I did not stop.

I came to the trench. I looked around. No one was there to look back at me. There were tower blocks in the distance, but their windows were blind. Too far away to pose a serious threat to my anonymity. A little closer were what looked like disused warehouses. Who could see me? What was I, after all? A tiny, pathetic figure, beachcombing the urban debris. I crouched down and looked over the edge of the ditch.

My first sensation was panic. I wanted to see the body. I wanted to see Anna's rain-soaked, crumpled form amid broken concrete, tyres and twisted metal. I wanted to see her. I wanted to see her where I had left her. But she was gone. She wasn't there. At the periphery of my senses, I caught the sound of a sibilant whisper and smelt the slightest scent of incense.

There is the London that you see, and the London that you don't see. There is London, and there is the other London. There are the people that you know, and the people that you don't know. The other people. Sometimes you see them, and sometimes you don't. But they are there.

What are the uses, I wonder, of a body? What do you do with the sodden, rotting corpse of a twenty-two-year-old woman? Would you keep her in your basement? Would you strip her naked and pump her decomposing carcass full of hot semen? Or, would you fashion her skin and bones into *objets d'art*? What strange delights are afforded to the man (or woman) with an interest in the dead? I cannot begin to imagine the extremities of behaviour that such a unique and irregular passion could produce.

That night, I slept the sleep of the saved. In the arms of the great, dark, cankered mother of all cities.

There was one more thing I decided to do. It was not planned, but spontaneous. I found the tape of Anna playing the Bach cello suite in D-minor. Listening to it did make me feel strange, I must admit. She finished playing, but the tape went on. We were talking, Anna and I, about this and that. It went on for quite some time.

I booked thirty minutes in the audio-visual suite of the media studies department. When I emerged, I had a tape in my Dictaphone. As the Tube rocked backwards and forwards, I listened to Anna's stilted, odd voice: 'Dave . . . I'm OK. Tell Tom – Don't worry.'

I I

Further Inquiries

Eventually, I had to report Anna missing. Two police officers arrived the same day. One was a rather remote man with a small moustache, the other was a WPC, who was strangely sympathetic. I wondered at her choice of profession. She would have made a far superior nurse. They asked me the obvious questions. Had I called Anna's mother? Where did Anna's brother live? How long had Anna and I lived together? Could I think of any reason why she would have run away? The WPC's questions were easy to answer: Yes, it was true that our relationship had deteriorated; yes, she had called a friend after her departure. Indeed, her departure was unexpected. And so on. The interview only lasted for about an hour.

Three days later, two more policemen arrived. They asked if they could search the flat. They did so, with some delicacy. I had expected them to ransack the place and spill my possessions everywhere. Instead, they rummaged around a bit and then asked if they could take a look inside the shed.

'What's all this, then?' said the senior party as he examined the remains of Locke's apparatus.

'It's part of a machine.'

'A machine? What kind of machine?'

'Well, one that was originally designed in the nineteenth century. It's a kind of electricity generator.'

'Anything to do with those gadgets under the bed?'

'Yeah. I was thinking of building a reconstruction.'

The senior officer looked around the shed. He was clearly disdainful of my collection.

'Why do you want to build an electricity generator?'

'Something to do. It's a hobby.'

'I would have thought you'd already got enough on your plate. What with your Ph.D., eh?'

'Yeah . . .'

'Will it work, when you put it all together?' He raised his eyebrows, to express incredulity.

'I think so.'

The senior officer then reached out and lifted the murder weapon from a box of loose parts. He weighed it in his hands for a few moments before putting it gently back.

'OK, that's all.'

The senior officer and his junior colleague departed without incident and, apart from one or two rather vague telephone conversations with someone from 'missing persons', they left me alone.

I met up with Dave the following week. We assumed our preferred places in the Nightingale. Dave was somewhat apologetic.

'Look, Tom, I'm really sorry. I told them what you said. You know, that things weren't going well for you and Anna. I hope I did the right thing.'

'You did, I'm sure.'

'I thought I'd better tell the truth. I assumed that you would come clean.'

'Of course. There's no point in lying, is there?'

'No. I didn't say that much though. Only that you had said you weren't getting on. And that you'd mentioned Anna *going off* before.'

'That's fine.'

'I felt like shit after they left my flat. I felt like I was dropping you in it.'

'Well, you weren't.'

I was surprised at Dave. He seemed jittery, nervous. I had never seen him like that before. His cool, together exterior seemed to have collapsed. He was smoking excessively and appeared to be unduly worried. Had a visit from the police really unsettled him so pro-foundly? I found that difficult to believe. Yet, there was no other explanation.

Again, our conversation failed to ignite. Things were made even worse by Dave's agitated state. We simply couldn't communicate. When I waved goodbye to Dave that night, I knew that our relation-ship was over, for ever. Things could never be the same again.

Curiously, I felt no hostility toward him. He seemed oddly diminished. Someone who had always appeared to me like James Dean had inexplicably taken on the mantle of my bank manager. A harassed man, chain-smoking in a desperate effort to ameliorate his stress levels. I couldn't understand it.

When Jean finally called, our conversation was extremely difficult.

'Hello, Tom, it's Jean.'

'Oh, hello, Jean, how are you?'

'Very worried, as you can imagine.' Her voice sounded brittle. I was reminded of the sound that ice makes when it cracks.

'Yes.'

'I presume there hasn't been any more news?'

'No, Jean, I'm sorry. There hasn't.'

There was then an uncomfortable pause.

'Look, Tom. I know that this will be as difficult for you as it is for me, but I think we need to talk.'

'Of course. I'm sorry I didn't call you earlier. But I thought it best to wait. I didn't want to alarm you unnecessarily.'

'I can understand that, and that was thoughtful of you, but I do wish you had let me know.'

I could feel the terrible, barely restrained anger.

'Yes, I was wrong not to call you. I realize that now. I am sorry.'

Silence.

'As you probably know, the police have spoken to me. I understand that Anna wasn't happy.'

I began to perspire.

'That's right. I don't think she was.'

'Why? Why wasn't she happy?'

'I don't know. It's so difficult to say. I suppose we weren't getting along. But she was working very hard too. I think that may have had an effect on her.'

'Had you started to argue?'

'No, not really. We had our disagreements, but it would be wrong to say that we were arguing.'

'What were you disagreeing over?'

'Stupid things. Who was going to do the cleaning. Nothing serious.'

There was a long pause.

'And you have no idea where she's gone?'

'No idea at all. If I had the faintest idea I would have told the police.'

'Yes. Of course.'

I swallowed, and waited for the next question. My mouth was quite dry. It felt like I was choking.

'She never said anything, anything that might be relevant? Anything that might help the police with their inquiries? Anything that might have suggested where she was thinking of going? Think, Tom, please.'

'Jean, I really don't know where she is.' I was telling the truth, and it sounded better as a result. 'Anna's disappearance was a complete surprise to me. I just . . . I just don't know.'

I listened to her breathing and continued, 'She hated London. Toward . . .' (I almost said 'the end') 'the end of the year, she became depressed about living here . . . She could have . . . but, I really don't know.'

There was nothing else to say. As I listened to Jean's breathing, it began to develop irregularities. Then I heard the sobbing. Slow, deep, repetitive stabs of grief which accelerated to become an almost animal bellowing. An uncontrolled wail of improbable volume. It was so raw, so primitive, I was utterly shocked. I thought I heard the word 'sorry', before the dialling tone. I replaced the receiver and had to sit down. Numb inside.

Evolutionary theory is very nearly all about sex. And the rest? Well, the rest is violence. Of course, I know all about the new Darwinians: 'kin selection', altruism, and all that. But in the end these theorists seem to me to be nothing more than a bunch of apologists. Really, if you have the courage to look at all animal and human behaviour – without flinching – and distil the essence, you are rewarded with a fine Darwinian draught of sex and violence.

Natural selection has always awarded men the lion's share of the latter. In all cultures, from the Congo basin to LA, men are more dangerous than women. Moreover, this asymmetry holds for nearly every species on the planet. You see, the male has been selected to compete for sexual resources. When sexual resources are scarce, he has to decommission the competition. And if he doesn't, well, that's it. The end. Gene-ocide. Non-replication.

The unfortunate thing is, genes don't think things through.

Violence is a means to an end. A tool, selected to help ensure replication. And, like any tool, it can be used indiscriminately. Once evolution had hard-wired violence into the subcortex, there was no guarantee that it would only be used against sexual competitors. Indeed, mankind has shown a conspicuous talent for exploiting the uses of violence.

When we condemn acts of violence, we condemn evolution. We condemn the very process that got us here in the first place. Some things that we do were actually determined several million years before we were born. Given the facts, it is no easy matter to discriminate right from wrong. Glib answers are seldom satisfactory. Not if you care to think about the broader issues, that is.

In the absence of any distraction I abandoned myself to academic life.

Day and night I worked on my thesis, and watched it develop into a fine and original contribution to human knowledge. I had no other existence. My world had become a series of simulated liquid convolutions on my computer screen. I even *dreamed* knots and whorls of fluidity. It was a splendid way of diminishing my own self-awareness. My personality ceased to exist and I became the organic interface linking my computer to the greater universe.

Béla had learned of Anna's disappearance when the police contacted the university. I strongly suspect that they interviewed Béla but, if they did, he didn't let on. In spite of his tirade against women, he was interested in my welfare and very supportive. He even suggested that I take a long holiday. I could hardly believe it. The old tyrant had feelings after all. Of course, I declined the offer. Without my work, I would have had to face myself.

Weeks became months. In the spring I invited Huntley over to collect Anna's things. Her clothes, her photographs, her cello. This was in response to a letter from Anna's mother, who had begun to accept that she might never see her daughter again. I had only met Huntley once before, in a pub in Covent Garden. Our reunion did little to make me regret our long-standing poverty of social intercourse.

He arrived with a friend who owned a battered, rusting Bedford van. Huntley was in a terrible state, as expected. His penchant for chemical stimulation had reduced him to a scrawny personage with glassy eyes and very few 'life signs'. His colleague, who rejoiced in the name of Jex, was also mentally and physically challenged. I offered them both tea, and they sat at the table, smoking. Clearly experiencing the most extreme discomfort.

'She ain't dead, man . . . I know. Don't you worry, she'll be back,' said Huntley.

'What makes you so sure?'

'Like, I know this woman. Like, she's psychic? Yeah?'

'Psychic?'

'And, she's got this guide. On the other side, you know?'

'The other side?'

'For sure . . .' interjected the cadaverous Jex, firmly, as though speaking from experience.

' . . . and, like,' Huntley continued, 'Anna's not there, man.'

'I see.'

The stupidity of what subsequently passed as a conversation between Huntley and Jex beggared belief. My awareness recoiled back into my skull like a salted mollusc retreating into a shell. After a hiatus punctuated only by the crackling inhalations and exhalations of my two unwelcome guests, I remarked on the afternoon's advance toward evening. Huntley and Jex took the hint, and bade me a cryptic adieu.

'Tom . . .'

' . . . yeah'

'Like . . . OK, then.'

What could I say to this? I nodded my head and replied, 'Hunt, Jex . . . OK, then.'

It had the desired effect. They rose like two bubbles of rank gas, released from a belching and restless quagmire.

At the door Huntley stopped and turned to look at me. Jex went to the van and, without looking back, took his place behind the wheel. My heart sank when Huntley began to have some last thoughts that he clearly wished to share.

'So sad, man.'

'What is?'

'You know, like. Why people split and that.'

'Yes, it is.'

'I never thought that she would do-the-off like this. Not with you. We used to worry about Anna. Me and me mum. You know, she never had boyfriends. To tell the truth, I didn't think she was interested. Then, you came along. I thought, well. Must mean something, this. Yeah? And to just fuck off like this . . .'

'She never had boyfriends.' I repeated those words, like a robot.

'No, man. Just you. It all seemed so right. You know?'

195

I could not reply. I simply nodded and closed the door. I took a deep, deep breath, turned and walked down the hallway. My steps were slow and careful because the floor seemed curiously accommodating, as though made of rubber. It seemed to yield, making the next step very difficult. By the time I was back at the kitchen table I could hear their van rattling and backfiring in the direction of south London.

A curious thing happened the following week. I was on my way in to see Béla and had arrived at Russell Square Tube station much earlier than expected. The morning was clear and crisp, the sky, a pale but lucid blue. I was feeling somewhat sleepy and wanted a coffee. I had not been to my old haunt in the square for nearly six months. Recollection of the eyes of the ancient mariner still sent a chill and shiver down my spine. Perhaps because of the extraordinary convalescent effect of the sunlight, I was content to risk returning to my table. I felt somehow stronger. Able to cope.

I stirred my cappuccino and inhaled the fresh air. Then, to my sudden horror, I noticed a figure walking toward Senate House. A rather intense figure, with a brisk, purposive stride. I felt sick. It was Richard Dawkins. I was sure that the mariner would soon appear, to pass some comment, and hold my attention. A cruel re-enactment of our previous encounter. However, as the figure approached, I looked again and questioned the accuracy of my initial observation. No, it wasn't Richard Dawkins. Definitely not. In fact, the rather plump, bespectacled man didn't look like Richard Dawkins at all. I heaved a sigh of relief and finished my cappuccino under a benign and warmly portentous sun. The world had changed.

I was awarded my doctoral thesis in mathematics by the University of London after a rather undemanding viva examination in late summer. My internal examiner was the pedestrian George Brill; however, my external was Béla's old mate from Harvard, Gabor Grzyzgy. So impressed was Grzyzgy that he offered me a junior lecturing post in his department. I accepted. I needed to get away from London.

When I was packing my things, I came across Locke's paper. I looked at the equations but, somehow, they had stopped making sense. That is, bar one – the one that I had borrowed and adapted for my Ph.D. The rest were nonsense. I was strongly tempted to throw it away but decided not to. It went in my case with the rest of my collection. My scientific antiques went in the dustbin. I had begun to question the value of many of these cherished items, particularly those that were acquired more recently.

I went to say goodbye to my parents. I don't know why I decided to. I had hardly spoken to them at all over the preceding year. Yet it seemed the right thing to do. It was more for me than for them. I wanted closure. I wanted an end to it. If I had had Bob's courage, I would have done it years ago.

We spent a typically frigid evening. An English meal. Two courses. Chicken, potatoes and peas, followed by treacle tart and custard. My mother said very little. The tartan-framed photograph of the *Flying Scotsman* was still positioned in the same place on the mantelpiece. Where other people might have displayed pictures of their sons and daughters, friends and relatives, my mother and father were content to have a locomotive steam-engine.

My father asked me a few questions about my new post; they were rather superficial questions. What salary would I be on? What opportunities were there for promotion? Did the university provide accommodation? That sort of thing. Nothing of consequence. Nothing about my work. Nothing about anything, or at least anything that mattered to me. It confirmed all my previous negative beliefs about them.

At about ten I said that I would be going. My parents both rose, a little too swiftly. Did I detect a certain eagerness in their alacrity?

'Well, then,' said my father. 'The very best of luck.'

He extended his hand. I could not believe it. He made me feel like a colleague at work who was leaving the company for a better position elsewhere. For a moment I thought of saying something. Pointing out that they had both been total failures as parents. That they had lost one son and were about to lose another. That I had never been loved. That it wasn't enough to be a biological mother and a biological father. That I would never see them again!

But, instead (and faithful to our family tradition to the very end) I extended my hand to meet his. Our weak, almost flaccid linkage did not last long. Like two autumn leaves, in brief collision. The embarrassment for both of us was almost painful. My mother's response was even worse. Deprived, by her gender, of the option of extending her hand, she merely looked at me and said, 'Do let us know that you've arrived safely.'

'I will, Mother,' I said, with absolutely no intention of doing so, before adding, 'Goodbye.'

I walked down the pathway, opened the gate and looked back at them. Two figures, separated by a swathe of hall light, with raised hands. I raised mine in response; a perfunctory gesture.

Before I had started to step away, my father had begun to close the door. On reflection, I think that they were as relieved as I was to bring our relationship to a close. Procreation was never *their thing*.

I had acquired very few possessions during my lifetime, and many of these I had thrown away. After everything was packed the flat seemed very still and empty. I wandered, from room to room, thinking. I did not see, or feel, any ghosts. I merely saw the furniture, the drab wallpaper, and smelt the damp. It was good to be moving on. I had not been happy in Wood Green. To tell the truth, by that time, I was beginning to feel quite excited. For the first time in a long while, I began to think about a future. My career.

It must have been only a few days before leaving for the States, no more than that. I was sitting in the kitchen, putting the finishing touches to one or two lectures (it seemed scarcely believable that in a matter of weeks I would be teaching undergraduates at Harvard), when there was a knock at the door. I was rather reluctant to open it. Nevertheless, I thought that I should. It might be some important document from Béla to be delivered by hand to Grzyzgy (or some such thought passed through my mind). I recall, my visitor was quite impatient. There were some more reports.

I left my work with more than a little reluctance and dragged my heels to the door. I opened it without thinking and was met with a sight that made my heart sink like a stone. In my mind, I was repeating one word. Just one word, again and again.

No, no, no, no.

The policeman was unaccompanied; however, beyond the row of parked cars behind him I could see a blue flashing light. My first instinct was to run – a stupid, almost animal instinct, to bolt past him and escape. It seemed like an eternity. Both of us, standing there, looking at each other. Remarkably, he didn't speak. He just looked at me and waited.

'Yes?' I finally ventured.

He could see I was deeply worried.

'Mr Jones.'

'Yes.'

'Mr Thomas Jones.'

'Yes.'

He flashed some identity in my face and started speaking. I could hear words, but somehow I couldn't grasp their meaning. It was as though he were speaking to me in Portuguese. I felt dizzy and hot. For a few seconds I thought I was going to be sick. Eventually I had to say, 'I'm sorry, I don't understand.'

He began again and, as my heart rate decelerated a little, I began to catch fragments: 'Accompany us . . . short drive . . . Highgate police station.'

Why? I can remember asking. *What for?*

Again, there were more words, more fragments: 'Your assistance . . . with respect to an investigation . . . would be most grateful if . . .'

Now? Right now?

'If at all possible.'

I don't know, I'm really not sure.

' . . . may cause considerable inconvenience at a later date . . . if there is any delay.'

I was in a state of utter terror. Harvard had felt very close only two minutes earlier. At that moment, it seemed to be receding at the velocity of light.

I heard the words come out of my mouth, but it was as though another person was saying them: 'Yes, very well. I'll just get my coat and my keys.'

The journey to Highgate was all but silent, apart from the occasional communication over the police radio. They were giving nothing away. I began to wonder, What's happened? What the fuck has happened? Have they found the body? Have they got forensics on me? What the fuck am I going to do? At times of extreme stress, you think the most idiotic things. I began to wonder how on earth the department at Harvard would find a replacement at such short notice.

When we got to Highgate I was taken into an office for questioning. Not one of those bare rooms possessed only of a desk, two chairs and an unshaded lightbulb swinging at the end of a cord, but a regular office. I was left alone for a few minutes, before a man in a suit came in. The suit was fairly crumpled, and he looked as though he could do with a shave. He was balding and had cropped his hair down to a fine, silver-grey stubble.

'Mr Jones,' he said before sitting down at what I presumed to be his desk.

I didn't reply.

He opened a file and spread a few sheets of paper out in front of him.

'Mr Thomas Jones? I suppose your friends call you Tom.'

'Yes, they do.'

'Tom Jones, eh?' He gave a broad, mischievous grin.

I don't know what compelled me to make conversation at that point. But I decided I would give it a try.

'It isn't as bad as my Ph.D. supervisor's name. His name is Béla Bartók.'

The inspector gave me a quizzical look. 'Pardon?'

'Béla Bartók. He was a famous Hungarian composer.'

'Oh yeah?' was the noncommittal reply.

He paused before speaking again. 'Do you have any idea why we've brought you in today, Mr Jones?'

'No, I haven't the faintest idea why I'm here.'

'*No idea* at all?'

'No.'

The inspector looked at his papers again, for a few moments. Then he leaned forward across his desk and stared directly into my eyes. He said nothing. I can remember how penetrating his stare was. I was so close to confessing at that point. I could barely restrain myself.

'You're a mathematics *student*? Is that right?' The word 'student' was pronounced in the same way as 'scum' or 'shit'.

'Well, not exactly, I've just finished my Ph.D. I'm about to go . . .'

I didn't know whether it was wise to mention Harvard. I didn't know what I should or shouldn't say.

'Yes. You're about to go where, Mr Jones?'

'Well, I'm about to go' – I decided I would have to tell, within reason, the truth – 'to the USA. I've been offered a teaching post there.'

'Very impressive, I must say.'

He began to drum his fingers on the desktop.

'So what was your Ph.D. on, exactly?'

'It's a little difficult to explain.'

'Why don't you try?'

'Because it was rather abstract.'

'You must be able to give the uneducated layman some idea of what you were doing?' His use of the term 'uneducated layman' was loaded with implications. He continued, 'I'm sure you've been asked that question before?'

'Well, I have. But I always find it difficult to answer.'

'Come, now, do try.'

I felt like I was walking on a sheet of glass.

'Very well, then. I suppose it was about the movement of liquids. Describing – in mathematical terms – how liquid moves and predicting patterns of liquid movement.'

'I think I can understand that. That wasn't too difficult for me, was it now?'

'No, but it wasn't a very detailed account of my work.' I tried to say this with good humour.

'Did I ask for a detailed account?'

'No.'

'Well, then.'

Again, he gave me a penetrating stare. The tension was intolerable.

'Your new job?'

'Yes?'

'Well-paid, is it? You'll do me the courtesy of answering in the conventional manner. It's amazing what Joe Public understands if you give him a chance.'

I shifted uncomfortably.

'Yes, it's a reasonably well-paid job. For someone who hasn't worked before.'

'Well, I'm glad to hear that. And that's true, I suppose. You haven't had a *proper* job before, have you?'

His unusual emphasis was puzzling. He seemed to communicate by the inflection he gave to certain words rather than through their actual meaning.

'You still have no idea why you're here today?'

'No.'

'Come, now, Mr Jones. Oh, I do beg your pardon. You must be *Doctor* Jones now.'

'It isn't something I insist on, being called Doctor.'

'Well, then, Mr Jones. I really don't believe that you have *absolutely* no idea why you might have been brought to this station – as a matter of some urgency.'

'No, I'm afraid I don't.'

Another dreadful pause. The fixed, unforgiving stare.

'I imagine that your income for the past three years has been quite low. It's very difficult, isn't it, living off a grant?'

I suddenly began to see a potential reason for my apprehension. A very good reason, in fact. One that might well explain my predicament.

'This isn't . . .'

'Yes?'

'This isn't anything to do with WRC-International, is it?'

'Bingo, Mr Jones.'

I almost laughed aloud with relief. The inspector noticed my sudden and prodigious joy and frowned.

'I don't see what there is to smile about, Mr Jones. I really don't.'

He pushed a rather grainy black-and-white photograph across the desktop. 'Do you know who that man is?'

'Yes. It's a chap called Tadweusz Wodiezko. He's a businessman.'

' . . . and you know him?'

'Yes. He used to employ me as a freelance programmer. He was in games. VR games. I haven't heard from him, though, recently. I was wondering what had . . .'

The inspector cut in. 'What sort of VR games?'

'All sorts.'

'No, Mr Jones. Not all sorts.'

I was still too relieved to bother with circumspect replies.

'You're right. He did seem to cater for a specialist market. Many of his games might have been considered pornographic.'

'Not "might have been considered". Many of his games *are* pornographic. And violent? Violent, wouldn't you say?'

'I honestly wouldn't know. Those ones I didn't see. But, I imagine that WRC would have probably handled that kind of material too.'

'Yes. Quite tasteless material, don't you think?'

'Indeed. But I was never asked to work on any of it.'

'I see.'

The inspector began to make a few notes. I was feeling much better.

'Where did you get my name from? May I ask?'

'You can. We found your name in one of Mr Wodiezko's diaries. These are now in our possession. You see, quite a lot of Mr Wodiezko's business documentation was confiscated recently.'

I played innocent.

'Are you saying that Tad was a criminal? His business was illegal?'

The inspector gave a wry smile. 'And how about this gentleman?'

He showed me another photograph. I didn't recognize the face.

'I'm sorry, I have no idea who this is.'

'Does the name Roland mean anything to you?'

'No, I can't say that it does. I only ever did work for Tad. Mr Wodiezko.'

'And how about this gentleman?'

He showed me another photograph, of a man who bore a strong resemblance to Mussolini.

'No. I don't know who he is. I'm sorry.'

The inspector looked at me again. Then, after quite a long silence, he said, 'Are you familiar with the term "snuff movie", Mr Jones?'

I swallowed.

'Yes.'

' . . . and the term, VirSnoo?'

'I haven't heard of that term before, no.'

'But I'm sure you can imagine what it means, a clever boy like you?'

'I presume . . . VirtualSnuff?'

'Bingo again, Mr Jones. Your friend Mr Wodiezko has been helping to arrange the most obscene, sometimes fatal acts of sexual brutality, which are then lovingly preserved in a virtual environment. He has made homicide a leisure activity.'

It was a murder inquiry after all.

I was detained for questioning for six hours. I had to make a statement, describing my involvement with WRC-International. I was scrupulously honest. I told them everything. I was sure that there was nothing to be frightened of. After all, I had done nothing wrong. Had I? I think, by the time I left Highgate police station, they agreed with me. Two days later, I caught my flight to the States. In September I was living in Boston. I had made it for their much celebrated *fall*.

12

Harvard, USA

One of the first people I got to know very well in the Harvard department was William Itō, a remarkably good-humoured Japanese-American. He had one of those open, boyish expressions. It took very little to make him smile. Moreover, he tended to find happiness in the simplest of things. He was fiercely proud of his oriental origins, and took great pleasure in quoting the haiku of Bashō. A great favourite of his was the enigmatic *Do not forget the plum blooming in the thicket*. Once, as we were sitting outside together, I asked him, 'Bill, what does it mean? That haiku you keep quoting?'

'Well,' he said, adopting a deeply thoughtful expression, that timeless expression, suggestive of age-old wisdom, that comes so easily to the oriental face, 'I've given this a great deal of consideration, Tom. And, I guess Bashō is telling his reader not to forget the plum blooming in the thicket.'

I didn't respond. I simply lazed in the soft glow of his inscrutability.

One might easily underestimate him. It would have been *oh so easy* to think him a rather simple person. An uncomplicated idiot savant – his talent, of course, being his mathematics. Yet to do so would have been a serious error.

After I had got to know him quite well, I raised the subject of Schwenck's problem and the second solution. The Bartók proofs.

'Wow,' he said, 'how d'you get to hear about that, over in England?'

'Bartók was my supervisor, remember? Gabor faxed him news of your work when I was his doctoral programme student.'

My Americanese was coming on fine.

'Ah, yes. I do remember. That was some problem. A real toughie.'

'It must have been. How long were you working on it?'

'Oh, must have been about two months.'

'That's pretty quick by most people's standards, Bill.'

'Well, that's very kind of you to say so, Tom.' He grinned at me. Nodding, not unlike one of those ridiculous mechanical dogs that plebeians were fond of placing at the back of their cars.

'So, tell me, Bill,' I continued. 'Why was it that you never published the second Schwenck solution?'

William Itō tilted his head to one side and looked at me with an expression of great kindness. 'I think Bashō can help me answer that one: *Winter downpour – even the monkey needs a raincoat.*'

In the stillness that we shared, you could have heard a cherry blossom dropping on to a koi pond.

After an extended silence, I ventured, 'If you get into a revolving door with a Hungarian behind you, he'll be in front of you by the time you get out.'

Itō nodded. I nodded. I think we both understood each other. Or, at least, that is what I choose to believe.

About four months after arriving in Boston I accessed the *London Underground* website. This is not, as some might believe, a repository of promotional material for London Regional Transport but, rather, the last vestiges of ViLP. A noticeboard for those who had once been involved with the project or who had developed a fixed and obsessional interest in it subsequent to its demise. Much of the noticeboard was coded, written in what has endearingly been called 'cockney'. Controversial contributions were coded in the most complex of the three cockney dialects: Bow, Bromley and Bethnal. Entries written in Bow are rare. The appearance of Bow on the Underground is the ViLP equivalent of a newsflash. It means that something very important has happened. Well, that is to say, something important as far as the ViLP community is concerned. The embedded sequence of Fibonacci numbers told me that I would have to use the Ackroyd rather than the Blake or Dickens translation grids. I clicked the mouse and waited. After two minutes – and let me tell you I have a pretty fast machine – the message blinked on to my blank screen: *Wodiezko, Tadweusz. Regret to inform. 25 years. Broadmoor.* Another door in my life had closed.

The good thing about America is that Americans have no fear of emotion. In fact, they are all emotion, and little else. Therefore, it was not in the least difficult to visit the campus counsellor, a 'girlish' middle-aged woman whose name was (aptly) Dr Peace. She insisted that I call her Sally Anne. I told her about the disappearance of my girlfriend back in London, and she helped me to *own* my grief. My loss. Apparently, I had been repressing my emotions, and it was now time for me to *get in touch* with them. She asked me to bring a memento of Anna with me to one of our sessions. I dutifully brought a picture of a young girl in a psychedelic dress, holding the hand of her protective, proud father, with his kind, intelligent eyes. Before I could finish explaining to Sally Anne who the people in the picture were, tears were rolling down my face. I cried for two hours. Sally Anne told me that I had been very courageous, and that it was her privilege to have shared my grief.

When I got back to my flat, I looked through a few other photographs of Anna. They reminded me of the daguerreotype. I don't know why, but I felt compelled to look at it again. The image had begun to fade and, to tell the truth, I'm really not sure what the remaining blobs and blotches represented. I snapped it in two, wrapped the pieces in a copy of *Scientific American*, and threw them in the bin. I sighed, leaned out of my window, and looked up at the Andromeda galaxy. It was such a long way away. Does anything really matter? I wondered.

I suppose my life began to turn around after this. Bill Itō began to become a more important figure for me. Our friendship developed and we spent many happy hours together, discussing our work. We even collaborated on a few very significant academic papers. Moreover, we formed something of an alliance in the department. A secure axis that was relatively immune to the political machinations of our colleagues. Eventually, even Grzyzgy backed off. He left us to it.

My friendship with Bill was very different to the friendship I had forged with Dave. It was cooler, in many ways a more pedestrian relationship, but nevertheless one that I felt was mature. I suppose Sally Anne would have described it as an Adult–Adult transaction (or some such term).

One day I walked into Bill's room, and he was looking intently at his monitor. He was examining the Dow-Jones.

'What are you doing, Bill?' I asked.

'Well, Tom, I'm looking at a chaotic system.'

I had never thought of finance as numbers. Ridiculous really. But it had just never occurred to me. We both stared at the screen, the changing digits, and I could tell that Bill was propositioning me, in his tangential, oriental way. Our last collaboration had involved the prediction of recurrent features in a quasi-four-dimensional Mandel-brot sculpture. Neither of us said a word, we both just stared at the screen, in deep meditation.

Then, almost inevitably, Bill broke the silence with his beloved Bashō: *Year's end, all corners of this floating world, swept.* For once, I knew exactly what he meant. He turned around grinning. 'This one's even got your name on it, Tom.'

We collected our data for exactly one year and examined the subtle ebb and flow of the commercial world. We modelled the chaos of the Dow and developed a set of prediction parameters. Of course, being a chaotic system, we never got it exactly right. There were significant discrepancies. However, as we refined our equations, as we fine-tuned our models, they began to correspond more and more with patterns and fluctuations in the market. Exactly one year later, our confidence estimate was at 78.236 per cent.

University life went on. Bill and I continued our academic work, encouraged our students and became familiar faces on the conference circuit. However, we never neglected our weekly financial meetings. Our programme, the 'Itō-Jo', was tirelessly gathering data, and our prediction equations were continuously subject to the most rigorous scrutiny and revision. Another year passed, and our confidence estimate reached 86.293 per cent. When those extraordinarily beautiful numbers came up on Bill's screen, he said, 'Small numbers, time for the harvest, big money.' I looked at him quizzically.

'Did Bashō really say that?'

'No, Tom, I did.'

'You think we should go with it now?'

'Yes. I can't see us getting much beyond 86, can you?'

'No. I guess not, Bill.'

'Well. It's time then.'

We started off with relatively small sums. But our return was consistently good. We were able to predict three 'corrections' and even got Black Tuesday.

Neither of us relinquished our academic posts. However, three years later neither of us really needed to work that much. We did maths because we enjoyed it, not because we had to. We did it because it was *our thing*.

It is remarkable how wealth increases your viability as a potential mate. There were times when I would recall my Cambridge years with disbelief. Was that really me? I could hardly believe that my memories of adolescence and Cambridge were my own. I started to entertain attractive, talented women. Some of them I dated. I was particularly fond of an orthodontist from New York. It didn't work out, but I took it well when we separated. I had acquired some of Bill's oriental calm. Such things didn't get to me any more. Besides, there was no shortage of attractive, talented women keen to make my acquaintance.

I suppose I started looking after myself more too. I started going to the gym every day. I became vegetarian. I drank a lot of orange juice. I wore fashionable spectacles. My favourite pair cost a thousand dollars. Life was good.

Eight years later, to my enormous surprise and disbelief, I ran into Dave. He had become a senior lecturer at Cambridge and had come to Harvard at the invitation of one of the big pharmaceutical companies. Once our initial astonishment had subsided, we shook hands and greeted each other with genuine warmth and affection. I, of course, invited him to the house, to meet my eccentric wife Lana (who still loves my accent) and our two beautiful children, Gail and Louise.

I insisted that Dave stay for a few days. He readily agreed. When he saw where I lived he almost passed out.

'Jesus, Tom!' was all that he could say.

Eventually he calmed down. 'How? I don't understand?'

'I made a few investments, Dave. I got lucky doing stocks and shares.'

'This lucky?'

'Yes, this lucky.'

He found the guest bedroom very comfortable.

Dave had changed so much. It was remarkable. He had become rather distinguished-looking. A proper academic. Traces of the old Dave, however, had survived. He had not married and, although he was taking his work very seriously these days, was still constitutionally unfit to settle down. He took an unhealthy interest in providing his female doctoral students with a broad education.

He was most distracted by my circumstances. He kept on looking around in disbelief, as though he had been transported to another world. I felt sorry for him. He was clearly overwhelmed. He kept on asking me what things were, like a child learning to name objects.

'What's this?'

'A Picasso, Dave. Lana's got a bit of a thing about Picasso.'

' . . . and what's this?'

'It's a tin-opener, Dave.'

'A tin-opener?'

'Sure. I'll show you how it works.'

It became almost embarrassing. Lana, being the absolute treasure that she is, found his curiosity endearing. She is such a kind, warm-spirited person.

On his last evening in Boston, we had a lot of time to ourselves. Lana had gone to her Feng Shui class, and the girls were asleep. Dave and I sat in the garden, by the pool, drinking a couple of chilled beers. We had come a long way since our days in the Nightingale.

I wanted to know more about his work. He had apparently remained in the field of biochemistry and genetics; however, I had no idea what he actually did. Indeed, I had formed the impression that he was rather evasive when subjected to close questioning.

'So, Dave, what is it – exactly – that you're working on at the moment? You know, I'm still not very clear what your current project is.'

He shifted in his seat. 'Well, to be honest, I've been asked not to disclose the exact nature of my work.'

'Oh, right.'

I could see that he felt uncomfortable, having given me the cold shoulder. I tried to reassure him. 'I understand. That's cool.'

His features twisted. 'No, fuck it. It's not cool. I should be able to tell you.'

'Well, Dave, that's up to you. But if you feel that there may be repercussions, then perhaps it's best you don't say anything.'

'No, fuck it. I will. But, Tom, you've got to keep this very, very quiet. OK?'

It was curious. After all these years, I found myself leaning forward. Ready to hear one of Dave's stories. 'OK.'

Dave took a sip of beer. Again, I was captured by old resonances. He would delay for a few more seconds, then begin.

'I've been working on a molecular warhead. It's designed to fuck up the genetic material in a newly identified retrovirus. Well, I say it's designed to fuck it over, but it can't yet. I'd say there's at least another five years' work to do, before it's anywhere near ready.'

'Ready for what? HIV-4?'

'No. A good guess though.'

'There's a more recent variant?'

'No, it's nothing to do with HIV variants. But, if my information is anything like accurate – which I believe it is – then the world is in for a pretty freaky ride.'

'Fuck. It's not an extraterrestrial, is it?'

'No. But, it might as well be.'

'Well, tell me for Christ's sake!'

Dave smiled. He was enjoying the audience reaction. And, perhaps I flatter myself, but I think he was happy to be letting his old mate in on some choice information. It was his turn to impress me. And he relished every moment.

'Do you know anything about temporal-lobe epilepsy, Tom?'

'No, nothing.'

'Well, it's one hell of a weird fuck. It's caused by abnormal electrical discharges in the temporal lobe. Individuals with TE have seizures, but they also experience changes in personality, emotion and beliefs. Moreover, TE can be subclinical. No fits, just the other stuff. So, you wouldn't know that there was something wrong with your brain. Not unless you happened to be wired up to an EEG machine. People like your friends and relatives would notice that you had undergone a "change", but it might not be a sufficiently dramatic change to warrant proper medical investigation.'

'So, what are the changes?'

'Odd. Very odd. People with TE tend to have frequent experiences of *déjà vu*. You know, thinking you've been somewhere before when you haven't. They get what might be described as altered states of consciousness. These are usually thought by the affected person to have some kind of spiritual significance.'

'You're kidding?'

213

'No, really. Spirituality is merely a disturbance in the temporal lobes. It's official now.'

'Well, I've always felt there was something wrong with believers. I suppose I should feel satisfied that my suspicions have been confirmed.'

'Yes, I can remember your views very clearly.' Dave sipped his beer again. 'Anyway, there are a load of other similar symptoms. Seeing auras, the odd vision, and a general willingness to accept the validity of paranormal phenomena.'

'So what's all this got to do with your warhead?'

'Not so fast, you need some background. Rewind four years. There was a neurologist doing epidemiological research at the Royal Free in Hampstead. Aaron Goldstein. And he noticed a rise in the number of patients showing temporal signs. He presented his findings at a few conferences, and it turned out that this rise was also evident in other hospitals around the UK. They were really puzzled by this and couldn't work out what was going on. However, when Goldstein took another look at his data and analysed it according to demographic variables, a curious pattern emerged. The trend had not affected Orthodox Jews.'

'So what does that mean?'

'Well, it could mean a lot of things. Some kind of inherited robustness, linked with race, for example. However, in the final reckoning, suspicion turned towards diet. And, in particular, the absence of pork.'

'There's something in the food-chain?'

'Yep. It took three years to confirm. But eventually they found the subclinical temporary epilepsy ALTH virus. STEALTH. ALTH refers to a neurotransmitter receptor site found in temporal-lobe fibres.'

'Shit! Why isn't this public knowledge?'

'Politics, Tom. Politics and economics. You remember the effect that CJD had on the beef industry. Well, the government wasn't prepared to have that happen again. It was such a fiasco. It didn't really amount to that much of a health hazard. Yet, the country lost

214

billions. The STEALTH virus could be far more damaging. So, a deal was struck with some major players in the meat industry. Goldstein and his cronies were paid off. I think he now lives in a luxury yacht moored off Cassis in the south of France. One of the team at the Royal Free – and this is where things get heavy – died in very mysterious circumstances. It's thought that he insisted on publication . . .'

'I see.'

'So, Tom. Please, keep this one quiet, eh?'

'Sure.'

'Funding was made available for a group of specialist units to work – in secrecy – on a molecular warhead. I was approached about a year ago. The idea is that by the time this shit surfaces we'll have the fucker licked. But who knows? The important thing is, if you ever visit the homeland, stay clear of the traditional English breakfast!' Dave's smile was grim.

'How infectious is it?'

'We don't know yet, but we think it's a whole lot more infectious than CJD. I've been keeping my eye on church attendance figures. They're going up. For the first time in fucking years. It could be a coincidence, but I doubt it.'

'Jesus.'

'Absolutely. Jesus and the whole fucking shebang!'

'What are the chances of success? With the warhead?'

'So-so. But I think the government is taking one hell of a risk. I wasn't sure that I really wanted to be part of it. You know, the secrecy and everything. But I was in pretty deep water before I knew it. And, I have to be honest, I'm promised some serious paycheques if progress is made. I won't be in your league, but I'll be very comfortable in a few years.'

I smiled inwardly. We had both done very well, in our separate ways. And how far, how very far, we seemed from the life that we both shared in London.

The evening drew on. Shadows lengthened and eventually

became indistinct. The birdsong, after a late flowering, diminished to nothing. The sky became a soft gradation of deepening blues, from horizon to zenith. It was a spectacular transition, which took us from day into night. Threads of cloud, webbing the celestial dome, captured the rays of an invisible sun, and fluoresced before evaporating. For a few minutes the sky had been marbled with a latticework of fire. Above us, the stars began to appear. The universe was revealing itself. Mocking our total insignificance. Pouring scorn on our transience and human frailty.

We talked on. About our lives. About our hopes and dreams. Dave's bold disclosures had created an atmosphere of intimacy – collusion, almost. However, as we became enveloped in darkness, it seemed that we were alone in the world. As though the vessel of space and time had bulged and the convexity become sealed off. We inhabited an aneurism in the cosmic vasculature. A bubble of impenetrable privacy.

We had talked about everything, except one subject. The obvious one. Indeed, we had been scrupulously avoiding it since our first encounter. I could not see Dave very clearly in the dark. Perhaps there was some subtle change in his posture that betrayed his intention. Whatever, I knew that the time had come. Neither of us spoke. The silence lasted for minutes. Dave took a deep breath. Eventually he exhaled. I braced myself, and he began to talk.

'Tom?'

'Dave?'

'Tom, I really don't know how to say this, but I have to. This is going to be so painful, for both of us, but, I've just got to do this. I really hope you'll understand.'

He paused, and leaned forward, resting his head in his hands. I could see his fingers, picked out in the starlight, encasing his skull.

'Dave, what is it?'

'Tom . . . I think I know what happened to Anna. I just can't live with myself any more. Please forgive me.'

I rested my hand on his arm.

216

'Look, Dave, if you know something, then say. It's all right.'

He released his head, and sat up. His umbrous presence was like a revenant's. 'You know, I could never have said this, if I hadn't seen you so happy. So happy with Lana and your daughters. So successful. It would have been out of the question. Tom, Anna must have killed herself. You see, she was riddled with guilt. You never did understand women, not then, anyway, but, she was having an affair. An affair with me . . . I'm so sorry.'

He paused and looked away. The quiet was intermittently broken by the sound of distant traffic. Staring at his shoes, he continued. 'I was too much of a coward to say what was going on, to the police. And after what happened, well, I couldn't really face you. Tom, I'm so sorry. Will you ever forgive me?'

I looked at Dave and shook his shoulder with my hand. A kind of masculine gesture of affection. His body had no resistance. He just moved backwards and forwards with each shake.

'It was a long time ago, Dave. Feels like two million years.' There was no sign of recognition, so I just continued, 'It doesn't matter any more . . . I don't think we need to discuss this, not really.'

The night was still and warm.

Dave said 'thank you' once, and once only. Thereafter, we spoke of other things. I even gave him a market tip. Just to tide him over.

After Lana came back from her class we had a few more drinks and then retired for the day. I didn't go straight to bed, though. I went to my study.

It is a curious and little-known fact that the human body contains ten to the power of twenty-five nitrogen atoms. This is a staggeringly large number. So large, that long after any single individual is dead, their liberated nitrogen is diffused into virtually every square metre of the atmosphere. We cannot escape the dead. We breathe them.

I sat, in my leather chair, in front of my mahogany desk, breathing Anna. Looking out of the window, I could not see the stars, only my reflection. I looked weary. Exhausted. I sat, listening to my breathing, and thinking. Thinking. Thinking.

Eventually, I turned the key in one of the lower drawers. I slid it open, and reached inside so that I could lift out a pile of yellowing photocopies. One of them was crumpled and circled with the stains of numerous coffee cups. I replaced the other papers in the drawer, and closed it gently.

I had not inspected Locke's paper for years.

I looked at the equations long and hard. And as I did so, I felt an unwelcome throbbing pain, behind my tired eyes. For a moment, they began to make sense again. For a moment, I thought I was back in London.